HOTEL MACABRE
VOL. 1

EDITED BY
JOE MYNHARDT

**PUBLISHED BY CRYSTAL LAKE PUBLISHING
WHERE STORIES COME ALIVE!**

**Crystal Lake Publishing
www.CrystalLakePub.com**

Copyright 2024 Crystal Lake Publishing
Join the Crystal Lake community today
on our newsletter and Patreon!
Download our latest catalog here.

All Rights Reserved

ISBN: 978-1-964398-33-4

Cover art: Rowan Rademan—1122Siren@gmail.com

Cover design: Ben Baldwin—www.benbaldwin.co.uk

Comic art: Mick Trimble—micktrimble74@sky.com

Comic letterer: Mindy Lopkin—mglopkin@yahoo.com

Layout Design Lori Michelle Booth—www.theauthorsalley.com

Proofreaders:
Charlene du Toit and Shane Nelson

This is a work of fiction. Names, characters, businesses, places, events and incidents are either the products of the authors' imagination or used in a fictitious manner. Any resemblance to actual persons, living or dead, or actual events is purely coincidental.

No part of this publication may be reproduced, stored in a retrieval system, or transmitted in any form or by any means, without the prior permission in writing of the publisher, nor be otherwise circulated in any form of binding or cover than that in which it is published and without a similar condition including this condition being imposed on the subsequent purchaser.

Follow us on Amazon:

WELCOME
TO ANOTHER

CRYSTAL LAKE PUBLISHING
CREATION

Join today at www.crystallakepub.com & www.patreon.com/CLP

TABLE OF CONTENTS

The Cage by Alessandro Manzetti 1
For Beth by Derek Odom 4
Anatomy of a Killer by Wil Dalton 8
Scritch, Scritch, Scritch by A.K. McCarthy 12
Night of Fevers by John Claude Smith 15
Room 636 by Bridgett Nelson 17
Summer People by Tom Deady 35
Wendigo Hunter by Colleen Anderson 38
Chain Smoking at Bus Stops by Devin M. Anderson 40
The Birdcage by Michael Lawrence 43
The Empath by John Palisano 48
Do Not Tempt Her with Apples by Diana Olney 65
The Lingering Taste of Your Last Supper
   by Matthew R. Davis 70
The Fear of Missing Out by Dylan Wells 74
Day Tripper by John Meachen 79
This Was Not the End We Were Promised
   by Maxwell I. Gold 85
—in case the chloroform wears off by Jennifer Osborn 87
The Red Tent by Chris Phelon 92
A Message from the Past, A Message from the Future
   by Jonathan Gensler 97

Burial Day by Stephanie M. Wytovich 100

Saving Face by Sean Eads and Joshua Viola 103

Vultures by Naching T. Kassa 144

A Clown at Midnight by Mia Dalia 146

Suspension by Brandon Wills 149

Hello by Karen Bayly 154

Philly's Little Boy by Linda D. Addison 157

Ashes in Wood by Jonathan Winn 159

A dramatic video reading of "Taking the Piss"
by Jasper Bark 172

All We Endure by Grant Longstaff 173

On a Swing by Patrick Malka 175

Hell Come Home by Amanda M. Blake 178

Nothing Funny About a Clown After Midnight
by Mark Allan Gunnells 183

Growing Gardens by Nick Roberts and Chrissy Winters 186

Unsolicited Advice from a Witch Who's Been There
by Diana Olney 214

Batsquatch Lives! by Larry Hinkle 218

All the Children are Inside by Jamal Hodge 223

Smile by Robin Brown 235

Goodbeak by Gregg Stewart 240

The Hug by Gary McMahon 244

The Dullahan's Reckoning by Claire Davon 253

The Little Thief by Esteban Vargas 257

Check-In/Check-out by Pixie Bruner 261

WELCOME TO HOTEL MACABRE, I'M YOUR HOST, JASPER BARK, BUT YOU CAN CALL ME UNCLE JASP. AND YOU ARE MR. AND MRS...?
...DARLING.
WELL, AREN'T YOU DARLING -- LITERALLY. ARE YOU HERE FOR THE CONVENTION?
NO, BUT WE ARE COLLECTORS AND WE WON'T BE STAYING LONG.
GRANDAD

I'LL TAKE YOU TO YOUR ROOM MYSELF. I'M AFRAID THAT, THANKS TO AN EXPERIMENT WITH A TRANSPORTER, OUR BELLHOP IS A LITTLE...TIED UP.
HELP ME! PLEASE HELP ME!

YOU'RE IN ROOM 635.
IT HAS GREAT VIEWS OF THE CEMETERY AND THE SLAUGHTER HOUSE. ON A GOOD DAY, YOU CAN'T SMELL EITHER.
635
HERE WE ARE.
OOPS!
OKAY, I'M GOING TO GO OUT ON A SEVERED LIMB AND SAY YOUR FAMILY HAS RATHER A LOT OF BAGGAGE.
WHEN YOU SAID YOU WERE COLLECTORS...

THAT'S RIGHT, WE COLLECT *VICTIMS.* WE'RE A FAMILY OF FAILED HORROR WRITERS.
CONSTANTLY REJECTED, WHILE LESSER TALENTS GET ALL THE GLORY! FINALLY WE DECIDED TO CUT THE COMPETITION OUT...*LITERALLY!*
AND NOW WE'RE ALONE WITH THE AUTHOR OF *BARK BITES HORROR* AND THE *DRAW YOU IN* TRILOGY.
OH, THE THINGS WE'RE GOING TO DO TO *YOU!*
WON'T BE ANY WORSE THAN MY LAST GOODREADS REVIEW. ACTUALLY, AS HORROR WRITERS, YOU'VE COME TO THE PERFECT PLACE.
WE HAVE?
OH YES. IT'S GREAT FOR MATERIAL. YOU SEE, EVERY ONE OF OUR GUESTS HAS A TERRIBLE TALE TO TELL OF THEIR PAST, PRESENT OR FUTURE.
WHY NOT TAKE NOTES, AS THEY RECOUNT THE SINISTER STORIES TO WHICH THEY'VE BEEN WITNESS...

THE CAGE

Alessandro Manzetti

When the show begins
a man is locked in a cage
next to the red-and-white striped skirt
of a suburban stinky circus,
one of those where hungry dogs
can't stop barking.

The knife-thrower is doing his job
with eyes shut, in a top hat painted with blood,
while the wooden wheel is turning
together with its beautiful fleshed skeleton:
a naked woman tied with ropes
—Dorina, the wife of the King of Knives—
with her breasts filled with poisoned milk.

She must be punished for her sins,
She's hatching a monster!
the knife-thrower thinks, humming a song
—I See a Darkness—
like a drunk ghost of Johnny Cash.
What people are seeing, sprayed on Dorina's skin
is not tomato, or paint; no tricks this time.
No encore.

The man in the cage,
the nameless King of the Crazy

ALESSANDRO MANZETTI

with his baggy pants
and the old Charlie Chaplin's shoes
hears the cries of the woman,
while the audience yells "Go for her throat!"
He knows that the motherfucker, after the show,
will cut her belly open to pull out the monster,
fishing in Dorina's paradise.
—A monster with his same funny red nose—

A little girl with a lollipop clutched in one hand
is approaching the cage
and the huddled shadow of the man.
She likes clowns, and the blue-eyed tigers
like the one, inside there
which is awakening, powering up
its predator engine.
Today must be its birthday:
the dinner walks on two legs, wow,
and smells good, like freedom
like some orange mirage of India.

When the tiger snaps forward,
pouncing on the King of Crazy,
the little girl drops her lollipop
jumping back like a doll, a puppet
when the master, back there
the King of Dead, masquerading as a butcher,
 pulls her thin strings.

She was never born, actually
so she disappears from the scene
flying away like a fake angel.
Dorina, her only warm house
was buried beneath a new shopping mall
with a soft human meatballs' rosary
around her so white fingers.
—what's left of the King of Crazy—
The knife-thrower, with his handlebar moustache,
is chased by the barking dogs
and by the ghost of Johnny Cash dressed in black;

THE CAGE

he runs around the imaginary tent
—a giant wheel which never stops turning—
of the Circus of the Dead,
over there . . . you can see it
if you get out of your colorful cage.

Alessandro Manzetti *is a three-time Bram Stoker Award-winning writer, editor, scriptwriter, and essayist. His work has been published extensively in English and Italian. His stories and poems have appeared in Italian, USA, UK, Australian, Canadian, Russian and Polish magazines. He received also the SFPA Elgin Award.*

Among his English publications: the novel Naraka—The Ultimate Human Breeding (2018); *the novella* The Keeper of Chernobyl (2019); *the collection* The Radioactive Bride (2020); *the poetry collections* Whitechapel Rhapsody (2020), The Place of Broken Things (2019), War (2018), Sacrificial Nights (2016), Eden Underground (2015); *the graphic novels* The Inhabitant of the Lake (2021), Calcutta Horror (2019); *the essay/guide* 150 Exquisite Horror Books (2021).

Manzetti edited the anthologies The Beauty of Death (2016), The Beauty of Death Vol. 2—Death by Water (2017), Monsters of Any Kind (2018), Rhysling Anthology (2021) *and* Enter Boogeyman (2024).

Website: www.battiago.com

FOR BETH...

Derek Odom

ONE

EACH YEAR, for nearly twenty years, I took Beth to the drive-in movies on Halloween night. Instead of the usual double feature, they played four movies, back-to-back. They did the same on Christmas Eve, but we liked to stay home then.

The first feature began promptly at six. I paid the attendant and he handed me tickets at fifteen before the hour. In previous years, we arrived earlier to get a good spot, but it didn't matter now. We weren't leaving, anyhow.

The theater was playing *Evil Dead II*, *Hellraiser*, *Creepshow 2*, and *The Lost Boys*. I figured if everything went to plan, we'd make it to the end of *Hellraiser* at least. But by then our cognitive processes may have slowed or stopped entirely, so we hoped *Evil Dead II* would be enjoyable.

I drove the station wagon past the screen, past the rows of cars, past the concession stand, and parked near the fence at the rear of the lot. I turned the key and flipped the headlight switch. Beth and I moved the seats back as far as they would go and reclined them. The popcorn and red licorice and extra-large drinks were missing, however; eating might slow things down, and we did not want that. We had brought with us one soda from home to share.

We chose to dress up in costume. I was a happy clown and Beth a fairy princess. We hoped the masks, which were sitting between us, might hide what was happening should someone walk by the car. Every other Halloween, we'd just gone as ourselves, and that had been good enough for us.

FOR BETH . . .

I put the window down and attached the speaker box, then rolled it up again. I sat back and Beth lightly grabbed my hand.
"Are you scared?"
"Me?" I said. "Nah. We'll do just fine."

TWO

Three years ago, Beth was diagnosed with an aggressive cancer. They said she wouldn't last six months, but they didn't know Beth. She's strong. Still, we were both aware it would be a losing battle. Since we received the news, we'd laughed until we cried and then laughed and then cried again so many times I'd lost count. But, like a freshly-planted tree, our love grew through the turmoil. We are soulmates, each incapable of living without the other.

Once all options had been exhausted and Beth's health declined to the point of no return, she had been handed a group of pills, to be taken only when she was sure and brave and ready. "Palliative sedation," they had called it, but it was really just soul dissolution in an amber bottle. The doctor told us they would be enough to end three healthy people, and it was done that way so there were no mistakes. That's when the idea came to me. It took convincing but, finally, Beth agreed and we began planning.

We updated our wills and sold or donated everything we didn't absolutely need. We took a cruise to Mexico. We gave money to the homeless outside restaurants and gas stations. We went to a rock concert. Beth, ever the horror film lover, got to meet Clive Barker in the flesh, and he'd signed her copy of *The Great and Secret Show*, her favorite novel. We made a deal that if she lasted, we'd go to the drive-in one last time on Halloween. And there we were.

We believed in spiritual energy, and that we turned into light after death. We looked forward to being together there, in the place we liked to call Home. We weren't God-fearing and we weren't atheists, but something in between, I guess. Each of us struggled with faith quite a bit after her diagnosis, but in the end, Home worked for us. We hoped it was enough to believe in *something*.

The overhead lights dimmed, and the speaker crackled to life. Beth squeezed my hand, hard, and I squeezed back.

THREE

"When do we put on the masks?" she asked.
"Not yet. Remember? After the previews."
"Oh. Right."
I smiled. "Don't worry, my love. We got this. Okay?" Beth nodded and I chuckled. "It's been quite a ride, huh?"
She managed a weak laugh. "You can say that again."

The screen lit up, promising good movies to come in the summertime of the following year. I pulled the tab on the soda can and it gave a pop and a hiss. We watched in silence as scenes from films we would never see flashed, one after the other. Then, darkness. I fished in the console for the pill bottle, found it, and put it in my lap. "Now," I said quietly. "Let's put them on."

Beth grabbed her fairy and I my clown, and we strapped them on, small elastic bands securing our facades. "Wait," she said, and lifted her mask up so it sat on her forehead. "A kiss?"

I cleared my throat. "Of course. Yes." I lifted mine and leaned toward her. With what must have taken all the strength she had, Beth leaned to me. When our lips touched, we broke down. Sobbing, I reached out and grabbed her shoulders, rubbed her there, told her how much I loved her and how proud of her I was.

We sat back and slid our masks down. "Oh, dammit," I said. "The pills."

Beth laughed nervously and raised her mask again. "Right. Those. I'm so sorry."

"Don't ever be sorry, my love. Don't ever say that."

We split the bottle and I offered the soda to her. "You first," she said. "I don't think I can do it knowing you hadn't yet."

"Sure, baby. Okay."

I took my half, and then she took hers.

We sat back in our seats, lowered the masks, and watched the features, her hand in mine, until we slept.

I awoke groggy, sick, my shirt wet with vomit. The screen was dark, the cars were gone, and Beth was dead.

Derek *has been reading and writing since he can remember, and has been interested in words and how they work since he was two years old. He loves the infinite number of ways they can be arranged to mean*

FOR BETH . . .

different things or even say the same thing. He is a huge fan of the writings of Stephen King, H.G. Wells, H.P. Lovecraft, Clive Barker, Dean Koontz, John Saul, and myriad other dark authors. He also collects issues of Weird Tales, both old and new. An animal lover, he has owned critters of all shapes and sizes, from dogs to cats to tarantulas and even a pet black widow named Sparkles. That didn't last long. Derek has dreams of one day writing from the loft of an isolated country home in Oregon. For now, he owns a home in southern California. He likes to laugh, love, and experience everything to the absolute fullest. He also plays a wicked game of chess. His motto: Don't aim for perfection; aim for better, you can do that.

ANATOMY OF A KILLER

Wil Dalton

WITH THIS WEEKEND'S release of George Lewis' tactlessly titled *David Dominic Dufour: Anatomy of a Killer*, America's recurrent interest in its most brutal children's most heinous crimes collides with its equally absurd fascination with revisiting late 1980s culture. Elevating this oft-explored corner of uniquely American crime is Lewis' longtime cinematographer and artistic collaborator Andi Michaels' truly visionary camera work. From the opening shot of Dufour's meticulously organized freezer to the closing montage of Ronald Reagan's assurances of American greatness, the power of the film's conflicting images batter the viewer beyond understandable shock and sadness into something more akin to utter defeat.

The film begins with a sampling of headlines before flashbacking to Dufour's troubled childhood:
FRANKENSTEIN KILLER SNAGS ANOTHER PART
FRANKENSTEIN KILLER MOVES TO SUBURBS
POLICE LACK LEADS, WILL KILLER COMPLETE COLLECTION?
HEARTLESS KILLER FINALLY CAUGHT

The obligatory humanization segment thankfully contains itself to ten brief, early minutes and a handful of interviews with former schoolteachers, Scout leaders, and a frankly too-twitchy-for-the-camera pastor. Anyone familiar with the genre knows this bit. John Wayne Gacy's alcoholic father beat his son with a belt; Richard Ramirez saw his cousin murder his wife; Ted Bundy was addicted to porn.

ANATOMY OF A KILLER

Mercifully, none of the reminiscence about Dufour's childhood attempts to justify the later monster known to the world. More interesting, Lewis and Michaels introduce a curious technique they revisit with subsequent interviews. After each speaker finishes, the camera zooms in for an awkward close-up. Lewis asks what they are doing next; grocery shopping, picking up kids, watching the news. The mundane but necessary acts of life. Only later in the documentary, when each of Dufour's victims' last known acts before their murders are shown to be eerily similar to the interviewees' responses, does it hit the viewer how near to death we all walk.

As other critics have noted, far too much of the movie dissects the role of how the media focus on whether Dufour would complete "his collection" before he was caught may have sped his escalating final kills. Laudably, *Anatomy of a Killer* highlights the early advantage Dufour had in operating undetected, because of the lack of interest in vanishing gay youth by the Chicago Police Department. But unlike Wayne Williams, once apprehended, the contents of Dufour's freezer prevented any defense by denial.

The other distinctive contribution to the genre is the inclusion of the era's advertisements between crime scene photos and concurrent news reports. Footage of dried blood on tile floors interrupted by Pac-Man; trial exhibit B of Dufour's many blades bookended by commercials for Cabbage Patch Kids and The Clapper; shots of how detectives found the victims interspersed with plugs for big shoulders and bigger hair. Like the neon cheetah prints that defined the decade, Lewis' vision is one of excess. It is technically impressive and frequently overwhelming. However, it is the film's closing interview that seizes the heart and refuses to leave.

Lewis speaks with Sophia—the sister of one of Dufour's victims, Theodore Heflin. She sits with her back straight, poised on a stool. A pretty blonde wearing a pink hoodie and grey sweatpants, wiping her watery eyes. Her voice is loud and clear and firm and kind—like a kindergarten teacher. Subtly employing a low angle shot, the camera zooms in until Sophia's face fills the screen. She calls her brother Teddy.

Sophia talks about the pressure Teddy felt from their dad to abandon acting. She speculates that her brother met Dufour under the guise of an audition. She doesn't understand why else his body would have been found at the Goodman Theatre.

WIL DALTON

Sophia says that her brother was the most ethical person she knew: always volunteering, always helping out. He believed that if he did good, his goodness would inspire others to also do good, and in that way, the world would slowly be filled with goodness. She says, "Teddy was really hard on himself. He always thought he could be doing better."

The sister pauses and, like with the previous subjects, the camera lingers on her, recording her sad silent face.

She says, "If there is a man like Dufour who is capable of such evil, doesn't that mean that there must also exist a man equally as good? I wish my brother could have met that man instead."

She looks up, then down, and the camera stays on her face. She is the only subject whom Lewis doesn't ask about her subsequent plans. In this moment, all of the film's conflicting images reveal themselves to be asking this larger question. The lemon next to the bag of sugar. The daisy breaking through the asphalt. The fanny packs and body bags. Where is the opposite of David Dominic Dufour?

In the extended silence that lingers on the sister's face, when she looks at the camera with tears in her eyes, for a brief moment you wonder if maybe the answer is simply that our math is wrong. Maybe Dufour isn't an outlier of humanity but rests only slightly lower than the mean; that the lack of an opposing positive person exposes the truth that all of us are so full of lies and overestimations of our own benevolence that we cannot comprehend that not a one of us is actually that good. If only we perceived our situation clearly, we would see that Dufour is not an abnormality, but merely a braver example of each of our own depraved potential.

But then the sister wipes her eyes and looks up at the ceiling, and we watch her gazing heavenward for a full forty seconds. Her head still upright, she clenches her eyes, and then her chin drops, her golden hair covers her face, and she sobs. And that's when we realize that no, the answer is not that David Dominic Dufour is an average representative of humanity. The answer is the sister is correct. As evil as he is evil, there must be those as equally good and kind, but just as Dufour and his fellow monsters need to be found and locked up and punished, the good ones need to be found and protected and nourished; and tragically, none of the police, none of the neighbors, none of the teachers, none of the Scout

ANATOMY OF A KILLER

leaders, none of the pastors, none of us were paying attention. We were all preoccupied with grocery shopping, picking up kids, watching the news. The sad, simple answer is that we do not know anyone as good as Dufour is bad because we failed to protect them.

Wil Dalton *is an AmeriCorps*NCCC and Peace Corps (Bulgaria) alum. He worked several years in residence life and currently parents three beautiful children. He studies the craft of fiction under the generous instruction of George Saunders and Chuck Palahniuk. Recent stories can be found in Crystal Lake's* Shallow Waters: Halloween Flash Fiction Anthology *and the Outcast Press diner noir anthology,* Turn Out the Lights and Cry. *You can find him at wildalton.substack.com*

SCRITCH, SCRITCH, SCRITCH

A.K. McCarthy

I'M NOT CRAZY, officers. You must believe me. You must listen to my story. Even you there, in the back.
I'm not mad. I'm more sure of that now than I have been in months. Since before I started seeing *them*.

They lurk in dark corners and in the reflections of mirrors. Always just a little bit out of view. At first I only caught glimpses of them, but I knew they were there.

I told my sister, and she told me to see a therapist. She said it would be good for me to "work my stuff out" and "reflect on my trauma." She saw a therapist and told them about our parents and our dirty laundry and it made her feel so much better.

So, whatever. I went. I saw Dr. Audra Carmody. I knew something was off with her right away, but I wanted to at least say I tried. So I lay on her couch and looked at the little statue of the horse on her table as I told her about my life.

She asked me this and that. My parents. My sister. My drinking. My divorce. When I got laid off. I've made my peace with all that stuff, but I humored her. I really wanted to tell her about *them*. The Lurkers, I call them.

I told her about their ice-blue eyes and the way their long fingers came to points. How they hunch over until you see them. Then they snap their heads up at you like you've caught a scavenger picking at roadkill.

Audra nodded along, her pen scratching away at her notepad. *Scritch scritch scritch*, reducing my life to shorthand. She said this was all completely normal, that I'd been through a lot and

SCRITCH, SCRITCH, SCRITCH

people who deal with a great deal of loss in a short period of time can hallucinate.

Are you writing this down, officers? You there, in the back, are you paying attention? You aren't even facing me, you're just hunched over your notepad.

Yes, yes, I'll get back to my statement. Dr. Carmody said precisely what I thought she'd say. That we'd talk about it in our next appointment. Of course. Why have me pay for one session when she could bring me in again and get me hooked?

I told her I'd think about it. I got up to leave and happened to walk by her full-length mirror near the door.

I saw her reflection in the mirror and tried not to gasp.

I saw the *real* her.

The Lurker that she was.

Her eyes, which were light brown when I'd first seen her, were ice-blue behind her glasses. Her hands were so dark they were almost black. Like they'd been burnt. The long fingers came to points. She was hunched over her notepad like she was guarding it.

I realized the *scritch*ing I'd heard wasn't from her pen at all. She'd been scratching her notes into her notepad with her sharp fingertips.

I kept it together. See, officers, a truly crazy person would have crumbled in that moment. They would have freaked out and cried and jumped out the window or something. No, I stayed calm. I smiled at her and nodded and said I'd see her at our next appointment.

I went out to her receptionist Clara and scheduled my next appointment. Obviously I didn't think I'd come back for it. I couldn't be in a room with that woman again. Maybe she was just harvesting my thoughts so that the rest of them could learn from me. *Scritch, scritch, scritch.* No, I wasn't going to let her back into my mind.

But the more I thought about it, the more I realized I had a chance to do something important. Something that would make up for the boozing and the things I said to my wife and the things I did at work. I had a chance at redemption here, to stand face-to-face with evil and loudly declare that I wasn't scared.

So I went back for my next appointment. I went in with a plan.

Are you writing this down? Is that officer in the back paying attention yet? Is he taking notes?

A.K. MCCARTHY

So, I waited until Dr. Carmody was settled in a little bit. Then, when her guard was down, I grabbed that horse statue and smashed it into the mirror. I snatched a shard of glass and slashed Dr. Carmody's throat with it.

Then I cut out her eyes. Her ice-blue eyes.

She slashed at me with her sharp fingers, and you can see the scratches all over me. I was lucky to make it out of there alive. She snarled and cursed me and called me all kinds of things until she couldn't speak anymore.

You know in movies, you can tell when someone dies when their eyes glaze over? Well, it's harder to tell when someone doesn't have their eyes anymore. I waited for her chest to stop heaving, then waited a little more. Then I got off her.

She'd gone back to her human form at that point, and I understand how it looks. Believe me, I understand it. Have you looked at her body in a mirror yet? No? You should do that. You have to believe me, officers.

The good news is, I haven't seen any Lurkers since I did it. Maybe it sent a message to them that I'm not someone to be messed with. Now they know I can hurt them. I don't think they'll be lurking around me anymore.

But you can tell I'm not crazy, can't you? Think about Clara, the receptionist. I didn't put a hand on her. I wouldn't have. I'm a killer, you see, but I'm not a monster. That's something I learned about myself during this therapy process.

You, there. Yes, you, officer in the back. You've been hunched over this whole time. What are you writing? What are you scribbling down back there?

Does nobody else see him? He's scratching away on his little notepad. That terrible *scritching*, I can't stand it. I can't bear it!

None of you see him? *Make him stop that scratching! MAKE HIM STOP!*

A.K. McCarthy *is a writer based in St. Louis, Missouri. In addition to his award-winning journalism, his short fiction has been published in numerous anthologies. He finds inspiration in hikes, giallo films, and frightened expressions from his cats Tulio and Henrietta. You can connect with him in Crystal Lake's Shadows & Ink community under the name Alex McCarthy.*

NIGHT OF FEVERS

John Claude Smith

.
. . .
again
relenting to a
night of fevers
breathing smoke
brand of misery singed
on sweat-soaked sheets
sleep a crematory dream

containing the mutation takes
concentration—I cannot let slumber
inspire combustion or the sleep of reason
to breed monsters

I am the monster

I am human—imbued
with the curse of the sun
body an impatient match
when the mind wanders
when control stumbles

my solitude is imperative
arid as the eternal desert
I wander dunes and mirages
inspire lizard brain

JOHN CLAUDE SMITH

circuitry to crackle
sleep on sand of fire
melting—a lava embrace

I am the monster

waking into the horror
of what I can't resist
my frenetic interior
I'm ready to burn
soul made flame
my name is
Arson
  . . .
.

John Claude Smith *has had three collections, four chapbooks, and two novels published, along with tales and/or poems in Vastarien, Pluto in Furs, and more magazines and anthologies. His debut novel,* Riding the Centipede, *was a Bram Stoker Award Finalist. He is presently shopping four novels, two short story collections, and a poetry collection. Busy is good. Reissues of his OOP earlier books are in progress as he types this sentence (one is out now!). He splits his time between the East Bay across from San Francisco, and Rome, Italy, where his heart resides always.*

ROOM 636

Bridgett Nelson

Prologue
2005

"**W**HY YA GOTTA be such an annoying little shit? Go find something else to do, will ya?"

My little brother thought he needed to be glued to my ass every minute of every day, and it rankled.

"Yeah, Troy, go hang out with kids your own age!" Erick pointed to a group of toddlers in the sandbox across the park, their mothers sitting on nearby benches, sipping drinks from their insulated stainless-steel mugs.

Our other friends laughed.

"Screw you!" Troy yelled at me, his lower lip protruding in a pout. "Screw all y'all! I'm nine! I ain't no baby."

I sighed, already knowing this was going to end with Troy tattling. If I never heard another, 'It doesn't hurt you to play with your brother, Will. He looks up to you, and you need to be a good role model,' from my dad, I'd be thrilled. I just wanted to spend the summer hanging out with friends, not babysitting my bratty sibling.

Trying to defuse the situation, I said, "Don't you know that kid on the jungle gym over there? Go hang out with him. We're trying to play basketball." I dribbled the textured orange and black ball to emphasize my point. "And you're in the way."

"You just won't let me because I'm a better player than you!" Troy lunged for the ball, going for the steal.

I anticipated the move and pulled it aside. He overcompensated and fell to his knees, then rolled, groaning, onto his back. Several layers of skin were missing from each knee, and blood bubbled through the abraded tissue.

"Nice move, twerp," I said, laughing. "You sure showed me."

"Yeah, way to go, dumbass," Erick added. "Now you're bleeding all over the basketball court. Gross."

"Just help me, you . . . you . . . buttholes!" Troy glared, but I could see he was proud of his word choice. "It hurts!"

A soft voice interrupted from behind. "Hey, do you need some help?"

I spun around, my heart thudding triple-time in my chest.

Kaia.

I passed the ball to Erick, who was annoyed by the interruption, but moved away.

"Oh, uh, hi, Kaia. Troy just . . . tripped . . . and stuff."

She glanced at him. "You okay?"

Unwilling to show weakness, Troy got unsteadily to his feet, trying not to cringe. "Sure, I'm good. This here ain't nothin'. One time, I was out hunting with my dad, and—"

"And we don't give a crap, Troy." I gave him my best 'stern big brother' look. "Go home and get cleaned up."

"I have some Band-Aids," Kaia said, then gave an embarrassed chuckle. "In my fanny pack." She slapped the coral-colored bag sitting on her hip. "My . . . mom . . . makes me carry this stupid thing everywhere."

I noticed the hesitation when she said 'mom.' Kaia had moved to our small Texas town last year when the Fierro's adopted her. She'd been in foster care since she was four, after her biological mother overdosed, or something, and she didn't know her father. I'd been secretly in love with her since the day she arrived.

Kaia handed over the Band-Aids, seemingly lost in thought. I took a moment to study her silky wheat-colored hair, expressive brown eyes, peaches and cream complexion, and delicate pink lips covered in a light sheen of cherry-flavored ChapStick—I'd watched her apply it enough times to know. She was the prettiest girl I'd ever laid eyes on and, lucky for me, we were in the same grade at school.

Troy yelped, catching the sticky part of the bandage on one of his wounds. Kaia crouched, looking to see what he'd done.

"Here, let me help," she said. He winced as she removed the ruined bandage. "Sorry, little man."

"I'm not *that* little," Troy grumbled.

Kaia giggled. "No, of course you aren't." She looked at me. "Got any water?"

I fetched my nearly empty water bottle from a wooden bench at the edge of the blacktop.

Jealousy rumbled through my gut as she rinsed Troy's raw skin, blew it dry, and tenderly placed fresh Band-Aids on his abrasions.

"There you go, *big* guy. You're good as new!" She stood, checking the cheap, plastic watch encircling her dainty wrist. "Oops. I told Misty—er, Mom—I'd be home by seven."

"Well, since you're already late, why not hang around a while?" I said, trying to sound cool and casual. "Then I'll walk you home."

Kaia hesitated.

"I can walk you home now," Troy piped up. "Will doesn't want me here anyway, so I'm leaving," He shot me a sly grin. "You can show your mom my knees and tell her how you helped me! She won't mind you being late then."

The little snot knew exactly what he was doing. I could have throttled him.

"Oh, that's a great idea!" she said, her relief palpable. "Are you sure you're okay to walk, though?"

"I think so, but maybe I could hold your hand? It'll help me keep my balance." He smirked at me, a devilish glint in his eye, as she took his hand.

"See you at school, Will!" Kaia said, waving goodbye.

Off they went, my crush and my obnoxious brat of a brother. God, I hated that little fucker.

Present Day

"Will?"

I heard the female voice behind me but ignored it and moved up a spot in line, determined to get my daily caffeine fix.

"Look, Luis," I said into my phone, making no attempt to lower my voice. "I neither want nor need your excuses. What I *do* want is for you to get off your lazy ass and get those papers filed *today*."

Hanging up, I slipped the phone into my pocket and angrily cracked my knuckles. *Fucking incompetent help.*

"Rough day?" the woman behind me teased.

My shoulders tensed. *She's still here? Can't she take a goddamn hint?* Agitated, I ran my fingers through my hair and continued to face forward, not acknowledging her quip.

"Tut, tut, Will Emerick. Such shameful behavior from my prom date."

Prom—?

I spun around so quickly, I lost my balance and nearly fell.

This wasn't just any 'her.'

Kaia.

A racing pulse pounded in my ears. My heart lodged into my throat, sucking up all the saliva, making it hard to breathe.

It *was* Kaia, more breathtaking than ever—her peachy skin glowed with sun-kissed good health and long, thick wheat-colored hair flowed in soft waves around a somewhat fuller heart-shaped face. Mocha eyes sparkled with curiosity and amusement.

God, she was so beautiful. I hadn't seen her since the summer after my sophomore year of college . . . the summer everything changed.

Standing there, in front of this girl whose virginity I'd taken—and who'd also claimed mine—I suddenly realized that everyone else I'd been with had fallen desperately short of her perfection. There never had been, and never would be, another girl for me . . . only Kaia.

"What are you doing here?" I realized, as soon as the words came from my mouth, how stupid and uninspired they were. Unexpectedly seeing somebody from my past had me flustered. The person I'd been before that summer, and the person I'd become after, were never meant to collide.

"I live here now," she said.

A man behind her cleared his throat, and I realized we hadn't shifted with the rest of the line. I stepped forward, and Kaia followed.

At the counter, I told the barista. "Espresso, extra shot, with soy milk . . . and whatever the lady would like."

Kaia looked at me with uncertainty, gave the barista a small grin, and said, "A large green tea with honey and mint, please."

Drinks in hand, we found an umbrella-covered table just

outside and settled in. Not sure where to start, I asked about her adoptive family.

"Misty was diagnosed with breast cancer," she said. "She and Tom moved to Oregon to be closer to her family."

"They just up and left you?"

"We haven't really talked in ages. You know they never felt like family to me. More like roommates pretending to be something else. Sure, they provided me with all the necessities and let me decorate my bedroom, but they never gave a shit. I was closer to your parents than my so-called family."

I knew all these things, of course, but it still hurt to hear her speak about their emotional neglect. "I know they weren't great parents, but they brought you into my life. I'll be forever grateful for that."

She paused, then quietly asked, "Where did you go, Will? After that summer? Why didn't we see or hear from you again?"

"You know why."

"No. I don't. I mean, yes, I was in the car with Troy when it crashed, but that doesn't seem reason enough to—"

"He nearly killed you, Kaia!" The words, pent up for years, burst from me. "He was drunk, risking every life on the road that night—including yours! Yet you all defended him afterward! My parents, okay, that wasn't a surprise. That shallow asshole's always been their 'baby.' But you . . . "

I choked up, remembering the sight of her in the hospital. A cervical collar stiff around her neck, one leg in traction, face black and blue with bruising—hearing her tell me it was all an accident . . . begging me not to blame Troy. To forgive him . . .

I studied her expression and saw only sadness.

"And then there were the pictures, Kaia."

Her brow furrowed with confusion. "What pictures?"

"From Troy's graduation party."

Her expression only became more baffled. "What are you talking about?"

Was she really going to deny it?

That fateful day flashed through my memory, bringing with it the same intense pain I'd felt back then. "At the end of the term, Dad picked me up at the dorm and drove me home. We unloaded my stuff, then I went to my room to shower and change clothes. The heat and humidity were horrible that day."

I paused, letting the recollection completely take hold.

"There was an envelope on the bed, with my name written on it." I chuckled ruefully. "At first, I was excited, thinking it was a gift from my folks, a little extra spending money. Instead, I pulled out a note from Troy."

I studied Kaia closely for any reaction. She seemed invested in the story, but she didn't appear to know where it was going.

"It said, 'My graduation party rocked, dude! Wish you could have been there!' And there were a few photos. Polaroids, you know? Troy and a few of his friends goofing off in the pool, that sort of thing. But then—" I ran my hands through my hair and tried to stifle the tears I could feel welling in the corners of my eyes.

"What, Will? My God, what? Are you okay?"

"Am I *okay*? You and Troy, in his bedroom? Kissing? Your shirt pushed up? Him licking your—Jesus, I can barely say it!"

Kaia's jaw dropped, and her eyes sparked with anger. "What?!"

"I thought you were mine . . . that we were happy together," I said brokenly. "How could you do something like that?"

"I . . . I didn't!"

"I saw the pictures!"

"Do you still have them?"

"No! I fucking burned them, couldn't bear having those images anywhere near me. I only wish I could have burned them from my mind! But I saw them, Kaia. I saw them. Then, just a few hours later, we got the call about the car accident."

"That son of a bitch!" she cried, her voice sharp with indignation. "Will, listen to me . . . that night, at his graduation party, I told Troy I had a headache and was going home. He offered me some ibuprofen . . . or, what I thought was ibuprofen. I don't remember anything else. I certainly don't remember making out with your brother!"

"Oh. Oh shit. Kaia . . . "

"The next thing I knew, I was in the hospital. I don't even know how I ended up in the car with him. All I knew was the hurt—my entire body was white-hot misery. Being so drugged up on painkillers, I barely recall your visit. I just remember being so happy you were home . . . never realizing I wouldn't ever see you again." Tears filled her eyes. "I've always thought my memories were messed up from the trauma of the crash. I couldn't figure out why you just . . . left. And I certainly had no idea about . . . "

She buried her face in her hands.

I noticed concerned glances from the other patrons, unclenched my fists and jaw, and, with effort, spoke more softly. "I'm so sorry to have dropped this on you, Kaia. Hell, I'm even more sorry it happened. I . . . I didn't know . . . I *should* have known."

She gasped a watery breath. "You and me both."

My phone had been vibrating constantly with texts, some from Luis, some from other business connections. I made a snap decision and turned it off.

"What do you say we go grab a bite to eat?" I suggested, striving for a lighter tone. "Catch up, start fresh, maybe spend some more time bitching about my piece-of-shit brother?" I held my hand out to her.

She smiled feebly and placed her hand inside mine. "Yes. Let's."

The next few weeks flew by in a blur of dinners, movies, parties, long strolls on the riverwalk, even a ghost tour around the city.

It didn't matter what we did, Kaia and I had fun together. Laughter came easily. Falling back in love with her was effortless . . . as if I'd never stopped. We even landed in some local entertainment/gossip rags, which enthusiastically discussed the 'mystery blonde' seen about town with 'eligible bachelor and perennial party boy, Will Emerick.'

Nobody knew who Kaia was, and I liked that just fine. I wanted her all to myself. Having her back in my life—especially after all this time—made me happier than I could have ever imagined.

When the time felt right, I drove her to The Gunter Hotel in downtown San Antonio, a beautiful, luxury building built in 1909.

Kaia looked at me in surprise as I pulled into the parking lot. "What are we doing here, Will?"

"I'm treating you to a vacation full of pampering, my love."

"Oh . . . how nice." Her voice was oddly subdued. She was obviously nervous about taking our relationship to the next level. We'd been playing it slow, not rushing into anything. I found it sweet and kind of cute.

"Come on! It'll be fun! We get the full spa experience . . . room service ice cream sundaes . . . anything we want!" I gave her a lingering kiss, took her hand, and led her into the hotel, where I'd booked us under assumed names, to prevent more unsolicited gossip.

When I opened the door to room 636, Kaia squealed in astonished delight.

"It's so beautiful!" She turned in circles, taking it all in.

Even I was taken aback by the extravagance. Espresso-colored wooden floors, a semi-circular wall of windows overlooking the riverwalk, a king-sized bed covered in a fluffy white duvet and more pillows than any two people could ever use, and a sectional sofa in a rich chocolate brown. The bathroom had a standalone soaking tub, a marble walk-in shower, and the biggest vanity I'd ever seen. The walls were a classy shade of muted blue-gray. A glass door led to a private balcony. It was perfect.

"And it's all ours! The spa has standing orders to give you the massage of your choice, a manicure and pedicure, hair styling, make-up application, whatever. We've got dinner reservations for eight o'clock. Sound good?"

"So good!" The smile on her lips lit up her lovely face. "But . . . I didn't bring anything fancy to wear, Will. I didn't know."

"Leave that to me."

Five hours later, we were seated at a private corner table at Bliss, my favorite fine-dining restaurant in the city. Kaia looked beautiful in the black Marchesa cocktail dress I'd chosen for her at Neiman Marcus.

"Gosh, this is some menu," Kaia said, scanning the leatherbound bill of fare. "I'm not sure I know what most of this is."

"Would you like me to order for you? I think I know exactly what you'd enjoy."

"Do it," she said, playfully. "Then I'll rate you on your choices."

I belly-laughed, causing nearby patrons to scowl. One of the things I loved most about Kaia was her ability to take me by complete surprise with her banter. "That's fair," I said. "Rate away."

"Can I interest you in some wine?" asked our waiter, French accent thick and unapologetic.

"I'd like a glass of the 1973 Chateau Montelena Chardonnay."

ROOM 636

He nodded his approval. "A most excellent choice. And for you, mademoiselle?"

"Oh, no wine for me, thanks," Kaia said, blushing. "Maybe a club soda?"

"Of course. Shall I get an appetizer started?"

"Let's start with the roasted bone marrow and beef tenderloin tartare, then cleanse our palates with some melon gazpacho." The waiter nodded, offering me a polite smile, so I continued. I didn't want him interrupting us all evening. "For the entrees, the lady will have the Mediterranean Branzino, and I'll have the duck breast and pan-seared foie gras. For dessert, hm." I pondered. "I think she'd most enjoy the chocolate bar. For me, the lavender goat cheese cheesecake."

"A refined palate, indeed. I shall get this started for you. Have a blissful evening."

Kaia gaped. "My God, I won't be able to eat all that!"

"You don't have to, but I guarantee you'll love every bite you *do* eat."

"You are a crazy, crazy man, Will Emerick."

After dinner, our limo driver—yes, I hired a limo—took us to Louis Vuitton, where I bought my sweet Kaia a new handbag.

"Will," she frantically whispered, "it's *four thousand dollars!*"

I patted her hand. "It's fine, love."

She fought me tooth and nail, but I won. She certainly looked elated when she carried the luxury French purse out of the store.

On our way back to the hotel, sitting in the privacy of our limousine, I said, "You never did rate my dinner choices. How'd I do?"

"Is it one to five stars?"

"Sure. That works."

"Hm," she mulled. "I'd give the bone marrow a 4.6, the melon gazpacho a 4.7, the branzino a 4.8, the chocolate bar a 4.9, and the company a full five stars!"

"I passed!"

"Undoubtedly."

I kissed the back of her hand, and smiled when I saw her cheeks redden. "Are you happy, Kaia?"

After a slight hesitation, she said, "So very much."

25

I pushed open the door to our hotel room, holding my breath in anticipation.

Flickering candles provided the only light, spread around the room, creating warm and mysterious shadows. Crimson rose petals covered the bed, dispersing their fresh and slightly spicy aroma. The music of a string quartet filtered through hidden speakers, and a bottle of champagne sat in a silver bucket of ice.

Kaia noticed the additions and paused, her back to me. I removed the box I'd carried with me all evening and got down on one knee.

"Wow," she said. "This sure is a fancy hotel. It's so beautiful!" Then she turned, seeing the shiny engagement ring. Gasping, she whispered a breathless, "Will . . . ?"

"I wanted the night I proposed to you to be perfect in every way."

"Oh my God." Dazed, she took a small step back.

"Kaia, I've realized something very important during these weeks we've spent so happily together. I've learned I'm still single because I have always, subconsciously, been searching for you. I fell in love with you when we were kids, and I've been in love with you ever since, even though we've lived apart. You're the only one I want to be with. Today, tomorrow, and for the rest of our lives. I love you, and I hope with all my heart you'll be my wife. Kaia . . . will you marry me?"

She stared at me, breathing heavily, her eyes wide with . . . was that . . . apprehension? Dismay?

"Oh." Tears trickled down her cheeks. "Oh, Will."

My chest felt heavy with sudden apprehension and dismay of my own. I'd never considered the possibility she might refuse. "Please say yes. *Please.*"

She hesitated a moment longer. I saw something like resignation cross her face. "Of course I'll marry you, Will."

I jumped up, pulling her into my arms. "Oh, thank God! Thank God for you, Kaia. I don't want to live without you anymore."

Her body felt limp against mine, making me wonder why she wasn't more excited. Surprise? Shock?

Placing my finger beneath her chin, I gently pushed up until

ROOM 636

our eyes met. "I love you," I said. "I will do anything for you. We don't need your so-called parents. We don't need *my* parents, who always played favorites. And we sure as hell don't need my pissant little brother. We can live on our own terms, Kaia, from this day forward. Okay?" I gently brushed some hair off her forehead and felt her relax into me.

"You're beautiful," I said, giving her a soft kiss.
"You're sweet and kind," I said, repeating the process.
"You're funny and smart." The kiss lasted longer.
"You're so goddamn sexy."

This time, as I kissed her, I picked her up and carried her to our gorgeous rose-strewn bed, tenderly placing her atop the plush duvet. Sliding onto the bed beside her, my lips made their way to her neck, dipping down to her chest and cleavage. Goosebumps covered her silky skin, and a soft moan escaped her throat.

She'd been reluctant to consummate our new relationship. I didn't know why, but I'd given her time without pressure. Sure, I wanted her desperately, but I'd do *anything* for Kaia.

Unzipping her dress, I slid it down over her breasts. Gazing at her nakedness, I noticed her breasts were fuller now, the nipples darker. Not surprising. A decade had passed since I'd last seen her body. She'd been a teenager then, and now she was a grown woman. I groaned, cupping both her breasts, while passionately kissing her lips. I could tell she wanted me too, as she squirmed and rubbed herself against my leg.

"Lift your hips, baby. This dress needs to go," I said, pushing it over her slightly wider hips, her knees, and her tiny, adorable feet, before wadding it up and tossing it on the floor.

"You naughty girl. No panties?" I asked, taking her in. I was delighted.

"No panties," she said, blushing. "The lines showed."

"Easy access," I said, burying my face between her thighs.

Neither of us spoke again until after her body stopped shuddering. "Jesus, Will . . . " she managed to murmur. "Had some practice at this, haven't ya?"

"Maybe a little."
"Do it some more."
I happily obliged.

Sometime later, we sprawled across the bed with various body parts intertwined, spent.

"Happy?" I asked, stroking her shoulder.

"Deliciously happy."

"I don't know what that means."

"Neither do I, but it sounded good."

"You're an imp."

"Maybe." She chuckled. "Probably."

"Fine. From now on, you're Imp to me."

"I won't argue." She rose from the tangled sheets. "I'm going to get a shower."

I admired the profile of her slender body in the candlelight—the body I'd just spent hours loving. The delicately curved neck, the narrow shoulders, the perky bottom I couldn't get enough of, and the long, lean legs that were wrapped around me just minutes ago.

There was also the cute little paunch of a belly, the sign of a woman who'd thoroughly enjoyed her engagement meal. I liked my women to be in shape, but *I* was the one who'd insisted on the decadent dinner, and we could always work out in the hotel exercise room tomorrow.

Except . . .

As her palm unconsciously caressed the bump, bitter reality became crystal clear. I nearly threw up.

Leaping from the bed, post-sex contentment vanished, I seized her arm and spun her around. She laughed, thinking I was still playing . . . until she saw my face.

"Whose baby are you carrying, Kaia? Because it sure as hell isn't mine!"

All color drained from her face, and I could see the pulse pounding in her neck. "I . . . I don't know what you mean," she finally said, using both hands to try and cover her protruding abdomen.

"Don't fuck with me right now. I mean it, Kaia. Do *not* fuck with me." I punched the blue wall, denting the drywall, but felt nothing. "Tell me who it was. NOW!"

Bursting into tears, she ran for the door.

That only infuriated me more.

ROOM 636

Grabbing a handful of golden hair, I yanked her back and tossed her onto the bed like a sack of potatoes.

"How the fuck could you come to me *tainted* like this? Did you think you could hide the little bastard forever?"

She tried to talk through the blubbers. "I'm . . . barely showing, and . . . and with the right clothes, it . . . "

I punched the mattress beside her head, causing her to scream. I'd never been so angry or felt so betrayed. Even seeing Troy's pictures hadn't made me feel this way. Covering her mouth with my hand, I pushed my face so close to hers, our noses touched.

"When I lift my hand," I snarled, spittle flying from my lips, "you're going to say one word. Just one word. A name. I don't want to hear anything else from your slut-hole mouth right now. Otherwise, I will put my hands around your throat and choke the life from you. *Both* of you. Do you understand?"

She nodded, her eyes wide with terror.

"Just a name," I coldly repeated, and lifted my hand from her mouth.

Instead of speaking, she lurched sideways and vomited the delicious meal we'd shared all over the floor. Then, still gagging, she screamed for help.

My backhand knocked her flat on the mattress.

"You bitch! You miserable, lying cunt! What did I tell you, huh? This is your last chance. Tell me who put that baby inside you."

"I can't," she said, sobs robbing her voice.

"You can, and you will."

"Please don't make me. I—"

I wrapped my hands around her neck and squeezed. Eyes bulging, her tongue protruded from her mouth as she choked and wheezed, trying to pull some air into her oxygen-starved lungs.

I released my grasp.

"The next time I put my hands around your neck will be the last, Kaia. You fucking sicken me. I asked you to be my wife, and you said yes, while carrying some other man's remnants in your belly? That's the lowest of low. Everything I thought I knew about you was wrong. Now, *who was it?*"

She mumbled something.

"What was that, Kaia? Speak up!"

"Troy!" she shrieked, "It was Troy, okay? I'm carrying your brother's baby!"

I recoiled in shock.

"And guess what?" she went on. "He's a fucking *phenomenal* lay! Are you happy to know that, Will?" A shuddering sob racked her body. "I knew Troy would make a terrible father. After everything I've learned in the last few weeks, my regrets are plentiful. But . . . you left me, Will."

Her voice was small, pitiful.

"You . . ."

"That's where you come in now. You're successful and wealthy, and you've always cared about me. I knew you'd give my baby everything."

Those were the last words she ever spoke.

Letting out a roar full of rage and despair, I did just as I'd promised.

She was cold.

Looking at the tortured, death grimace on her pale face, the evidence of a violent death, I felt numb.

How could this night—this lovely, special occasion I'd planned so meticulously—have gone so horrifically wrong?

How could the girl I'd loved so passionately for most of my life, the girl I'd never treated with anything except kindness and respect, sleep with that cretin I had nothing more than a biological connection to?

I'd wanted to spend the rest of my life making her happy, but instead, I had to figure out what to do with her body.

Her body, with the gently rounded curve of pregnant belly.

A familiar fury worked its way through my core. By the time the sun had risen, I had a plan.

I strolled the streets of San Antonio, wearing a baseball cap and aviator sunglasses. A bell jingled as I entered a kitchenware supply store and casually greeted the homely woman standing behind the check-out counter.

I'd placed the 'do not disturb' sign on the hotel room door before I left, but for extra security, I'd also placed a pillow under

ROOM 636

Kaia's head and covered her with the duvet to make it look like she was asleep. Unable to get her eyelids to remain closed, I'd slipped a complimentary, black satin eye mask into place.

"I'm looking for a heavy-duty piece of equipment and the sharpest cutlery you offer," I told the woman at the counter.

An hour later, after catching a ride with an Uber driver, I was back in my room, sitting on the bathroom floor, constructing the meat grinder I'd purchased. Beneath the cool-toned lighting, a large cleaver gleamed. Beside it, a chef's cutlery set waited, wrapped in a pristine cloth.

When the grinder was ready, I chose a knife and went to the bed. Pulling back the duvet,

I tentatively rubbed my hand over the baby bump, caressing my niece or nephew. It gave me a momentary pang. Hardly the baby's fault its parents were loathsome humans.

"Sorry, baby," I said, before plunging the knife into Kaia's abdomen.

Cutting the fetus from the womb was surprisingly easy, the blade slicing through tissue and muscle with little effort.

Turns out, it was a niece. Her head was enormous in relation to her body, her skin so thin, I could see the shadows of her tiny organs and the network of blood vessels. Using Google, I determined Kaia had likely been around four months pregnant.

Tearing open the box surrounding my other purchase—something I hadn't expected to find in a corner mini-mart, but which seemed perfectly serendipitous—I loaded the film packet into my new Polaroid camera.

I placed the baby on Kaia's chest but was unable to wrap her arms around it—she was stiff with rigor mortis. After snapping some photos, I took the baby into the bathroom.

I stuffed the fetus' fragile body into the grinder head, used the stopper to push it down into the neck, and started cranking.

A little while later, the toilet flushed it away.

I realized I needed to drain the blood from Kaia's body before I started cutting parts off, so I dragged her into the bathroom and hoisted her into the tub. She seemed heavier dead than alive.

I'd love to say it was hard slicing through the throat I'd kissed so many times before, but she'd become nothing more than meat to me. I rolled her over, disarticulated the shoulder joint, and cut off her arm.

More grinding.
More flushing.
I worked throughout the night.

My red, swollen eyes gazed wondrously at the vibrant pinks and oranges of the sunrise. A new day had dawned, but lack of sleep and rivers of shed tears had aged me.

I wasn't crying for Kaia. Nor for her unborn child. And certainly not for Troy.

No. The tears were for me.

Two short days ago, an amazing life lay before me . . . true love, marriage, a family, a successful career.

Today, that life was over.

But, as I'd sent the remains of my one-and-only into the dark, fetid sewers of San Antonio, it became clear how this story needed to end.

Taking one final look around the hotel room, I smiled. The coppery scent that permeated the room despite the constant hum of the air conditioner . . . the meat grinder sitting in the bathroom amid splattered, sticky blood . . . the red rings circling the interiors of the otherwise pristine bathtub and toilet bowl . . . the bigger pieces I hadn't bothered trying to flush . . . and . . .

The finishing tableau: Kaia's decapitated head sitting on a pillow, the hellish expression and broken capillaries on her face hinting at her brutal death.

Also on the pillow, her left hand, a huge diamond ring glinting on the fourth finger.

Propped against the pillow, a standard white envelope, holding Polaroid photos and a note.

My engagement party rocked, dude! Wish you could have been there!

Satisfied with my preparations, I picked up Kaia's phone, scrolled through her contacts, and sent a text:

ROOM 636

Gunter Hotel, San Antonio. Room 636. Key in the potted plant outside the door. I'll be waiting!

As an afterthought, I added the winky emoji, then laughed. The Troy I knew would race to the hotel, hard-on raging.

Dropping the phone on the floor, I made sure the 'do not disturb' sign was still in place, and walked out, leaving everything behind.

Including my Kaia.

Epilogue

The St. Anthony Hotel was located just one block from the Gunter. I checked into room 636, using another assumed name.

On the balcony, gazing out at the twinkling San Antonio skyline, I withdrew a gun from my coat pocket, placed it in my mouth, and pulled the trigger.

Author's Note: This past winter, while attending the Ghoulish Book Festival in San Antonio, I went on a ghost tour of the city. By far, the best story I heard that night involved the Gunter Hotel—which now sits vacant—Walter Emerick, a mysterious blonde, and a grisly, unsolved murder.

"Room 636" is based on that true story.

Once an operating room registered nurse, **Bridgett Nelson** *so enjoyed playing with human organs, she decided to turn her macabre interest into a horror writing career. She loves bubble baths (because nothing says spooooky writer like orange-scented bubbles), hates not knowing what's swimming in the water with her, lives for Halloween season (but loathes chainsaw-wielding dudes in haunted houses), adores her West Virginia University Mountaineers, is very pro-Oxford comma, and thinks bananas are absolutely disgusting. Her first collection,* A Bouquet of Viscera, *is a two-time Splatterpunk Award winner, recognized both for the collection itself and its standout story, "Jinx." She is also the author of* Poisoned Pink, What the Fuck Was That?, Sweet, Sour, & Spicy, *and her first novella,* Red Inside, *is now available! Her work has appeared in many anthologies, including the iconic* Deathrealm Spirits, Hotel Macabre Volume 1: Tales of Horror, Edward Lee's Erotic Horror for

BRIDGETT NELSON

Horny Housewives, The Rack, To Hell and Back, Evil Little Fucks, Y'all Ain't Right, Splatterpunk's Basement of Horror, Dark Disasters, October Screams, American Cannibal, *and* A Woman Unbecoming. *Bridgett is working on her first original novel, a brand new collection, a collaboration with a very funny writer, and has been contracted by Encyclopocalypse Publications to write a novelization of the cult classic film Deadgirl. When Edward Lee read her story "Giggly," available in Poison Pink, he said to her: "Giggly kicked my ass. Outstanding job! I need therapy now."* She is mom to Parker and Autumn, a 2022 Michael Knost WINGS award nominee, and she also won second-place in the '22 Gross-Out contest at KillerCon in Austin, Texas, and third-place in the '23 Gross-Out contest. Bridgett currently lives in Duluth, Minnesota, with Bram Stoker Award-winning author, Jeff Strand, and their ball python, Indie Hellspawn McFangy Serenity Strand.

SUMMER PEOPLE

Tom Deady

I WALK THE deserted streets of Sandy Cove, enjoying the silent solitude. The town is waking up from its sleepy winter slumber, the shops and beaches crowded on the weekends. Not all the summer people have arrived, but the off-season is pretty much over. It's the third week of June, just a few days shy of the summer solstice. By the time July Fourth rolls around, these same streets will *never* be deserted, even at the no-hour of 3 AM. I sigh, at once dreading the crowds but also relieved at how much easier they make things.

I push thoughts of drunken teenagers, wine-drinking Karens, and rich BMW drivers away for the moment as I turn up Spyglass Hill. I've lived in Sandy Cove for a long, long time. My entire life. I could probably take my nightly walk with my eyes closed. After all these years, though, the sights never cease to bring me joy. Nor do the memories. So many memories.

I pause at the Williams place trying to recall what year it was that Katie died. I think it was '80 but I can't be sure. Suicide is always a tragedy, but she'd been so young. So happy. Her parents put the house up for sale and moved away the day after the funeral. The image of Katie hanging from the garage rafters would never leave them, I suspect. I continue on, cresting the hill to the great relief of my tired knees.

I reach the sea wall at the bottom of the hill just as the waning crescent moon rises above the ocean, casting an eerie silver-blue glow on the boats bobbing in the harbor. Last year, one of the summer people—he had an Irish name . . . O'Bannon or Malone, maybe—made the ill-advised decision to take his boat to Castle Island after a night of drinking. He was unfamiliar with the tricky tides around the island. And the fog, of course. The boat was reduced to splinters and the driver washed up a few days later, at least what was left of him. The sea critters make quick work of tender human flesh in these waters. Sometimes, there's nothing left at all save for the memories.

That was the case with little Lucy Ashcroft. It was during a heatwave back in '74. Lucy was only seven, but a strong swimmer according to her parents. She was at the water's edge playing chicken with the tide. She'd run away giggling when a whitecap crashed to shore, then chased the receding wave back to the ocean. The sea was calm, but a rogue wave caught her, breaking over Lucy's head and knocking her flat, then pulling her back out to the deep water. Her little game was over.

Dozens of people saw it happen and rushed into the water, but Lucy was never seen again. They say there was a riptide that day. Rare, but not impossible even in relatively tranquil water. Lucy's mother, Sarah, shot her husband in their rented cottage on Heron Run later that week, then turned the gun on herself. Sarah had made quite a scene on the beach that day, berating her husband for not watching Lucy closely. He'd dozed off for just a few minutes, and that was long enough.

I follow the sea wall for a few blocks, cutting up Weeping Willow Lane toward what passed for downtown Sandy Cove. Up ahead, the streetlight flashes yellow at the intersection of Main Street. The Snapdragon Tavern, the most popular bar in town, occupies the corner spot, its rooftop deck lit only by a handful of security lights. In a couple weeks when the 'Dragon is in full swing, that deck will sway under the weight of dancing tourists, festooned with multi-colored lights. Speakers will crank out a cringeworthy mix of the summer's hottest new tracks and moldy oldies.

In the summer just before 9/11, a man named Simms threw the mayor's son, Stu Wayne, off that deck, allegedly over a woman. Stu had died instantly, neck broken and brains spilling out on the sidewalk. Simms swore he'd never spoken to Wayne but there were witnesses. I was one, of course. Now, there's a higher safety railing surrounding the deck.

I reach my house and pause on the small front porch. The moon is high now, a few lazy clouds sailing by, painting the street

SUMMER PEOPLE

with odd shadows. A light breeze carries the soothing sound of the surf along with the pleasant scent of cool, salty air. I breathe deeply, savoring the moment.

My hand itches and I absently rub it, the scar from the rope burn still acts up after all these years. Katie had been heavier than she looked. Malone, that was the Irishman's name, I'm sure of it. There were rumors that he hadn't been alone when his boat left the harbor but his was the only body found. I'm a much stronger swimmer than Lucy Ashcroft was.

I think of Lucy's dad, how inconsolable he'd been, burdened with the guilt of letting his own child slip away. I'd come close to admitting I slipped Valium in his drink but what good would that have done? Sarah had done us both a favor.

I slap my palm on the sturdy deck of my house. The house that Mayor Wayne had tried to take from me to turn into a home for the Sandy Cove Historical Society. I know more of this town's history than those old crones. I guess poor Stu did die over a woman after all. Mayor Wayne had always looked at me funny after that night. But I'm used to the looks. Mayor Wayne finished drinking himself to death a few years back, but I'm still here.

Sheriff Wallace has been asking a lot of questions lately. He, too, gives me those looks. He likes to fish off the rocks by Baxter Point early in the morning. Those rocks get pretty slippery, and the waves come in hard there.

Yes, the summer people do disturb the tranquility I so enjoy. But they are necessary. They serve a purpose. They're a hindrance but also a convenience. Like I said, I've lived in Sandy Cove for a long, *long* time.

Tom Deady's *first novel,* Haven, *won the 2016 Bram Stoker Award for Superior Achievement in a First Novel. He has since published several novels, novellas, a short story collection, and the first book in his middle-grade horror series. He has a Master's Degree in English and Creative Writing and is a member of both the Horror Writers Association and the New England Horror Writers Association.*

WENDIGO HUNTER

Colleen Anderson

Algonquian

Long the nights
longer the hunt
starving to end
this vengeful vigil
ice fangs and smothering snow
my breath's spirit
wisping away

It hides so well
in night's dark skull
when it tore the flesh
from my children's bones
limbs cracked and marrow sucked
a trail of blood
frozen drops telling all

With nothing to hold
me to the earth
it gnaws and tears
destroys my loves
renders me numb
with a chilled heart
daring to go as far as I must

WEDNDIGO HUNTER

Untethered I shift
from man to trapper
trapped in the woods
with winter's howl dogging my heels
I trudge deeper, away from light
seeking the monster
that devoured my life

Weeks spent blown about
through blizzard days
and withering frost
away from the living
my supplies run low
hunger chews but my purpose holds
freezing, I follow footprints north

I dream of meat turning on a spit
its sizzling scent draws me close
and saliva drips, chilling my chin
I awake from pain to searing truth
sucking the marrow
from tiny bones

My children's skulls
watch from the cold

Colleen Anderson is multiple nominated and award-winning author with works widely published in seven countries in such venues as Weird Tales, Cemetery Dance, *and the award-winning* Shadow Atlas. *Her Rhysling winning poem "Machine (r)Evolution" is in Tenebrous Press's Brave New Weird, and she has won SFPA's dwarf poetry contest for two years. Colleen lives in Vancouver, BC, and her poetry collections* The Lore of Inscrutable Dreams, I Dreamed a World, *and recently launched* Weird Worlds, *plus fiction collections* A Body of Work *and* Embers Amongst the Fallen *are available online.*

CHAIN SMOKING AT BUS STOPS

Devin M. Anderson

GARRY LIT A CIGARETTE.
The man standing next to Garry wrinkled his nose and gave him a sideways glance.

Garry lit another cigarette. Now holding two in one hand, he took a slow drag from the cancerous twins. The smoke executed a surgical strike deep within the nasal passage of the stranger, engorging his ire. This was war.

The stranger's hand ascended like lightning to his mouth. Yet Gary could have sworn it was in slow motion. It shook visibly, that pale hand. Nearly vibrating with the telltale sign of incipient alcoholism. Withdrawal tremors masquerading as adrenaline shakes. Or perhaps it was something even more insidious.

Garry lit two cigarettes and added them to the party. The four coffin nails dangled from his moistened lips, taunting the stranger.

Spider-like, the stranger's hand crawled until it reached the razor-burned jowls, then back up to his rather mundane face. The face attached itself to the head, that in turn attached itself to the neck, that attached to the body, to the arm, to that quaking fucking hand, that attached to five dainty little digits. Fat digits. Like a big man baby.

The baby digits cupped the mouth, and so began the great spiral of hand to mouth to hand again. Forever into infinity. One could become lost in that spiral. One could go mad.

Then came the cough. That annoyingly rude 'I don't really need to cough but I'm going to anyway, because you obviously must not be in on the ubiquitous little factoid that smoking is bad, are you?

CHAIN SMOKING AT BUS STOPS

Are you? Huh? Well, are you??' kind of cough. You know the one. That judgmental ex-smoker cough.

Garry lit up three more cigarettes. Now seven little cherries burned brightly from between long piano fingers. Bluish smoke hung in the air between the two men, thick enough to cut with a knife. Thick like marmalade.

The stranger turned his frowning, pinkish face to stare directly at Garry. Garry and his seven repugnant cigarettes.

Garry lit up another five cigarettes. Now he had to use both hands to smoke them all, like some kind of burning pan flute out of a meth-induced fever dream.

The stranger quirked a caterpillar eyebrow at Garry. He was flabbergasted. Flabbergasted!

Garry watched the stranger take a picture and post it to Instagram without even looking at his iPhone. It was an action of habit. A rote gesture.

Garry zealously supported artistic expression, so he struck an interpretive pose just in time for the flash. The stranger didn't seem to notice, too busy aggressively hash-tagging his disapproval all over the interweb.

Garry lit up another eight cigarettes. His manly fists looked like birthday cakes made of meat and knuckles.

Understanding dawned on the stranger's face. Epiphany made flesh.

"Are you . . . " The stranger hesitated.

"Are you smoking the Fibonacci sequence?" he asked.

Garry turned once more to the stranger and their eyes met. Tears of joy shimmered in the stranger's eyes. Tears of love.

The stranger reached slowly into his trendy 90's messenger bag and pulled a worn copy of the latest Fibonacci Quarterly, a mathematical journal of some prestige. The stranger's face stared back at Garry from the cover art.

The resemblance was uncanny. It was too good to be true. It was the ghost of the great Leonardo of Pisa Fibonacci!

Before either of them had a chance to consider the repercussions to the space-time continuum, they were wrapped tightly in each other's arms. Cigarettes tumbled to the ground beneath their feet like smoldering confetti. It was an embrace written in the spiraling cosmos above and below.

All at once, they began to blur together as one spiraling swatch

DEVIN M. ANDERSON

of pure carbon, oxygen, hydrogen, and nitrogen. Energy in its purest, most effulgent expression. Now perfected in the insanity of the cosmos.

Garry dreamt of spirals as he ceased to be, and became again. Into forever.

Devin M. Anderson *is a writer, poet, and stay at home dad to two beautifully brilliant autistic kiddos. A mental health advocate, he himself battles with Borderline Personality Disorder, and PTSD. Balancing between psychosis, and depression; he writes to combat the voices in his head. His work has previously been featured by* Three Minute Plastic. *To find more by Devin check out his author page at* https://devmanderson.wordpress.com

THE BIRDCAGE

Michael Lawrence

11/16/94

THE GLARE OF the flames lights up the night sky, staining it red and transforming the rain into fat, semi-frozen drops of blood.
    Jarrod watches his father rush toward the house, watches his mother hold his father back, watches the two of them collapse on the front lawn clinging to each other. Janet is standing beside Jarrod, tears streaming down her horror-stricken face. She is screaming "Elea! Elea!" over and over.
    Jarrod sinks to his knees and stares through the red, bloody rain as the second floor of their house collapses in a deadly nightshade bloom of drifting embers and shooting sparks.

11/17/94

Sifting through the ashes, Jarrod is first to find Elea.
    The family dog—a German Shepard with a perpetual grin—is barely recognizable, a blackened skeleton twisted by heat and fire. Jarrod chokes on a sob. Janet, standing nearby and examining a melted glob with a row of buttons, drops the remains of the portable phone and comes running.
    Elea lies curled up in front of the contorted, jagged remains of the birdcage. The two parakeets within are little more than lumps of ashy charcoal.
    After his initial sob, Jarrod is silent. Tears fall from distant, inward-peering eyes.

Did Elea die in front of the birdcage because she wanted to protect the parakeets? Or was she looking for comfort in the face of imminent death?

11/20/94

Wearing donated clothes doesn't feel right. They don't fit right; they don't have the same familiar smell or feel against the skin. Jarrod can sense someone else's memories and experiences woven into the fibers of the red Harvard sweater. They crawl across his skin with curious, questing fingers.

11/24/94

The shelter is a big brick building with bars on the windows of the first two floors. Ms. Dumfries serves a small, modest Thanksgiving dinner for the residents with nowhere else to go.

Sitting across from Janet is a man with a giant, cauliflowered mass of warts and misshapen cartilage in place of a nose. A woman across from Jarrod is missing her right eye. Every few minutes the woman lifts the patch covering the eye and rubs at the raw-edged hole beneath. After each rub, she wipes stringy, blood-flecked mucus onto a napkin.

Afterward, they sit and watch *A Charlie Brown Thanksgiving* on the television in the community room. In the past, someone must have placed a magnet too close to the TV set, because now the right corner of the picture is oddly discolored. In some shots, the Peanuts find themselves under a patch of blue sky stained red.

It looks to Jarrod like the sky above his burning home.

12/07/94

Police find Mom's car in the parking lot of The Corner Pharmacy with the keys locked inside, tucked up underneath the visor.

Two cops—one of them has a tattoo of a dragon on his forearm—come to the shelter and ask Dad, Janet, and Jarrod dozens of questions. Janet mostly just cries. Dad says Mom must have run away. She'd talked about leaving before; with them staying in the shelter, it must have all been too much for her.

THE BIRDCAGE

Jarrod says nothing.

12/12/94

Jarrod ghosts through the school hallways, his mind a blank fog of shock. Janet drifts as well, her eyes ever more hollowed and black-ringed.

At the shelter, Dad drinks, hiding in the bathroom so Ms. Dumfries doesn't catch him and kick them out.

That night, they watch *How the Grinch Stole Christmas* on the discolored tube TV.

Jarrod finds the story unrelatable. The Whos of Whoville have a tight community; even with everything taken from them, they sing and find comfort in each other. And the Grinch, seeing this, gives back the presents and their stolen feast, and the Whos reward the Grinch and let him carve the roast beast.

Fire doesn't do that.

What fire takes, it keeps. It leaves behind plenty of ashy crumbs, but not a single answer.

Was Elea seeking comfort *from* the birds? Or trying to *give* comfort *to* them?

Fire doesn't care to answer. Fire doesn't see Jarrod's grief and change its mind. Fire's heart is—and will always be—three sizes too small.

12/19/94

Ms. Dumfries pulls into the driveway with a large pine tied to the top of her car. All the residents, including the silent Jarrod and hollow-eyed Janet, assist in pulling the tree off her car and hauling it to the community room where, as a group, they decorate it.

When they finish, Ms. Dumfries turns off the lights and plugs in the tree.

Everyone but Jarrod bursts into cheers and applause.

The lights are all red, and the glow spreads like a bloody stain across the wall behind the tree. In the pattern made by the shadows thrown by the tree branches, Jarrod can see the chaotic twists of melted birdcage wire.

He doesn't hear clapping. He hears the snapping crackle of fire.

Jarrod throws his hands over his ears and screams.

MICHAEL LAWRENCE

12/24/94

The two cops come back, asking more questions. Some of them are a little scary: "Would anyone have any reason to hurt Mommy?" "Did Mommy and Daddy ever have bad arguments?" "Did you ever see Daddy hitting Mommy?"

Janet comes to the door while Jarrod is brushing his teeth before bed. "They found blood in the car. That's what Ms. Dumfries says. I heard her telling Mr. Crawford. That's why the cops came back. They told Ms. Dumfries it looks like someone tried to clean it up. They think someone hurt her. Or worse."

Janet stares at him for a minute, tears streaming down her face. "They think Dad did it."

Jarrod turns back to the sink and rinses his toothbrush.

12/25/94

A bad dream wakes Jarrod in the early hours of the morning.

He goes downstairs to the lockers and finds Dad's. He opens the locker and searches through his father's few belongings. Pushing a jacket aside, he finds the seam in the back wall. He pokes at the seam, and a small door pops open. Jarrod reaches into the revealed compartment and pulls out a long-handled fire axe.

The wood where the handle and axe head join is stained red.

In the community room, Jarrod plugs in the Christmas tree, and the melted birdcage jumps into view on the blood-colored wall. He stares at the shadows for a minute, then pulls a zippo from the waistband of his underwear. He flips open the lighter and lights the lowest hanging tree branches on fire.

When the tree is a burning red candle, Jarrod throws the couch cushions onto the blaze.

Ms. Dumfries comes to investigate the noise, bleary-eyed and confused. Jarrod hits her in the stomach with the axe as hard as he can. When he pulls the axe back, ribbons of intestine entwine the axe head, fat and bloated like shiny, red sausage links. Ms. Dumfries's eyes roll back in her head, and she falls to the floor. Her stomach leaks blood and other stuff, stuff that is red and purple and yellow.

Despite the hour, Ms. Dumfries still wears her work pants.

THE BIRDCAGE

When Jarrod checks her pockets, he finds her keys. He uses them to lock the front and back doors, then throws the keyring on the fire, the tongues of which now lick the walls hungrily. The fire alarm finally starts to shriek in panic.
    Gripping the axe, Jarrod sits in front of the burning tree and waits for the others.
        Will they bring comfort? Or seek to take it?
        Why did Elea die in front of the birdcage?

Michael Lawrence *lives in Maine with his wife and daughter, where he writes stories, novellas, screenplays, and whatever other project makes itself known to him. When he is not writing, he is thinking about writing.* Hotel Macabre *marks his first time in print, but certainly won't be his last. He can be reached for inquiry or discussion at* author.michaellawrence2@gmail.com

THE EMPATH

A PLAY IN ONE ACT

John Palisano

CAST OF CHARACTERS

JUDITH JOY: An agreeable woman, on the conservative side, approaching middle age.

VIRGINIA EVANS: Within striking distance of 30 and still wearing the same jeans and blouse as ever.

<u>Scene</u>
A hotel in San Antonio.

<u>Time</u>
The present.

<u>ACT 1</u>
<u>Scene 1</u>

SETTING: We are in JUDITH JOY's spare hotel room. The bed is still made.

THE EMPATH

> There is a chair in the center. A Lamp shines from a desk.
>
> She is welcoming VIRGINIA EVANS.
>
> Their body language is that of those who are about to duel.

VIRGINIA
Can you tell me what makes you an empath?

JUDITH
Usually I'm the one asking most of the questions.

VIRGINIA
I just want to be sure. This is . . . different. It would make me more comfortable if I knew more about you.

> JUDITH puts her hands out in a gesture of warmth and openness.

JUDITH
Of course. I work as an assistant at the San Antonio Library. You know that because that's where we met.

VIRGINIA
You didn't always want to be an assistant.

JUDITH
No. I wanted to be a doctor. But these . . .

> JUDITH raises her hands. Regards them.

JUDITH
. . . these got in the way. I have to reserve them for very special times.

VIRGINIA
Is this a very special time?

JUDITH
Why, yes. It is and you are. I can sense it.

VIRGINIA
How is that? Why is that?

Walking past Virginia, JUDITH makes her way to the windows and draws the curtains.

JUDITH
I almost drowned as a little girl. We were on the Cape. Hyannis. A bad storm was coming so we couldn't swim in the ocean and were in the pool, instead. The rain started and I went underwater. I couldn't swim up. My aunt Chris dove in and pulled me out. When I was on my back looking up at the angry grey sky, raindrops tickling my face, she took my hand in hers. That's when I first felt it.

JUDITH takes two steps toward a chair. Runs a hand along its back.

JUDITH
Something was wrong with my aunt. Dark as pitch. I felt it travel inside me. I felt it like little bombs inside me. Cold on the outside. Warm on the inside. It was going to destroy her bit by bit.

THE EMPATH

VIRGINIA
Did you tell her? Tell your parents? Or did you keep it to yourself?

JUDITH
I told her right away. She knew. Said she had lung cancer. Never smoked. Never did drugs. She was young. 45.

JUDITH wipes away tears.
VIRGINIA approaches.

VIRGINIA
I woke memories of losing her. I didn't mean to.

JUDITH
That's the crazy part, though. I didn't lose her. She did so much better. No one knew how. She wasn't supposed to. But I knew. It was me.

VIRGINIA is close and JUDITH grabs her hand.

VIRGINIA
That seems impossible.

JUDITH
It made me sick. I took it on. It felt like it'd overtake me.

VIRGINIA
It didn't.

JUDITH
No. It didn't stick. I was a vessel it passed through.

VIRGINIA
Where'd it go?

JUDITH
To the great void where awful things go, I imagine.

VIRGINIA
It was gone? For good?

> VIRGINIA circles JUDITH. Turning to face her, JUDITH folds her hands in front of her.

JUDITH
Cast out of her. Cast out of me.

VIRGINIA
You ate her cancer and vomited it out.

> JUDITH can't help but look surprised.

JUDITH
That's one way of putting it.

> JUDITH gestures toward the chair.

JUDITH
Why don't you have a seat?

> VIRGINIA pauses . . . regards JUDITH'S ask for a moment. Accepts.

VIRGINIA
Of course. That's why we're here.

> VIRGINIA sits.

THE EMPATH

JUDITH
Your turn to tell me about your history and your stomach problems.

VIRGINIA
I can't eat anything without feeling sick. Everything tastes like metal. Nothing has flavor. Just texture. Food is so disgusting. I can only eat simple things like Cheerios or macaroni and cheese. Everything else makes me want to throw up.

JUDITH steps away from the chair and stands where Virginia can see her.

JUDITH
What do you think is causing this? I'm sure you've seen a doctor.

VIRGINIA
Several specialists, actually. One thought it was IBS. Another told me it's a gluten allergy. The worst told me it was a female thing . . . hysteria! A young, handsome man. Can you believe people still believe such awful things?

JUDITH
Nothing surprises me anymore.

VIRGINIA
Maybe things should surprise you. Long story short, none of them were right. I tried medicines. Changing my diet. Tried toughing it out, just to prove to that last man he was as wrong as pineapple on pizza. But nothing worked.

VIRGINIA looks right at JUDITH.

VIRGINIA
I'm desperate. I can't live with this anymore. It's affecting every part of me twenty-four hours a day.

JUDITH
I understand and I'm sorry.

VIRGINIA
So, how does this work? What do we do?

JUDITH steps closer.
Raises a hand.

JUDITH
There needs to be contact. Not for long. Just long enough.

VIRGINIA
And you can just take it away . . . just like that?

JUDITH
When it works and the connection is there, yes. That's how.

VIRGINIA
How long until I feel better?

JUDITH
A few moments. Pain lifts quickly, I'm told. It can take time for the echoes of what you're feeling to dissipate.

VIRGINIA
Like aftershocks.

JUDITH
Exactly.

THE EMPATH

VIRGINIA
What happens to you?

JUDITH
I wait here until it works through me. Then I go back to my normal life.

VIRGINIA
No one helps? You're alone? Does anyone know what you're doing?

JUDITH
Nope. I keep this on the down low. Most people I've told think I'm crazy.

VIRGINIA
What if something bad happens to you? Won't someone miss you?

JUDITH
My cats would. It's been hard getting close to anyone.

JUDITH holds up her hands again.

JUDITH
These always get in the way, whether the other person knows it or not.

VIRGINIA
That's tragic.

JUDITH
I don't know. It's kept my life simple.

VIRGINIA
Simple. I like that.

                    JUDITH
Me, too.

                    VIRGINIA
What about paying for the hotel room? Let me at least cover that.

                    JUDITH
It's all in kind. My way of giving.

                    VIRGINIA
You're sure?

                    JUDITH
Absolutely.

          VIRGINIA gestures toward the
          bed.

                    VIRGINIA
Should I lay down?

                    JUDITH
You don't have to.

          VIRGINIA shrugs.

                    VIRGINIA
Here is fine.

          JUDITH places her hands on
          VIRGINIA'S shoulders. They
          both shut their eyes.

                    JUDITH
Tell me where it hurts.

          VIRGINIA eases back.

THE EMPATH

                    VIRGINIA
Bottom of my stomach area.

              JUDITH tilts her head back.

              A moment passes.

              VIRGINIA opens her eyes.

                    VIRGINIA
Anything?

                    JUDITH
Your pulse . . . there's a counter rhythm.

                    VIRGINIA
What does that mean?

                    JUDITH
Maybe something with your heart like tachycardia.

                    VIRGINIA
Could that be what's wrong?

                    JUDITH
Possible. Do you mind showing me exactly where it hurts?

                    VIRGINIA
Sure.

              Putting her hand to the bottom
              of her blouse, VIRGINIA
              hesitates. Have things gone in
              a direction that is too
              intimate? Can she trust
              Judith?

              She places a hand on her abdomen.

57

                    VIRGINIA
Here. This is the worst part.

                    JUDITH
All right. Do you mind if I put my hand there?

                    VIRGINIA
Sure.

          Lifting a hand off VIRGINIA's
          shoulder, JUDITH carefully
          lowers it to her abdomen and
          places it.

                    JUDITH
There we go.

          JUDITH lets out a breath,
          steeling herself. Shuts her
          eyes.

          VIRGINIA looks down at
          JUDITH's hand.

                    VIRGINIA
I hope this works.

                    JUDITH
It should.

          Another moment passes.

          Then another.

          JUDITH doesn't seem to move.

          VIRGINIA looks like she's
          going to melt.

THE EMPATH

                VIRGINIA
Judith?

           VIRGINIA goes woozy.

                JUDITH
Virginia . . .

           VIRGINIA puts up her hands, tries steadying herself.

                VIRGINIA
Judith . . .

                JUDITH
It's taking.

                VIRGINIA
I don't feel so good.

           JUDITH lifts her hand, staggers back.

                JUDITH
It worked.

           VIRGINIA slinks off the chair and curls up on the floor.

           JUDITH steps toward the bed and sits. Puts a hand to her head.

                JUDITH
I can feel it inside me. It's very cold. And very hot, too.

                VIRGINIA
My stomach is sore but not like before. Now I'm starving.

VIRGINIA rises up to sitting.

JUDITH
I feel full.

VIRGINIA
It worked.

JUDITH crawls up onto the bed.

JUDITH
It's in me.

VIRGINIA rises. Puts her hands on her stomach. Her chest. Her head. On her stomach again.

VIRGINIA
I don't believe it.

JUDITH
You never told me about yourself.

Judith sounds ill.

JUDITH
When did this begin?

VIRGINIA
Little less than a year ago. That strange feeling is gone. I can think clearer than I have in a long time.

JUDITH reclines, hands crossed on her middle, eyes closed.

JUDITH
Tell me.

THE EMPATH

VIRGINIA
I fell in love. Fast. It wasn't reciprocated. He used me. It crushed me. Maybe it was all in my mind. Psychosomatic. They say when you're brokenhearted that you can really make yourself sick. Amazing, the power of the mind.

JUDITH
True.

VIRGINIA
I couldn't stop thinking about him. He was this close in my head all the time. Now, though? The grief has lifted. I'm so hungry. I should get a pizza. Maybe a cheeseburger. Tacos?

JUDITH puts up a hand.

JUDITH
Stop. I can't hear it. I feel nauseous.

VIRGINIA
Oh. Right. Sorry.

She eyes Judith.

VIRGINIA
So, now what? Do I just leave you here? This took no time at all.

JUDITH
It's always been fast. Just a blink. You can go.

JUDITH turns and moans.

JUDITH
Working through me will take time. I'd rather not have company for that, no offense.

VIRGINIA
None taken. Understood.

> She pauses.

VIRGINIA
Well, thank you for giving me back my body and my freedom.

JUDITH
Of course.

VIRGINIA
There is something I brought for you, in case you wouldn't accept money. A small token. A crystal that catches unwanted things.

> She withdraws a small bag from her side pocket. She places it on the edge of the bed.

VIRGINIA
I'll leave this with you, Judith.

> JUDITH doesn't reply. She's blacked out.
>
> VIRGINIA stares. Waves a hand in front of her face to see if she responds. She doesn't.
>
> Her steps light, VIRGINIA makes her way out.

VIRGINIA
I think I'll have a big breakfast. Eggs. Bacon. Toast. Orange juice. Coffee. Lots and lots of coffee.

> She hums as she saunters out.

THE EMPATH

The door shuts.
LIGHT dims. Night falls.

JUDITH slumbers.

The BAG on the bed glows an otherworldly purple.

GLOWS until it is blinding.

After a moment, it dies down.

THREE HOODED FIGURES stand over the bed. We cannot see their faces, but we hear a sound like crackling burning wood.

          FIGURE
We are here to collect what is ours.

JUDITH wakes hearing the voice.

          FIGURE
What is ours and ours alone will be taken from this vessel.

          JUDITH
No. No. No. What's happening?

The FIGURES reach out and place their hands on her stomach.

JUDITH cannot move.

JOHN PALISANO

                    FIGURES
    Let it be brought forth in our hands.

              The room goes black.

              We hear a CRY like that of a
              newborn, only it is not just
              that of a human, but of
              something other . . . something
              dark and evil has come forth.

              JUDITH screams her last.

                             CURTAIN.

John Palisano's writing has won the Bram Stoker Award®, the Yog Soggoth Award, and he has been published and appeared in such notable venues as Vanity Fair, The Log Angeles Times, Blumhouse Online, Cemetery Dance, Fangoria, and more. His screenplays have won acclaim as finalists in Shriekfest, Project Greenlight, Latent Image, and more. His professional career started with an internship and work with Ridley Scott & Associates, then with director Marcus Nispel, Tony Bon Jovi, and more. www.johnpalisano.com

DO NOT TEMPT HER WITH APPLES

Diana Olney

Night falls
like a guillotine:
that sharp, singing blade,
heavy with need,
with want;
heaven-sent, hell-bent,
and dark as a hollow
heart,
every sinking beat
a dying star
doomed to asphyxiate
all that it loves.

In shadow, she lies,
not a woman, not a girl.
Just a silhouette
of the desperate, shrunken
shapes to come;
a lunar phase
caught in the corseted web
spun between dusk and dawn.

She does not love
anymore.

DIANA OLNEY

Most nights, she starves,
wilts, waits;
flesh coiled fetal and crescent
while the insatiable city
eats itself alive.
But not
this time.

For once, in so many moons
the waxing state
is more than equal
to the sum of its parts;
a Fibonacci sequence written in blood.
In twilight's wake, rows of red and white soldiers
multiply, divide and conquer,
deep in the trenches of civil war.

As the battle rages,
through muscle, vein, and sinew,
she dreams
only of the spoils.

Yet when victory comes,
there is no reprieve, no fanfare,
only the struggle
for domination,
coursing electric
through restless anatomy.

It is not
a pleasant way to wake up.

Pain consumes,
blinds,
deafens.
An aria
silver and gilded with agony,
wailing in every chamber
of this crumbling temple
she calls home.

DO NOT TEMPT HER WITH APPLES

But it is only temporary,
the sting of each open sore
a rite of passage on the path to growth.

Through it all, she never forgets:
whether by chaos or design
change does not come cheap—
it comes with violence,
with knives, with fury,
eviscerating the line between vice and virtue,
saint and sinner,
wretched and holy.
And at the end of the road,
this
is what's left over.

She is not
a monster,
a mistake,
an aberration.
Diamond skin, lizard brain,
serrated, Glasgow grin—
these are merely accoutrements.
She bares the teeth
of demons,
but they do not
belong to her.

Not the way
the hunger does.

It is her birthright:
bloodborne, marrow-deep.
But it is older than flesh,
older
than bone.
An appetite of ancients
plucked from Paradise
by a greased palm
and a silver tongue.

One bite
was all it took
to bring the lust for eternal youth
crashing in abject hysteria
down to Earth,
falling like Autumn
from Eve's withered limbs
into the ripe, budding ribs
that held the hearts of her daughters.

That's how the story went,
once upon a time—
a time when the faithful
still believed in blasphemy.
But these days, the doctrine of men
has no room for heroines.
Especially one who was born
motherless.

Living
with this gift is not easy.
But she keeps it
close to the chest,
so close that sometimes,
in the long, empty hours
between midnight and morning
she can hear it:
a ragged arrhythmia,
strident and saw-toothed,
biting, scratching,
chewing and gnawing
on the soft, fatty tissue
stretched between heartbeats.

But she has nothing
to fear;
a hungry heart may bend,
and crack,
and bleed,
but it will never break—

DO NOT TEMPT HER WITH APPLES

as long as it is fed.

Do not tempt her with apples,
or any such unoriginal
sin.
This city
has so much more to offer,
and tonight
is all-you-can-eat.

Diana Olney *is a Seattle based author, but she is most at home in the shadows, exploring the dark paths between dreams and nightmares. Her stories and poems have appeared in publications by Small Wonders Magazine, Crystal Lake Publishing, Worldstone Publishing, Critical Blast, and more. She is also a columnist at Memento Mori Ink Magazine, as well as the creator of Siren's Song, an original comic series that will debut this winter. Her influences include Gwendolyn Kiste, Cassandra Khaw, Richard Kadrey, Jack Skillingstead, and her furry assistants, black cats Dolce and Gabbana. Visit her website dianaolney.com or her Instagram @dianaolneyauthor for updates on her latest tales.*

THE LINGERING TASTE OF YOUR LAST SUPPER

Matthew R. Davis

YOU OPEN YOUR eyes and nothing changes. All is as pitch black as the back of your eyelids. It takes a few seconds to realise there's no sheet draped over you, and the surface beneath is too harsh and ungiving to be a mattress.

You are not in your bed.

This wrongness shocks you out of your sluggish sleep, and you sit up. You barely rise six inches before your forehead thumps against something hard and sends you crashing back into your prone position. Shocked, you reach up and find the ceiling so close that your elbows scarcely leave the floor.

Are you beneath your bed, then? It wouldn't be the first time you've sought safety there. But when you stretch your arms out, you discover the walls scant inches away. You're so closely confined on all sides you can barely move, and it's full dark.

Terror snake-strikes as you understand what this means. She's finally done it. After all her threats, Ma has made good on her promise.

You're in the Box.

You lie still, struggling not to panic. Your mouth is cotton-dry, haunted by the lingering taste of your last supper. The one you spent withering beneath Ma's furious gaze.

I warned you, wretched child! Rebellion must be punished.

Your palms slap against the lid of the Box. The casket she keeps in the shed alongside the firepit out back of the house, where—you'd dimly noticed as Ma tore into you with words like jagged ice—the dirt had been dug up in an oblong hole roughly the size of a–

THE LINGERING TASTE OF YOUR LAST SUPPER

You're grounded.
You scream, knowing it won't help. The earth is packed four feet deep above you. No-one will hear a sound, even if anyone ever came out to Ma's property this far from town.
You can't waste a single lungful of air. You're lucky not to have used it up as you slept—a slumber too deep to be natural. No wonder Ma insisted you finish your supper, miserable as your appetite was with her fury filling your stomach with dread instead. You'd thought the metallic undertaste was your own anxiety.
How could she *do* this? She's always so angry, no matter what you do or don't, like you're to blame for all that's bad in her life. Your cries mean nothing to her. Soon, they will be stifled forever.
Wait! What's this poking through the lid of the Box, just to the side of your head? A pipe of some sort? You wrench your face over to peer up its length. The small round window of the pipe's mouth shows you a circle of lesser darkness at the far end.
The night sky, four feet and a million miles away.
Your breath comes fast, but that's okay. She doesn't mean for you to suffocate down here. A small mercy, one you grasp with desperate relief. But how long does Ma intend to keep you grounded? What else did she say as you forced down that sickly soup, as your head grew too heavy to hold up?
You remember, and your limbs tremble anew.
For a week.
She can't mean that! You were all set to go away and visit Uncle Randy, so any minute now that tiny circle of lesser dark will be filled by a glaring eye, by bitter lips as Ma tells you you'd better behave in future–
No. She keenly anticipates these visits, where mean Randy makes you scrub the floors while they cackle and moan in his room. She'd never miss this brief escape from her cold, loveless home.
Ma's already gone. Without you.
For a week.
You try to stay calm. It's impossible. The magnitude of this punishment is so extreme your mind can scarcely encompass it. No food! No toilet! No water, and your mouth is so *dry*–
Something chill dashes into your eye. You flinch, blink it away.
A drop of water?
You turn your ear to the pipe. You can hear the rising wind

blowing a doleful note across the other end of your breathing tube. Another drop of water falls into the waiting bucket of your ear.

A storm.

Rain! You manage to get your mouth beneath the pipe, and one, two, three drops fall upon your waiting tongue. Another small mercy.

Your relief doesn't last long. The storm is building, and the raindrops come faster and faster. Soon you've drunk your fill, and you crane your aching neck away. Still the rain dribbles in.

The pipe is narrow, you tell yourself. Barely any water will find its way down here. But you can hear trees thrashing as the storm escalates, can hear the hastening rhythm of raindrops pattering onto the bottom of the Box beside your ear, hear the discordant creaking of the house's gutters beneath the wind's buffeting blows—

Oh.

Oh, *no*.

The gutters are almost rusted through. Ma's been meaning to replace them for as long as you can remember. The gutter over the firepit, in particular, is so decrepit that it might give way any day now, creating a dangling chute that would channel the rain down upon the ground below—right where the pipe waits like a greedy straw.

Where you lie buried in a shallow Box that's already almost filled by your small body.

The storm grows wilder, wetter. The machine-gun drips down the pipe become a steady trickle; a puddle spreads beneath your head. Ma is one week and a million miles away, and above you the frail old gutter screeches, beseeching mercy.

You gave up when it became clear no-one was listening, but you used to pray for Ma to go away and never come back. Now you pray fervently for her merciful return, desperate to drown only in her rage and her blame and her cold, cold eyes, and each kiss from the rain upon your face is one she never gave you, a million chilly kisses now come all at once and far too late.

Matthew R. Davis *is an author and musician based in Adelaide, South Australia, with over seventy short stories published around the world thus far. He's been shortlisted for a Shirley Jackson Award, the WSFA Small Press Award, and multiple Aurealis and Australian Shadows*

THE LINGERING TASTE OF YOUR LAST SUPPER

Awards, winning two Shadows for 2019—the only author other than Kaaron Warren to have done so. His books include If Only Tonight We Could Sleep *(collection, Things in the Well, 2020),* Midnight in the Chapel of Love *(novel, JournalStone, 2021),* The Dark Matter of Natasha *(novella, Grey Matter Press, 2022), and* Bites Eyes: 13 Macabre Morsels *(flash chapbook, Brain Jar Press, 2023). Find out more at matthewrdavisfiction.wordpress.com*

THE FEAR OF MISSING OUT

Dylan Wells

I WATCH MY gumdrop-shaped ginger cat drag his ass on the carpet and decide to call it quits. It's the perfect finale to this miserable night. I give Booger an assist, then eat enough of the otherwise untouched candy to give myself a stomach ache and comfort my disappointment.

I grew up spending Halloween deep in prayer, so I'm late to enjoying it free from guilt. I'm late to a lot of things. A house, a family, a career. I tell myself, "It's not too late, Cassie!" Thirty-three is boring but it's not too late. Maybe it's too late to be a trick-or-treater—I don't want the authorities called on me—but being the trick-or-treatee is just as exciting.

Except no one came.

My debate between tossing the candy because I'll just eat it, or saving it because I'll get to eat it, is interrupted by a text. It's from Meg.

"Hey girl! Going to a haunted house, please come!"

Meg is ten years younger than me but she's fun to share a cubicle with. This isn't the first time she's invited me somewhere, but I've always declined. I dread being the crone of an outing. Besides, it's already nine o'clock. I should be in my pajamas with a toothbrush in my mouth.

"What time?" I force myself to send.

"Five minutes! I'll pick you up!"

Knowing Meg, it'll be an hour, well past my usual bedtime. I look to Booger for advice. He stares at me, copper eyes unblinking, all-knowing, but silent.

THE FEAR OF MISSING OUT

It's probably expensive and I don't want to go, but I've never been to a haunted house. My younger self would have had an aneurysm at the thought. Now, I can do it. I can survive one late night. It won't move me out of my shit apartment, it won't pay my bills, but I can celebrate Halloween.

I spend the ride wishing I'd listened to myself and Booger's sudden howls for me to stay. Meg spilled a pumpkin spice latte on the passenger seat just before she arrived. I'm too old, tall, and fat to be squished in the back of her Maserati, especially with her younger brother, Matt.

Annoyance plummets into apprehension as we arrive. There are no cars, no lights, no music, no lines, nothing. It's just a house. It's about twice my age, one story, and clearly vacant with dying foliage that spreads to distant lights.

We are alone.

"Are you going to murder me?" I pretend to joke. "I thought we were going to a haunted house."

"Oh, it's haunted. The previous owner died of a heart attack while she was being kicked out," Meg says.

I'm too unnerved to respond. I have a heartburn-like feeling that if we enter, we'll never leave. And even if we do, a trespassing charge at my age would be really embarrassing. I'm suddenly aware I'm the only one here with a fully formed frontal lobe and that lobe is telling me to go home.

"I thought we were going to the other kind of haunted house," I say.

"Nope, this kind," Meg says, walking to the door. Matt, surprisingly, takes pity on me.

"Nothing's going to happen," he says. "It's not really haunted, just creepy. She'll get bored soon if you want to wait outside."

"And if the cops come?"

"Our dad owns it." He winces. "But don't think we're awful. He got it for back taxes to develop the land, barely anything, and the lady that died was almost eighty and dying anyway."

Meg yells for us to hurry. If only I'd done this stuff when I was younger, I wouldn't be subjected to the geriatric FOMO that forces my steps across the threshold.

Immediately, figures press themselves out from the walls as if trapped by wet silk. I turn the lights on and the figures are just hanging coats.

"Ugh," Meg says. "It smells like old lady and cat piss."

We're in the living room, the dining room is just beyond, the kitchen to the right, and a hallway to the left. There's a plate with a dried crust of bread and a mug on an end table. A paperback is open and face down on the arm of a chair. If it weren't for the dust, the old lady could just be in the bathroom.

Asthma tightens my already fear-tightened chest further. It does smell strongly of cat pee and mold.

"I swear, if I am alone and living like this at her age, someone better shoot me," Meg says, heading for the hallway. "No offense, Cassie."

It's a joke but I don't laugh. I find I don't like Meg as much out of the office, though I still follow her. At the end of the hallway is a hunched figure. I turn the light on and it's just an antique chair.

The walls show a life's frozen moments: a gray-haired woman on a beach at sunset. A fluffy black kitten asleep under a window. The inside of a cathedral lit by stained glass. The photographs continue. They're of herself, different cats, places overseas, but no other people. She had no one. No one to adorn her walls, no one to pack up her things. I can't help thinking this is my future.

Meg stops at a slightly open door. An ominous feeling crackles through my limbs.

"Scariest part first." She grins and pushes the door open to reveal stairs into a basement. The light from the hallway doesn't illuminate much beyond the stairs. Where light gives way to shadow, there's a pair of age-spotted legs and gnarled feet.

Hand shaking, I reach through the doorway and hit the light switch.

Nothing.

I do it again.

Nothing.

Fuck.

Still, it has to just be a trick of the light.

"One minute, alone, no light," Matt dares. "Twenty dollars you can't do it."

"Fifty I can and you can't," Meg says. They turn to me, but I've reached my limit.

"I'm not going down there," I say. This is stupid. What are they doing? What am I doing? I should be in bed, Booger curled in the

THE FEAR OF MISSING OUT

crook of my leg. I should've waited outside. I'm too scared to stay with them, too terrified to leave alone.

Fearless, Meg bounds down just as a small shadow darts up. There's an inhuman scream followed by a human yelp, and Meg falls, a blur of limbs and thumps.

"Fucking cat," Meg groans over a shuffling sound as she gets up. The gnarled feet seem to move toward her.

"Are you okay?" Matt asks.

"Yeah, my arm is-" She cuts off with a wet crunch.

Silence steals my breath.

"Meg?" Matt's voice shakes, making the name two syllables.

We are insignificant in the quiet, the stillness.

He fumbles with his phone's flashlight as he goes down the stairs. The light's movement highlights Meg in horrifying snapshots. When it steadies, the warmth drains from my body. Surrounded by darkness, she's kneeling, so motionless she looks stiff. Her neck is at a right angle and twisted so I see her vacant eyes, relaxed pupils manic in the light.

"Meg!" Matt's shout elongates into a scream as he slams into the ceiling, flung by an unseen force. He's wrenched down, his head cracking on the stairs. His phone lands on its back, smothering the flashlight. Dark blood expands beneath him.

I should help him, but I'm frozen. I need to run. I need to help him. Though, that's a lot of blood. He might already be dead. I lower one foot onto the first stair and something presses against my calf. I scream before I recognize the feeling. A ragged black cat weaves through my legs, scrawny and bulbous with matted fur. It looks up at me, green eyes wide and all-knowing. Its meow is just a whisper.

They left it here to starve. They left it to starve and they'd rather a house sit abandoned than let an old woman die in her sleep. Now, what's left of that old woman steps closer to the stairs in an unspoken ultimatum: I can join the bodies or let her keep them.

I run down the hallway and out of the house, leaving the lights on and the door open. Meg's car is in the driveway but the key is with her body. The nearest Uber is almost an hour away and costs more than I can afford. I should call the cops. I should stay to give a report. But my instincts say flee and, for once, I listen.

After my adrenaline wanes, it's just one foot in front of the other. Thirty minutes pass before I notice a ragged four-legged shadow following me. Another hour passes before it lets me touch it. By the time I can afford the ride, it's in my arms. My apartment is small but there's a sunny window and a friend named Booger. And, who knows, maybe I'll haunt it one day.

Dylan Wells *is a social worker by day and a writer by the darkest nights. She lives in Wisconsin with her feline roommate.*

DAY TRIPPER

John Meachen

RICHARD DUNCAN STOOD at the bus-stop and lifted the rucksack from his shoulders.
He placed it on the ground between his hiking boots. The sheer weight of the damn thing was beginning to play havoc with the osteoarthritis in his neck and shoulders.

Still, he wasn't in too bad a shape for a man of 73.

He sighed as he observed Margaret Taylor and Sheila Blake approach the stop. They looked him up and down with an unsavoury glance and went inside the plastic shelter to park their sagging buttocks onto the bench. In Richard's opinion they were nothing but a couple of vicious gossips who thought they were better than everyone else.

He had lived in the rural Burnsford all his life and knew he had a reputation of being a bit of a 'queerhawk,' mainly because he kept himself to himself and didn't choose to gossip about other people's business.

His mother, God rest her soul, had told him 'if you can't say anything nice, then don't say anything at all,' and throughout his life he'd always tried to live by that rule.

The irony was of course that there wasn't one of the so-called community that didn't have a metaphorical 'skeleton' in their own cupboard, including Taylor and Blake, sitting in the shelter like butter wouldn't melt in their ugly mouths.

He knew for a fact that Taylor had been caught years previously in a more than uncompromising situation with local butcher Fred Johnson behind the Co-op building.

JOHN MEACHEN

He took a deep breath and sighed, deciding not to let them ruin what was the highlight of his year.

He had attended every Senior Citizen bus trip since turning 65 and really looked forward to it for a change of scenery.

It was arranged through the library, a place where Richard felt at home. He consumed books the way other men did alcohol or wasted their time trying to find a winner at the bookmakers.

That was the thing with gamblers, they tended to shout it from the rooftops when they got a winner, but were never so forthright in declaring the losers they had backed.

Today's trip was The Lake District. If the previous ones were anything to go by, he knew once they reached their destination his fellow passengers would make a beeline toward the pubs, tearooms, and shops, like sheep not thinking about what they were doing.

This however wasn't for him; he would have a long walk in the hills, enjoy the scenery, and immerse himself in his surroundings.

He'd carefully packed his rucksack earlier that morning with all the essentials: a camera, flask of soup, banana, sandwiches, a Kagool, and a spare set of clothing in case of rain. He doubted very much if he would need them. It was a glorious morning.

The previous year's excursion had been Blackpool. He'd given serious consideration to not going. Blackpool just wasn't his idea of fun. Compared to Burnsford, it was a thriving metropolis and a hard place to find solitude, but he'd gone just the same, surprisingly finding what he'd been looking for.

No Pleasure Beach or Tower for him, he'd walked along the magnificent stretch of beach between Blackpool and Fleetwood and made the coach rendezvous pickup point with five minutes to spare.

Granted, the driver did do head counts, and would have probably given him an extra half-hour, but he hadn't wanted any sarcastic remarks from his fellow travellers for keeping them waiting.

There had been a sing-along on the return journey with everything from 'I Do Like To Be Beside The Seaside' to 'Yellow Submarine,' Richard however, hadn't joined in; they were just singing because they were drunk, and he wasn't going to lower himself to their level.

He had never been a huge fan of alcohol and couldn't

DAY TRIPPER

understand its appeal. All it did was dull the senses and make one feel ill the following morning.

Every trip he liked to bring home a souvenir, and he wondered what he would be bringing home with him that night.

That was part of the fun, the unpredictability of what may or may not happen. It was an adventure.

He lifted his rucksack as he saw the bus coming towards him.

It was a local company called Johnstone's. He had gone to school with its owner, Sinclair Johnstone, who had done really well for himself. It was rumoured he was a millionaire.

Johnstone had a fleet of coaches and mini-buses, and both him and his wife Ellen drove a top-of-the-range Mercedes.

Johnstone had been one of the few who hadn't bullied Richard all through primary and secondary school just because they sensed he was a little different. Johnstone himself had actually been the target of the bully-boys, and his nickname had eventually become 'chocolate,' as in chocolate eclair (due to his first name) which Richard had always found particularly unimaginative.

Richard didn't wish harm on anyone, but part of him couldn't help the feeling of schadenfreude when hearing about the misfortunes that had befallen some of his ex-tormentors.

Three were dead, two were alcoholics, and the other one was currently serving a thirty year jail sentence for interfering with children.

He was glad he was a 'little different' if that was *their* idea of normality.

"What the fu . . . ?" he stood there flabbergasted as Taylor and Blake rushed from the bus shelter and barged in front of him, almost knocking him over to get their choice of seats on the coach as it pulled up.

He decided not to comment further as their fat arses mounted the steps. What was the point? People like them had neither manners nor scruples.

As he climbed on board the driver gave him a pleasant nod and he chose a seat near the front of the coach.

The doors hissed closed, and the engine started up. Richard shut his eyes and let himself drift away.

JOHN MEACHEN

They arrived at Windermere at 10.05 A.M. and the journey up had been a pleasant one. He'd spent most of it consulting his 'Tourist walking guide' brochure and enjoying the continual change of scenery as the coach whizzed by different locations.

As predicted, most of his travelling companions had alighted the coach and headed straight towards the shops and tearooms.

Half a dozen even elected to stand in the ridiculous queue for the sight-seeing boat tour of the lakes. As if on cue the sun began to burn its way through the clouds, announcing to everyone it was going to be a scorcher. That made him extremely happy.

Pickup time was 8P.M, which gave him approximately ten hours to explore his surroundings. He checked his camera and took a shot of the sun glistening against the cold, dark surface of the lake.

That was the miracle of the digital age; no more waiting for spools to be developed and ending up disappointed at the results.

With modern technology, it was just a case of deleting and starting again.

He was almost three hours into the walk when he decided to stop and consume his cheese sandwiches and banana. He decided to save the flask of soup till later.

He breathed a sigh of contentment. The scenery was stunning.

According to the map, his current location was Moss Eccles Tarn, which afforded a splendid panoramic sweep of all of Windermere.

From his vantage point of the top of the hill, he could see a couple of fellow trekkers who resembled ants as they scurried across the landscape.

He always wondered about other people, what their lives were like. Where were they going. What their opinions and views were.

Sometimes he would come across other walkers, mainly couples, and they would stop and talk to him. The conversation always tended to be exclusively about the weather.

He knew he was lonely. He had tried to find himself a partner, but he was no spring chicken, and more often than not when he'd arrange a date through a dating website, when they'd turned up and saw him, they made their excuses and left.

He consulted his watch. It was almost 3 P.M. Had he really been there all that time?

It never ceased to amaze him how this one day of the year seemed to pass so quickly.

DAY TRIPPER

'Tempus Fugit,' as his old English teacher Mrs. Marshall had always said.
He decided he would try and reach the adjacent peak. He had five hours left and could easily achieve this, plus, it would give him a different perspective, and of course there was also the chance he would meet someone.

He got home around 10.30 P.M. exhausted but content.
It had been a particularly good trip.
He threw his rucksack onto the bed and opened the small zipped compartment at the front.
He liked to look at his mementoes first thing when he got home; it helped him relive the day.
The necklace was made of the finest silver, the letters attached spelling out "Ashley." He held it in his hand, examining it as if it were some ancient priceless artefact.
He moved over to the bedside cabinet and opened the drawer, carefully placing the necklace beside the collection of rings and bracelets already there. He closed the drawer and returned to the rucksack, removing the black leather gloves. He would dispose of them along with the bloodstained clothing first thing in the morning.
He removed the hammer next, remnants of blonde hair, skull fragments, and brain tissue still attached to the end of its flat nose.
He took out the camera and flicked through the images on the small screen.
She hadn't known what hit her. Just as he'd resigned himself to the fact that it wasn't going to be his day, she'd appeared from over the grassy incline.
She'd smiled at him as he'd walked past her, a beautiful smile.
He kept on walking and so had she, not occurring to her to look back to see if he was following her.
It was so easy. She'd been wearing earphones and didn't have a care in the world. He hit her with the hammer three times, twice on the back of the head and once on the cheekbone as she'd swivelled around.
Once he'd finished with her, he weighed her body down with some rocks and waded into the cold water of the lake.

JOHN MEACHEN

He imagined from the distance he must have looked like a Baptist preacher converting a new member, but this had been no re-birth.

He'd watched with wonderment as her sightless eyes had stared at him as her pretty face had disappeared under the water.

With a bit luck he would see that face again and learn who 'Ashley' was when she was eventually reported missing.

A pretty girl like that would always make front page headlines. If he was particularly lucky, he may even get to see an interview with her distraught parents on the news. The police were absolute buffoons, even with the aid of forensics and D.N.A. no one had come knocking at his door thus far, and this was his eighth.

All they had to do was tie in the murders with the annual coach trips, but this was apparently too complex for them.

Granted, at least four of the bodies hadn't been found until months later, so none of the morons on the coach had put two and two together either.

It frustrated him sometimes that he hadn't received the recognition he deserved, and he had even given serious consideration to writing to the police and dropping them a few clues.

But then again why should he?

Besides, he'd heard someone comment on the coach that next year's destination would be Bournemouth, and he'd have needed to be crazy to deny himself another excursion to look forward to.

John Meachen lives near Glasgow in Scotland. He has accumulated a number of his own horror/thriller stories over the past few years and would like one day to release them as an anthology. John is delighted and thrilled to be included by Crystal Lake Publishers for inclusion in their Hotel Macabre Vol 1 collection.

THIS WAS NOT THE END WE WERE PROMISED (SILVER WINGS)

Maxwell I. Gold

TOWARDS THE EDGE of a bright and hazy dawn, I saw silver wings flap across a scarlet horizon. Perhaps, confined inside this room by a nameless overlook, the end was anything else but quiet with these dreams of mine soon made real by fire and blood. Tangible nightmares spun together by webs of congruent dread, fed through cyber-reels, liquid screens, and trash-talks on replay was the end we were promised, a simulated vision-vault where everything was possible and punctured through our skulls like some vile machine. It became our manufactured apocalypse, a world writhing in wired-up beauty but instead I was slave to silver wings and laughing faces covered in flames.

An altered fate built by plastic gods who ushered in the finality of tomorrow where the only refuge I managed to find was huddled in the dark, musty confines of an old hotel without the immutable curses and voices of a putrescent world. Only the music of silver wings filled my ears. All at once, the heat and pressure of my reality collapsed, while my brain, floating within an ocean of blood and water, saw the last visions of a million tired souls; clamoring to escape indifferent cataclysms, and I sighed *this was not the end we were promised.*

Maxwell I. Gold *is a Jewish-American prose poet, author, and editor, with an extensive body of work comprising over 300 poems since 2017.*

MAXWELL I. GOLD

His writings have earned a place alongside many literary luminaries in the speculative fiction genres and his work has garnered nominations for multiple awards including the Pushcart Prize, the Eric Hoffer Awards, Rhysling Awards, and the Bram Stoker Awards. His work has appeared in numerous literary journals, magazines, and anthologies such as Weird Tales Magazine, Startling Stories, the recent Horror Writers Association anthology Other Terrors: An Inclusive Anthology, Chiral Mad 5, *and many more. Maxwell has taught several poetry workshops and co-edited several anthologies. He's the author of the Bram Stoker nominated poetry collection* Bleeding Rainbows and Other Broken Spectrums.

—IN CASE THE CHLOROFORM WEARS OFF

Jennifer Osborn

I DIDN'T MEAN to bake my best friends into a cherry pie, but what choice did I have? Okay, I had a choice, everyone has a choice and I made mine—but it was a matter of life or death and I sure as hell wasn't ready to die.

I felt just sick about it at the time, of course. I still do. That pie will forever remain the hardest thing I've ever made. Not just because I had to mince Margo & Claire up before puréeing their eyeballs, lips, and organs . . . before reducing them to liquid and folding them into cherry filling . . . but also because of the sheer amount of self-loathing and guilt that went into it. I think that's exactly what He *loved* about it though, and why that pie will always be His favorite.

I guess most things get easier with time, or maybe one just becomes desensitized, but I'm quite the baker these days. I'd have called the bakery 'no remorse pastries' but I suppose that doesn't sound very welcoming, so instead I call it Sinfully Sweet Treats, and the poor bastards are none the wiser.

While I'll never forgive her for what she did to our town, I understand Daphne on a much deeper level now. I understand *why* she did what she did and why it was easier to start over with a clean slate every so often, instead of remaining in any one place for too long. I've started over five times now. He always takes care of the little details, making it all possible—as long as I live up to my end of the deal.

With anything, trial and error go a long way and at this point I've tried all sorts of recipes, techniques, and ingredients. I learned quickly that He doesn't like animals. Stray dogs and cats are unacceptable substitutions for the human sacrifices He craves. He doesn't seem to have a preference when it comes to age or gender, but I think somehow the treats taste sweeter when they're baked with hints of sadness and guilt. I always feel guilty, but I don't feel sad anymore. I don't feel *anything* . . . except grateful to still be alive.

The rules are the same as they've always been. A deal is a deal. Every six months, on the sixth day, the hypothetical clock starts ticking and it's time to make six sacrifices again. You may not know this, but The Devil has a sweet tooth. Rather than splayed out on some bloodied boulder in the middle of the woods, He prefers these offerings presented to Him in the form of delectable little treats. I wouldn't have fancied Him for such a fellow, but I've seen the pure delight in His eyes when He savors that first bite, and the hellfire rage that washes over them if it's not to His liking. I've felt the flames of Hell lick my skin when I teeter on the edge of failure. *Failure is not an option.* So, I continue to hone my craft, to save my own soul. I bake and I bake, and I bake. And The Devil eats and he eats, and he eats. I have to make the sixth sacrifice tonight.

"How bout' a pack of smokes, pretty lady?"
"You plan to pay for those tonight, George?"
"Ahhh, you know I'm good for 'em."
"You're holding up the line, you gotta go. Be safe tonight. Go get some sleep, would ya?" Shelly said from behind the plexiglass window. It was just past 10 PM and George had been loitering at the gas station for hours. He'd also asked the tired cashier three times now for a pack of cigarettes without realizing he'd been repeating himself. She was doing him a favor by not calling the cops, but if he didn't move along, she'd have to get them involved.

"Yeah. Yeah, okay. Goodnight, Sherry." George did his best to flash the woman a sexy grin, but his toothless smirk, framed by an unwashed, matted beard only made her recoil.

"Come on, buddy, let's go," the man behind him mumbled, getting annoyed. George stumbled to the side, bumping into the sunglass rack. His baggy plaid shirt caught on one of the hooks and

—IN CASE THE CHLOROFORM WEARS OFF

ripped as he stepped forward, tearing a large hole in the fabric. The patrons in line stared at him without saying a word.

His uneven footfalls continued as he left the gas station, rounded the corner, and made his way toward the alley out back. Broken glass crunched beneath the soles of his shoes. Two cats hissed at each other, fighting over food scraps near the dumpster where he decided to sit down. A nearly empty bottle of vodka lay on the asphalt beside him. Without a second thought he slid it closer, unscrewed the cap and finished it off. Bits of loose tobacco, which had been floating in it, caught in the open holes in his mouth. George moved his tongue around, trying to dislodge them. The liquor washed over him, warming him. He passed out there, seated against the back alley dumpster.

⚷

Laura pulled her car into the alley and shut off the headlights, parking in a way that blocked the view of the dumpster from the main road. A homeless man was passed out on the filth-covered ground; the sound of the car approaching hadn't fazed him in the slightest. Of course, he was the reason she'd stopped.

For the last few years Laura had been abducting the homeless for her obligatory sacrifices. It seemed to ruffle the least feathers, cause the least amount of disturbance. Most often, no one even recognized that they were gone.

His arm fell heavily to his side as Laura picked it up and let it fall, testing his awareness. He coughed and mumbled something into the collar of his shirt but stayed asleep. The booze on his breath suggested he'd drank himself to the brink of unconsciousness.

"Thank you," Laura whispered as she grabbed him beneath both armpits and pulled him up and into the backseat of her car. There she slid a white cloth, doused in chloroform, gently over his nose and mouth until he went fully limp. She bound his wrists together with not one but three extra strength zip-ties before spinning the dial. *Isn't It Ironic* by Alanis Morisette played on the radio. Her headlights flicked on as she pulled out of the alley and into the flow of traffic.

Initially, when this all began, she'd wanted to lay low and do her baking in the comfort of her own home, without bringing attention to any type of storefront, but she quickly realized that the mess was inconceivable, and she'd need a much larger space to work. The same evening a targeted ad popped up on her phone for a rental space, which she pursued. Then, the exact dollar amount, right down to the penny, showed up in her savings account, allowing her to pay the first month's rent and deposit. Though she'd only briefly mentioned to the landlord that she'd intended to use the space for a bakery, she found it fully furnished with top-of-the-line baking appliances when she stepped inside. The Devil provided *everything* she needed, both in opportunity and tools for her craft, and He always did. Time after time when she would move and start over somewhere new, almost identical circumstances would unfold, allowing her to slip seamlessly into a new storefront and become a town favorite, never anyone the wiser. It bothered her a little though, how similar her life mirrored Daphne's at this point, but Daphne was dead, and she was alive—and that was always enough to shake the thought from her tainted mind.

The clock on the dashboard read 10:38 PM when she pulled up to the bakery. She needed to work quickly to finish up this last sacrifice, and then she could breathe easy for another six months. But now, it was time to get to work.

Large canvas tarps covered the floor and walls, easy to replace, easy to incinerate. Laura wore goggles on her face but preferred to work barehanded, as she found gloves too restrictive. A steel barrel of acid sat in the corner for the bits she didn't need, and the sound of an electric saw echoed through the room as blood splattered the floor. She sawed George's head off first (she knew his name was George, because she'd found his wallet.) *Always off with the head first—in case the chloroform wears off.* Laura glanced over to her tablet, where Pinterest was pulled up. She was trying a new recipe tonight:

Raspberry Crumble Cookies

INGREDIENTS
- 1 cup unsalted butter softened
- 1/4 cup granulated sugar

—IN CASE THE CHLOROFORM WEARS OFF

- 1/3 cup powdered sugar
- 3/4 cup puréed George
- 1 teaspoon vanilla extract
- 1 teaspoon almond extract
- 2 1/4 cups all-purpose flour
- 1/4 teaspoon kosher salt
- 1/2 cup seedless raspberry jam
- 1/4 cup strained blood

Jennifer Osborn, *author of* Intrusive Thoughts and Other Dark & Unusual Tales, *resides in the Midwest with her husband, three children, and random assortment of pets. She's currently hibernating until spring. Luckily that means she's working on several new projects, in between the noisy chaos of her life.*
   Follow her on FB @
https://www.facebook.com/profile.php?id=100088572137944&mibextid=9R9pXO

THE RED TENT

CHRIS PHELON

JACK SAT IN his garden on the wooden bench that he had helped his father build thirty years before and watched the sun finally emerge for the first time in what felt like weeks. It looked as though it would be the perfect weather to go camping with Bill and Jamie. In his hand was the letter from the Parish Council that Charlie Anderson had brought round a few days before; waiting respectfully whilst Jack read it, Charlie had given him an awkward hug and then quickly left. Jack checked again that he had committed the details to memory, then folded it up. Back in the kitchen, he opened a drawer and slid the letter beneath the cutlery tray.

'Bill? Jamie?' he called up the stairs. 'Pack some clothes. We're going camping for the weekend.'

He listened to the excited cheer and chatter from the boys' room for a few moments, then grabbed his wallet and car keys from the kitchen table. He'd be able to pick up what he needed from the camping shop in town, assuming they hadn't gone out of business like so many others had in recent months.

It was still open, just; a 'Closing Down Sale' sign hung in the window. Jack didn't make conversation with the owner, who just nodded dourly when he pointed to the two identical one-person tents—one blue, one red. He bought a camping stove and some bamboo skewers so they could roast marshmallows. He'd grab a few packs of them from the corner shop, along with a bottle of whiskey and some cigarettes for himself. He hadn't smoked or drank in years. Not since Allison had gone.

THE RED TENT

The boys were running around the garden playing when he got back. Jack dropped his purchases onto the kitchen counter and shouted out the window.

'Bill? Are you all packed up like I asked?'

Bill looked up at him. 'Not yet, Dad. We're playing war.'

Jack's eyes narrowed. 'What did I say? Get upstairs now. Help your brother get packed, too. Do as you're told or we'll stay in all weekend instead.'

Bill pouted. 'But Jamie wanted to play.'

Jack glared back, silently pointing towards the stairs. Bill reluctantly dragged his younger brother inside. Jack watched them climb the stairs, then began to pack his rucksack.

They had been only driving for twenty minutes, and already Bill was acting up. 'How much longer?' he whined as Jamie snatched back from him the toy car that Bill had taken.

'We're here,' said Jack. He saw the sign for the campsite and turned off of the main road, onto the dirt path. They soon reached a large field, surrounded by trees. There was an old rusty standpipe off to the left. There were no patches of charred grass where any recent campfires had been lit; it seemed that the recent weather had put anyone off coming here for months.

'Grab your bags, boys. I'll carry the tents,' said Jack.

'Aren't we staying here?' asked Bill.

Always a question with him these days, thought Jack.

'No. We'll pitch further in the woods. It's not far. Don't start complaining.'

They walked for ten minutes. Jack was starting to worry that the directions he'd been given were wrong, or that maybe he had missed the sign. Then he saw the collection of sticks, arranged about ten feet off the ground, hanging from a beech tree.

'Here we are, boys. Let's get the tents up.'

Bill stared at the muddy, leaf-strewn ground, frowning. 'Aren't we sleeping together, Dad?'

Jack pulled all three tent bags from the large rucksack he had been carrying. 'No, not this time. You're both too big for that. You get to have your own tent now.'

Jack rolled out both of the smaller tents he had bought earlier that day. He looked around until he spotted the small triangle of sticks arranged on the ground about twenty feet away. He set up the red tent on top of it; it was a simple construction, with just two metal poles running across each other at right angles, and some pegs to stop it blowing away. Then he walked twenty paces or so across the clearing, and put up the blue tent. 'Now, which tent do you want to sleep in, Jamie?' he asked.

Bill, looking wary, cut in. 'I don't want to sleep in a tent on my own. Why can't we sleep in with you?'

Jack took a deep breath and smiled. 'It's all part of growing up, son. You'll love it once you're inside. All that room to yourself.' Bill didn't look convinced. Jamie continued playing happily with his toy car on the muddy ground.

Jack turned to him. 'Jamie? Which tent do you want to sleep in, son?'

Jamie looked over at the two tents. 'That one,' he said, pointing at the blue one.

Jack glanced over at Bill. 'Okay?' he asked, still smiling. Bill nodded reluctantly.

For the rest of the day, they played football in a field a mile or so from their camp, fished in a stream with a rod and net that Jack had borrowed from a friend, and collected wood for a campfire and cooked some sausages. Jack sat down and opened one of the bags of marshmallows he had bought earlier. 'Who wants one of these?' he grinned. They worked their way through all three packs in no time at all.

'Time for bed,' said Jack, and yawned theatrically. Jamie raced off to the blue tent, and clambered into his sleeping bag.

'Don't we have to brush our teeth?' asked Bill, still sat by the fire.

'No, son. Missing one night isn't going to do you any harm,' replied Jack.

Once he had tucked Bill into his sleeping bag and said goodnight, Jack sat back down in front of the campfire, staring into the flames. Just before midnight, by which time he was halfway through the bottle of whiskey and had smoked all of the cigarettes, he heard the first sound.

THE RED TENT

He looked up, eyes wide. It had come from the red tent, in which Bill was sound asleep, snoring softly. Jack took another gulp of whiskey. Even though there was little light from the crescent moon, he could already see something emerging from the earth around Bill's tent. Jack, suddenly panicked, looked over at Jamie's tent; he hadn't thought about what he would do if Jamie woke up now, disturbed by the noise. But when he looked back, it was already over. The red tent had disappeared. It had happened in an instant; all that remained was a roughly circular patch of what looked like newly dug earth, as if prepared for planting. A flash of movement caught Jack's eye, and for a second he saw a long tendril, as fat as a finger, that tapered to a jagged thorn, the shape of a canine tooth, emerge and hang in the air. Then he watched as it sank back into the earth where the red tent had been moments before.

When the sun rose, Jack was still staring into the remains of the campfire, the bottle at his feet. When Jamie woke up, Jack made breakfast. When Jamie asked where Bill was, Jack sat down next to him and reminded him about the day his mum had died, and how sad they had all been. He explained that they were going to be sad again, because Bill had gone to the same place that their mum had, and they weren't going to see him again for a long, long time. But then it would be okay, he said as the tears flowed down Jamie's face, because then they would all be together again.

The sun shone down as Jack sat on the bench in his back garden, watching Jamie play with his toy cars on the grass. Charlie, from the Parish Council, sat beside him.

'How's the restaurant now?' Jack asked quietly.

'Great,' replied Charlie. 'The high street is really picking back up. Had four or five businesses reopen already. Takings are through the roof again. We're all very grateful,' he added, awkwardly.

'How is Mary these days?' asked Jack. Charlie didn't answer for a second.

'The same,' he said, eventually. 'Been five years this winter. Not easy for a mother, losing a daughter.'

They sat in silence for a few more minutes.

'If you don't want to say, of course . . . ' asked Charlie abruptly, 'but . . . how did you choose? Which one, I mean? Elizabeth was our only child . . . '

Jack stared at his son, playing in the grass. 'I didn't,' he said softly. 'I left it up to them. Or, chance, maybe. But I couldn't choose between my boys.'

They watched Jamie play with his toy cars contentedly in the sun. 'He really likes those cars, doesn't he?' smiled Charlie.

'Yeah,' Jack replied. 'The blue ones. He loves them. They're his favourites.'

Chris Phelon *writes ghost stories and weird fiction in his windswept and rain-battered terraced house in the sunny British seaside resort of Brighton.*

A MESSAGE FROM THE PAST, A MESSAGE FROM THE FUTURE

Jonathan Gensler

IT WASN'T THE sound of rustling leaves or trampling footsteps rushing up from behind that scared Becky. Not the faint echo of screams carried by the wind through the bone-bare trees.

It was the sudden silence when she turned toward the forest, expecting to see *something*. But the space between the trees was empty. Of faces, of bodies, of life; devoid of birdsong, of crickets chirping, of even the scuttle of a squirrel burying a soon-to-be forgotten acorn for the coming winter.

Only silence.

"Dad? Mamaw? Something weird's going on out here."

Becky turned away from the forest and walked back toward a brick two-story house, glancing to her left and right at the concrete foundation and stone outcroppings where the previous week sat two houses much like her Mamaw's.

Now, gone.

Her boots, crunching down plant detritus, kicked up a smell of rot and decay. Her own thumping rhythm once more became one of running feet behind her, merging into the memory of a scream as she stopped, closed her eyes.

"Who is it?" she asked in a whisper above a whisper, still facing the house.

The crackle of leaves became a quiet murmur again, and through its mumblings, the crinkling hiss slurred into:

JONATHAN GENSLER

go, forever
leave, or never

She whipped around with a childish fury, fists balled up, ponytail flailing out, brown eyes wide open. "I said, who is—"

Silence.

A body's length away the reds and yellows of fallen maple leaves spelled out the simple word *GO*.

She didn't scream, though her lips trembled to do so. The absence of sound was too oppressive; if she broke it, she knew something terrible might happen. Ripples of energy flowed through her. Her spine vibrated with a miniscule pulse. Her fingers and toes tingled with not-quite electricity. An intrusion of singed hair and smoky ash overwhelmed her sense of smell. Even her eyesight wavered with the unfamiliar frequencies in front of her.

She stood facing the trees again and scanned up the hill toward a slate gray building at the top of the slope. The factory where Poppy had worked. The Tower. The building itself was remarkably tall with gun-metal siding and no windows. It perched over the small hamlet of Doodletown, a tombstone over an empty grave.

From the corner of her vision, she could swear the neighbors' house was still standing, the family milling around at their normal weekend barbecue. Her friend Jimmy, who'd always played with her when she would come to Mamaw and Poppy's for their own Sunday dinners, should have been here for her eleventh birthday. Echoes of their voices floated to her ears, Jimmy calling to her to come look at what his daddy had showed him up by the Tower.

A flash of light and a tremendous wind blew them away in slow motion, ash and dust whorls left in its wake.

Jimmy's voice melted into the same screaming of *nonononononogogogogogoGOOOOOO!*

And as she turned to face it, the neighbors' house was once more gone. The voices replaced by the pressing emptiness, the air heavier and difficult to breathe, like on the hottest, sunniest days of summer.

The strange vibrations shook her body up and down, and she called out, "Dad! Where are you?"

Becky mentally marked the "Woody" station wagon in the driveway and glanced back at the foundation of Jimmy's old house. It looked like something had simply lifted it away. No debris, no trash, no nothing. A concrete pad the only evidence the house had ever existed.

A MESSAGE FROM THE PAST . . .

Becky turned back to Mamaw's as she walked up the stairs to the back door, and read the leaves spelling out *GO NOW* and thought to herself, *Did that change?*

The screen door slammed behind her after she entered the house, her face screwed up trying to sort out whatever was happening here.

"Dad! Come on! I'm serious!"

Becky floated through the kitchen, stirred the pot of "sketty" sauce on the stovetop, and called out with growing impatience, "Mamaw? Dad?"

The creak of muffled footsteps above told her they must be upstairs in the bedroom. She headed out of the kitchen and into the hallway, calling up, "Is everything OK, Dad? Is something wrong with Mamaw?"

Becky rushed to the stairwell, losing her nerve as the reality of what was going on outside started to crash into her sense of the present. The odd vibrations came rushing back into her bones and she stumbled into a large wooden dresser at the foot of the stairs, knocking over a picture frame.

"Oh shit," she said, catching it right before it fell off the edge.

WAR DEPARTMENT and *Army Corps of Engineers* printed in scrolling letters across the top. *Manhattan District* below that. And then *For work essential to the production of the Atomic Bomb.*

Replacing it carefully, a smile crossed her face, remembering the stories Poppy had told her about working at the Tower. The wartime years were all he ever talked about as his mind faded over his final months.

From upstairs, a scratchy, faded voice said, "Becky, that you? Stop! You'd better get—"

"Dad? What is wrong with your voice?"

She bounded up the stairs two at a time. As she made the upper landing, a blindingly white light flowed like water from the crack below the bedroom door down the hall.

"Dad! Mamaw!"

She sprinted down the hall to the door and opened it.

Stepping through she found herself in the woods staring up at the Tower, now seeping that impossibly bright light from gaps in its corners. Turning back to face Mamaw's house, she saw a girl with a dark ponytail staring at her. With a sudden realization,

JONATHAN GENSLER

Becky was shouting at the younger version of herself to go, to leave, to stop.

She kneeled to spell it out in the leaves, hoping against hope that this time, it wasn't too late.

Jonathan Gensler (he/him) grew up in a haunted house in West Virginia, and now writes dark, speculative fiction. Over the last twenty-odd years, he has served as an officer in the US Army, worked with his hands as a laborer in Aotearoa New Zealand, and helped build companies as a cleantech entrepreneur. He is an Affiliate Member of the Horror Writers Association, has degrees from West Point, MIT, and Harvard, and lives in Nashville with his partner and three children. You can connect with him on Twitter @jgensler.

BURIAL DAY

Stephanie M. Wytovich

Six feet deep, the dance of conqueror worms
around me, I sleep in a blanket of marigold
and mullein, the taste of dying stars
wet on my lips—

>see: there's a humming in the ground
>an echo

>>*it begs*
>>*it pleads*

I wipe a fistful of poppies across
my chest, feel the syrup of pomegranate
seeds slide down my throat, the velvet
hands of death choke me—

>>*I cough*
>>*I gasp*

I exit the grave in a shower of filth,
flesh bathed in yew, motherwort stuffed
in my cheeks like acorns, the air of burial
still clinging to my eyes—

>see: the dirt calls to me
>an invitation

STEPHANIE M. WYTOVICH

I answer
I submit

Stephanie M. Wytovich *is an American poet, novelist, and essayist. Her work has been featured in magazines and anthologies, such as Weird Tales, Nightmare Magazine, Southwest Review, Year's Best Hardcore Horror: Volume 2, and The Best Horror of the Year: Volumes 8 & 15. Wytovich is the Poetry Editor for Raw Dog Screaming Press and an adjunct at Western Connecticut State University, Southern New Hampshire University, and Point Park University. She has received the Elizabeth Matchett Stover Memorial Award, the 2021 Ladies of Horror Fiction Writers Grant, and the Rocky Wood Memorial Scholarship for nonfiction writing. Wytovich is a member of the Science Fiction and Fantasy Poetry Association, an active member of the Horror Writers Association, and a graduate of Seton Hill University's MFA program for Writing Popular Fiction. She is a two-time Bram Stoker Award-winning poet, and her debut novel,* The Eighth, *is published with Dark Regions Press. Her nonfiction craft book for speculative poetry,* Writing Poetry in the Dark, *is available now from Raw Dog Screaming Press. Follow Wytovich at https://www.stephaniemwytovich.com/ and on Twitter, Threads, and Instagram @SWytovich and @thehauntedbookshelf. You can also sign up for her newsletter at https://stephaniemwytovich.substack.com/.*

SAVING FACE

Sean Eads and Joshua Viola

NOT THE NECK, you're not taking the neck, Mark thought, lifting his chin to place the end of a tailor's measuring tape just below the base of his throat. He aligned it with the tip of a purple scar that had been climbing up from his left clavicle the past couple of weeks. Its course had been uncertain, but now it seemed aimed for his jugular.

A little mole near his Adam's Apple served as the measuring point. The last five days, he'd recorded a gap of 3.2 inches between it and the scar. Mark's fingers shook a little as he drew the measuring tape up his neck. His pulse couldn't be quicker, his breath less shallow as he held the tape to inspect the results.

3.1.

Mark threw the measuring tape onto the floor and scowled, leaning his face toward the vanity. Can't be right, he thought. There hadn't even been an itch. But he didn't try remeasuring. Blinking away tears, he uncapped a little bottle of cream that cost $200 per ounce and squeezed a dollop onto the tip of his index finger. "Not the neck, not the neck."

He jabbed his finger against the stretch mark, working the cream in like drywall spackling.

It's not going to do any good, he thought. It never does.

Mark straightened his shoulders and gave his reflection a hard stare. "*Not* the neck."

He went into his bedroom and pulled a red T-shirt over his lean torso. The shirt was almost a size too large and made of heavy cotton, but Mark felt the ruts in his skin as he smoothed the fabric over his chest and stomach. They seemed even more pronounced today. *Deeper.* He made a fist of his right hand and punched the wall twice, sending a jolt of pain up his arm.

Calm down, he told himself. Get a hold of yourself.

Mark returned to the bathroom mirror and found the edge of the stretch mark was just visible above the neckline. He gaped at the discovery. "Fuck you!" He tore the shirt off as he stormed back to his closet to grab a blue Oxford dress shirt. He started at the topmost button, cinching the collar tight around his neck, and moved down. At the second button from the bottom, he stopped and sat at the edge of the bed, head bowed.

It won't stop, he thought. *They never do. My neck and then my chin and then my whole face. Cheeks and nose and lips and even my goddamn ears.*

Today is not tomorrow and it's not yesterday.

It was a mantra a telehealth therapist had encouraged him to repeat in these dark moments. Mark closed his eyes and muttered it a few times. He stood up and shuffled back to the bathroom mirror. Covered up, he looked so nice. A good, angular face and floppy brown hair, though right now it was wet and clingy from the shower. His face pics never failed to attract female attention, but that's as far as he could let it go.

Only Gisella had seen the freak show.

He left the bathroom and started to pace his apartment, his thoughts a white noise. It was 10 PM and he'd intended to go out to a bar and at least chat up a girl. Anything to feel like a normal 26-year-old guy. But those plans were dashed.

3.1.

His cell phone buzzed. Mark grabbed it off the table and gave a quizzical smile when he saw the caller ID.

Gisella.

"Hey," he said, grinning a little more at how he sounded.

Was that a note of *confidence* in his voice?

"Been thinking about you."

Mark went to the living room and sat down in front of his computer. "I'm always thinking about you."

She answered with a sexy little chuckle he wished was genuine. Some things required you to be a realist.

"I hate to be rude about it, but I'm a little short right now. Payday is next Friday. But I could—I could Venmo you $30 for, you know—"

He winced at her laughter.

"Would you really write *phone sex* as the description?"

"I'd be a little more discreet than—"

"Besides, $30 would only get you sexting. So, if you want my voice, you better be willing to pay the big bucks."

"You're the one who called me."

There was a pause. He didn't feel he'd said anything wrong, but maybe it'd come across in a bad way. Had he hurt her feelings? Did prostitutes get offended?

"That's because I want to see you."

Mark hunched forward, frowning. "Payday really is next—"

"It's okay."

"What do you mean?"

"What do you think I mean? Can I come over?"

"For free?" He cringed again. But Gisella's little laugh showed she wasn't upset.

"I'm not too far away. A 10-minute walk."

Mark had no idea where she lived, and for the first time, he found himself caring. A 10-minute walk couldn't be more than a mile. How had she come to be so close? Discouraging suspicions abounded.

"I'd really like that."

"You sound a little down, Mark."

"Just tired."

"Not *too* tired, I hope."

He looked at the ceiling and smiled. "Nothing an energy drink won't fix."

The call ended and he went scrambling to clean up his place a little bit, taking a stack of dirty plates to the dishwasher and then picking up a pile of clothes and pushing them into the closet. Then he hurried to make the bed, smoothing the sheets flat, enjoying how the wrinkles and lumps faded under his touch. Mark didn't think it'd been more than five minutes before Gisella knocked on the door.

He opened it and said, "Hey there, beautiful."

She was just a little shorter than him at 5'8, with hair that must have been dyed black. It gleamed even under the dull hallway lighting. Gisella wore it long, almost to the small of her back, and he liked the way it spread out like a cape when they were in bed. Her nails were always a different color. Last payday, they'd been emerald green. Tonight, they were very red, and he found himself stirring.

"So are we going to do it in the hallway?"

"Sorry," he said, stepping aside. Gisella moved past him, giving him a whiff of her strange perfume, something herbal and a little earthy. He liked it a little more each time. She was wearing a blue mesh halter top that showed much of her chest. Her breasts had several puckered scars that resembled hash marks. They'd gotten together about ten times in the last six months, and he still hadn't worked up the nerve to ask her about them. Was she a cutter? Had some pimp done it to her? Mark could only admire how bold she was in revealing them.

"Have you had a good night?" he said.

"Getting better now."

She kissed his mouth and he damn near melted against her. One hand pressed against his shirt and he winced at a pain that wasn't there. The pressure of her palm pressed fabric into the skein of stretch marks on his stomach, making every purple, waxy depression acute in his mind. But they didn't matter. Not with her. Before it had been about the money, appearances didn't matter, disgust wasn't an issue. Tonight was different.

Today is not tomorrow and it's not yesterday.

He moaned a little—almost a whimper. Gisella's hand moved up his body, massaging, pinching. When she reached his neck, Gisella began working on the tight top button. Mark was so lost in feelings of being desired he didn't realize what she was doing until the collar fell open. It felt like she'd unfastened the one thing holding him together and he pulled back, clenching the fabric tight around his Adam's Apple.

"What's wrong with you?"

"Nothing."

"Aren't we past the bullshit? I've seen you naked."

He nodded, welling up at the same time. Mark went to the living room and sat down on his computer chair. He was astonished when Gisella perched herself on his lap and stroked his hair.

"Show me."

He sighed and pulled back the left collar to expose more skin. Gisella's brows knitted and she shook her head.

"Same hot guy as last time."

Mark put his finger on his throat. "This is new. Broke off from the really big one on my shoulder. It's going to take my face."

"Quit fidgeting and let me look."

He tensed as she spread his shirt wide all the way to the sternum, revealing a crisscross network of furrows, as if a small child had drawn all over him with a bright purple marker. Mark focused on Gisella's face, seeking any trace of disgust now that she was here without payment. He instead found fascination. She seemed to marvel at the gross ruin of his torso, enthralled by the network of narrow violet lines that sprang like spokes around the axle of his nipples, nosing along their various pathways from shoulders to armpits and down his abs. The first time they'd gotten together, she'd even licked the wide and dark stretch marks on his flanks as if they were lines of chocolate syrup to savor, the tip of her tongue gliding along the waxy furrows.

"I'm pretty sure it's always been there, Mark."

"It *wasn't*," he said, fighting not to snap at her. "Trust me."

"Okay."

"I swear to God, if I get them on my face, I'm going to kill myself."

"Don't talk like that! You're a beautiful guy, not a freak."

"I sure as fuck feel like one."

"There are so many people worse off."

"Yeah, yeah. Burn victims, people with severe neurofibromatosis–"

"Quit being vain. You're healthy. Someone with kidney failure or stage four cancer would trade places with you in a second."

"You sound like my therapist."

"Whores are therapists," Gisella said.

Mark grimaced. "Don't call yourself that."

"I'll call myself whatever I want, thank you very much. You're lucky I'm feeling kinky tonight, otherwise I'd be so pissed off at you I'd leave."

For a moment, he found it difficult to lift his head. He was being so damn stupid. Then she nudged and poked him into a smile.

"You said you're feeling kinky?"

Gisella clicked her teeth together in a playful bite. "Yeah."

She pulled him out of the chair and led him to the bedroom, where she broke the shirt's buttons, tearing it off him. Mark went rigid.

"Goddamn, if this isn't perfection," she said, those red

fingernails like ten teasing daggers. Then she gave both nipples a twist and used them to pull him against her.

"Say it," she said.

"What?"

"I'm perfection."

"You're perfection—"

"*No*," Gisella said, twisting until he gritted his teeth. Their gazes were locked. "*I'm* perfection."

Pain and excitement made it difficult to breathe. He could only stutter. "I'm—I'm per-perfection."

"Good boy. It's a judgment on me if I'm fucking a man with no self-esteem."

"I never thought about it that way—"

She twisted again, leaving him panting.

"Don't think. Just do."

Mark nodded.

She pushed him onto the bed, ruining those smooth sheets in an instant. Gisella had never been so enthusiastic, ecstatic even. And she's not being paid, he thought. Was he hallucinating this? He looked down at his torso and saw the ugly scars that had started destroying him in the last year, since his 25th birthday. They wouldn't be there if he were fantasizing, even knowing Gisella's seeming fetish for them. She was still kissing along each stretch mark, regardless of size.

The largest was an inch wide and ran from the top of his navel to the middle of his chest like some sort of surgical scar. It was also the first to appear. He'd gone to the gym on his birthday and taken off his shirt in the locker room to snap a few pictures he'd text out later. At the time, it was just a little purple spot. He thought it might be a pimple. By the end of the week, it was about ¼ of an inch long. Its presence annoyed Mark and made him cringe a little, but he shrugged it off. Lots of muscle heads walked around with stretch marks all over their shoulders and biceps. Nothing to fret over. They faded. Big deal.

Gisella pushed him onto the bed and put her tongue into his belly button. Then she moved onto the big stretch mark. "Time to take a drive down Main Street," she said, lapping her way up. Mark shivered. Her breath was hot and tickling, making him squirm a little. Her fingers gripped his thighs tight in response. "I see you. No, you can't get away from me," she said. "Don't even try."

SAVING FACE

Mark groaned as she bit him hard enough to draw blood. Gisella rose up, smiling as she watched a red trickle rise and run along the track of the big stretch mark, filling it as rainwater fills ruts in a road. She slid herself up on the bed and kissed his mouth. Was that the taste of his own blood on her lips?

She pulled back and nestled her head on the pillow beside him, smiling.

"That was a nice ending."

He looked down at himself, eyes widening. He'd come. A lot. The mix of pain and desire must have made him lose his mind.

"Yeah," he said, adding a nervous laugh. "Better clean myself up."

Gisella grabbed his arm when he tried to sit up. She shook her head. "Just relax and let it dry, baby. Go to sleep."

He *was* tired. In the last hour, his emotions had see-sawed him into exhaustion.

"Will you be here when I wake up?"

She kissed his lips. "No promises."

Gisella's morning absence didn't bother him. Last night was magic and magic never lasts. He showered looking straight at the wall except for one quick glance down at the bite mark. It was a dark bruise that made the surrounding stretch marks look even angrier. But he felt no pain.

He dried himself and then began applying a variety of lotions and creams over the bulk of the scars. StriVectin, TriLASTIN, cocoa butter. Moisturizers and collagens and vitamins, until his torso gleamed and felt as slippery as an eel. Twenty minutes later, he took up the measuring tape, lifted his head, and braced himself.

3.1.

"Thank God," he said.

He put on shorts and the T-shirt he'd rejected last night. He'd always favored V-necks until the stretch marks reached his pecs. The top edge of the new stretch mark was still visible, and he spent a few minutes pulling down on the back of the shirt until the neckline rested higher on his collar bone. But it slipped back into place right away.

"To hell with it," he said, grabbing his wallet and his keys. He had Gisella and she thought he was hot. Why waste time worrying?

He felt good as he drove down to the local library's podcasting studio, where Charlie Morris had made a ninety-minute reservation to record episode 190 of *Sinister Cities,* the 562nd most popular paranormal-themed podcast on the Internet. Mark had been listening to Charlie since he was fifteen, discovering him as a guest on *Coast to Coast.* That they lived in the same city and had become friends and colleagues despite a thirty-three-year age difference still blew his mind.

Charlie was already in the studio when Mark arrived to find him scowling at his laptop.

"What's wrong?"

"Solti just messaged me."

"Is that son of a bitch canceling on us *again*?"

"He said something unforeseen came up."

"Pretty damning indictment of his psychic powers," Mark said, sitting down in the adjacent chair. "I wonder who gave him a better offer."

"He promised to be here next time."

"He said that last time."

"Just be patient, okay? A guest appearance by Solti would boost us up to—"

"560? 559?"

Charlie shook his head and for a moment it seemed that age and bad habits had caught up to him all at once. Charlie was always doing something, always nosing around, never down. He had a full head of vivid white hair and laughter lines around his blue eyes. He wore untucked Hawaiian shirts that seemed like merry maternity gowns on his 300lb frame. His stomach was a full, round girth that Mark had seen in the flesh. There wasn't a blemish on it, a fact that of late filled Mark with unkind thoughts.

"Sorry," Mark said. "You know I believe in the podcast. I'm your biggest fan. But what's the next episode about if we don't have Solti—*again*?"

"I think I've got something. Of all the paranormal city stories I've explored over the years, there's never been one based right here in our backyard."

Mark laughed. "That's because this is the most boring place on Earth. We don't even have an urban legend."

"True, but there *is* something going on around here. Something–dare I say–*sinister*."

"Tell me."

Charlie ran his tongue along his bottom lip, a sure sign of excitement. He looked at his laptop, though the screen was blank.

"Two weeks ago, a man and a woman were found in their apartment, mauled from head to toe. Every inch."

"Mauled? Like by a dog?"

"No," Charlie said. "The bite marks were human."

His tone was very serious, even grim—so at odds with the fascinating amusement that characterized his podcast persona. This was the same man who'd never lost a boyish grin while prodding New Jersey Detective Alexander Tumlock for exhaustive details on the Satanic cannibal couple from Teaneck, who believed eating the flesh of children before sex would help them conceive the Antichrist.

"How long would it take someone to *maul* another person, much less two?"

"Mauled isn't even the correct word. Chewed is the better adjective. Chewed and spat out whole."

"I didn't hear about that on the—" Mark cut himself off. Rebutting the bizarre with appeals to media authority was the play of the standard skeptical rube.

"Rick and Theresa Pennington. The news did report their deaths, just not the details. I doubt any of the reporters even asked. The paper doesn't exactly have an army of Kolchaks on their staff."

"But you found out more. Have you been wining and dining Detective Warren again?"

Charlie winked. "Adele's the chief investigator on the case."

"So more wine and less dine."

"The price of insider information is seldom as cheap as a bottle of Bordeaux. Adele's a good detective even when she's drunk. The problem with this crime is it requires a great detective. The difference between good and great is imagination."

Mark's eyes widened a little. There was a little itch near his collarbone, the sensation of a single ant probing along one stretch mark.

I won't scratch it, Mark thought. *I will not.*

Charlie meanwhile stared at the ceiling like he was looking through it toward some dreamy cloud.

"Adele told me something else. Two weeks prior to that, a man was found drowned in his car."

Mark shifted in his seat. A second ant had joined the procession. And now a third. "Was it Lake Thompson? They've pulled a few cars out of it before."

"It was the Sweetwater."

"Never heard of Lake Sweetwater. Is it by the hotel?"

"No, Mark. I mean the Sweetwater Hotel itself. Or rather its parking garage."

Mark fidgeted. Lots of marching ants now. He begrudged a swift, quick rub. Anything to appease the itch.

"So he drowned and someone . . . fished him out . . . Then put him in the car . . . and . . . and . . ."

"Are you okay?"

Mark tried to formulate an answer but ended up snarling "God!" before scrubbing at the itch, aware of Charlie's growing scrutiny. "Sorry–just a rash. Really itchy."

"I see. No, nothing as mundane as some murderer's idiotic attempt at a coverup. Too ordinary. Not *sinister* enough."

Mark's fingertips pressed harder. The friction wasn't enough. He had to surrender.

He always did.

He began to use his nails.

"Fine," Mark said, sighing from a little relief. "Don't keep me in suspense."

"Adele says the car was found completely filled with fluid. If the man weren't belted down, he'd have been floating. It flooded out once the attending officers broke a window. Sounds impossible, right?"

The itching ended. Mark sat back feeling like a spent man.

"I used the word 'fluid' on purpose. Lab tests showed the substance was a mix of water, proteins, and salt. What's that sound like?"

"I don't know. Saliva, I guess."

"That's right, Mark. The man died in a car filled to the roof in *spit*."

"No, no, no," he said, fingers shaking as he took up the measuring tape. Mark dropped it again without even trying. The mirror showed all the empirical evidence he needed.

The stretch mark had advanced above the edge of the shirt collar. The fabric didn't come close to concealing it now. Why, *why* had he surrendered to the itch? Scratching always made the stretch marks spread, like he was helping to rip the fibers of his skin.

He applied the regimen of creams and lotions along his neck like smears of paste until he couldn't stand it anymore and started crying. "What can I do?" he said, whispering at his reflection, finding no hope in his haunted eyes. He leaned in closer, obsessed with the delicate network of capillaries in the whites. Tiny purple lines moving everywhere, expanding, pulsing.

Itching.

Mark screamed.

"I've seen cases of severity approaching yours."

Dr. Mortelli's tone maintained a professional keel, but Mark could tell he was disturbed.

"You have?"

Mortelli answered with a noncommittal grunt, "Have you ever been tested for Cush–"

"Cushing's Disease? That was the first thing that came up on Google. Multiple tests say I don't have it. None of it makes sense. The first stretch mark showed up on my 25th birthday. Now here I am 14 months later."

Mortelli frowned. "Did you lose a lot of–"

"I've been exactly the same weight. I'm a *fit* guy. There's no explanation. *None.* So let's talk about treatments."

"You say you've tried nothing so far?"

"I wanted to do laser sessions, but they're just too expensive when it comes to the sheer number of sessions I'd need. I did try microneedling, but had to stop after a minute. It hurt so damn bad."

Mortelli's eyebrows lifted. "There should be minimum discomfort."

"It was agony. I felt like I was getting shanked."

"I'd like to try laser therapy."

"I already told you, I can't afford them. Not for the total number of treatments to see any difference–"

"I'm prepared to offer them for free."

Mark's voice broke once he was able to answer. "You're serious?"

"Very much so. This situation is unique, and I know how psychologically damaging stretch marks can be."

"They've ruined my life. How soon can we start?"

"Now, if you're ready."

Mark fought back tears. "I've never wanted to hug someone so much in my life."

"Would you consider being the subject of a paper I might want to write if we succeed?"

"Doctor, feel free to do a whole book on me."

Mortelli smiled. "Very well. We'll start slow. Target a small area and see how you respond."

Mark pointed to his throat. "Can we start with this one?"

"Of course."

Mark followed Mortelli into another room and followed his instructions to rest on the exam table. Mortelli applied a cool gel to Mark's neck as he explained the procedure. Then he showed Mark a handheld device.

"This is an ablative laser. It will shear off the upper layer of skin."

"Shear away!"

"Just relax. There may be a little pain."

"This time I don't care how bad it hurts."

Mortelli finished his preparations and activated the laser. The first small jolt had Mark clamping down against a scream. When the second pulse fired, he thought he was going out of his mind. There were shrieks in his head, a blend of voices. It felt like Mortelli was branding him and despite himself he cried out for mercy.

Just as he did, Mortelli dropped the laser and fell back. His mouth was agape.

"Impossible," he whispered.

"What?" Mark said.

"It's growing. Right in front of me. It *grew*."

Mark left the table and went to the wall mirror. He stood there frozen by his reflection, fingers on his neck as if trying to find a pulse.

Today is not tomorrow and it's not yesterday.

That's right, he thought. Today is worse than yesterday. And tomorrow will be worse than today.

SAVING FACE

The stretch mark was an inch longer than it had been a few minutes ago.
It now reached his Adam's Apple.

⚷

"I'm sorry. I'm so embarrassed."
"Don't be."
"It was such a pathetic cry for help."
"I'm just glad you reached out."

Mark leaned over and put his head on Gisella's shoulder, plunging into her herbal scent. They were sitting on the edge of his bed, each holding their cell phones. The screens showed a thread of text messages—his threat of suicide, her compassionate response.

She'd arrived in less than half an hour, after taking a Lyft. He wanted to reimburse her, but she wouldn't hear it. As soon as she'd come into the apartment, she noticed his neck and gasped.

"What did you do?"
"I tried laser therapy."
"You mustn't!" Her horror was as genuine as anything Mark had ever heard. "Love yourself for who you are, Mark!"
"I can't. Not—not like this."
"Yes, you can. Let me show you how."

She started undressing him, and though he wasn't in the mood, she soon aroused him. Made him forget his appearance. Scratched a deep itch inside for acceptance. Her own clothes didn't even come off in her haste to go down on him. There'd been no trace of her usual kinkiness, just a passion that made him come very hard and filled him with the most wonderful sentiment.

She really loves me.

His foolishness shamed him. After fleeing Mortelli's office, he'd come home and swallowed whatever pills he had in the medicine cabinet—Tylenol, Gas-X, probiotics, and the last One-a-Day vitamin from a jar that expired last year. Anxiety made him so nervous that he threw them up within a minute and then he sat sobbing and holding his neck while he texted Gisella about killing himself.

But she was beside him now. All was well.

"I never allowed myself to think it would happen. Knowing they were hidden under my shirt was like a psychic pressure valve. I could pretend to be normal—"

"You are normal, Mark."

He fingered the purple indentation along his throat and shook his head. Gisella squeezed his hand in response.

"There's stuff you can put on it," she said.

"I've tried every lotion, every cream."

"I mean to conceal it. I know it looks terrible to you, but I'm telling you it's not very noticeable."

He squeezed back. "I only feel better about what's happening because of you. Thanks for coming over."

"I'm the whore with the heart of gold."

"Don't say that. I know, I know, call yourself whatever you want. But you're not a whore."

Her expression was a little quizzical, as if she were trying to decipher the gibberish of a toddler. Did she pity him for his squeamishness? Did she *like* being a prostitute? Was it just like any gig economy job to her? Then he thought of something that made him laugh.

She smiled. "What is it?"

"I was thinking of something like Uber except for sex. There should be an app called Hookr."

Considering how chill she'd been, Mark expected her to laugh. But a darkness flashed through her expression. A moment later, she was pocketing her phone and saying, "I think my job here is done. Don't go killing yourself any time soon."

She left the room. Mark followed, shaking and fumbling an apology. "Please don't go. I'm sorry, I'm an idiot. You get me nervous–"

"You're not nervous when you pay."

He looked at his feet.

"Because I'm just a commodity when you pay, right?"

"*No.*"

"You feel better when you pay, because then it's not about your body, it's about the money. That's what you think *my* interest is, right?"

Mark held up his hands. "Gisella, I'm so sorry. I'm just really awkward and stupid and I wasn't thinking. Please stay. I need you to stay."

She looked him up and down, then came forward and put her right hand flat against his stomach. Her fingernails were light as they skimmed along the stretch marks. She seemed determined to touch them all, like a rat following an elaborate maze that led to his throat. Her fingertips came to rest on his Adam's Apple as they met each other's gaze.

Gisella smiled.

"You really are a work of art."

She took off her blouse and bra. Mark's attention went to the scars on her breast. He started to touch them and she stepped back.

"What are you doing?"

"Sorry," he said. "I just wanted you to feel good about your scars the way you make me feel good about mine."

"A little presumptuous, don't you think? Do I seem embarrassed?"

His face went hot and he knew he deserved a slap that never came. "I'm really being a dumbass tonight."

"I did this to myself, Mark. I'm proud of them. They were a learning experience."

"Learning experience?"

"Everything is if you have the right mindset."

"Goddamn," he said. "You're just about perfect, Gisella."

She led him back to the bedroom and pushed him onto the mattress.

"I don't think I can go again so soon," he said.

"Do you trust me?"

"Totally."

"Good. I'm going to make you a drink."

"I don't have any alcohol—"

"It's not a cocktail, Mark. More of a tea."

"I don't have any tea, either."

Gisella offered a slight smile. "Let me take care of it. You just rest here. I want you to relax. Don't pick up your phone. Just stare at the ceiling and let your mind go blank."

"You're serious?"

"It's meditation. Give it a shot. I'll be back in about ten minutes."

Mark watched her leave and then put his head on a pillow and looked up, listening to her rummaging around the kitchen. *Just stare at the ceiling.* The drywall texture reminded him of looking at satellite topography photos. He saw dunes of white sand. He saw canyons.

Gisella started singing. Singing or humming, he couldn't be sure. The words were indistinct, almost murmurs, like the sound of running water.

I have to hold on to her, he thought. It doesn't matter how we met, it matters what we are together. It doesn't matter who she is, it matters who she is with me. She's great. Gisella's just great.

The dunes and the canyons went away. He saw words emerging from their hiding places, like in subliminal ads.

Hope.

Love.

Happiness.

They might have been lyrics to Gisella's song.

Mark's head lolled a little. Heaviness touched his eyelids. The ceiling texture became indistinct, a blurred, smooth white surface. He thought of skin, taut and flawless, and smiled. He touched his stomach, expecting to find equal perfection. Tracing the familiar grooves darkened his vision. The texture began reasserting itself. Lines emerged. Crevices. Dark, purple distinctions.

Why, why had this happened to him? Why was he being punished?

Gisella's singing was stronger. Mark knew she was in the room with him but couldn't quite see her until she sat down beside him.

"Here you go. This will make you feel so much better."

He felt her hand behind his head, lifting him while the other brought the cup to his lips. The tea was not good. He started to cough at its bitterness but she did not relent. Gulping it by the mouthful made it better. So much better.

She put the cup on the nightstand and brushed the hair back from his eyes.

"Never forget how perfect you are."

He was hard again. Hard like he hadn't done anything in days. Gisella straddled him. He felt her warmth and tightness. Her face occupied the center of his vision, but the ceiling that framed her face had become wet flesh, riddled with bright purple lines expanding in all directions. He screamed once–into her mouth. He screamed all of himself into her and she swallowed it.

She swallowed it all.

Gisella left him a text in the morning.

Hope you don't feel too out of it. I'll be busy for a couple of

SAVING FACE

days but I want to meet up on Saturday. So don't go killing yourself.

Mark had only been up a few minutes, but he'd already read the message several times, already eager for Saturday to come. Police sirens blared from some distant point outside. He didn't give them much thought until another text message flashed on his screen.

Charlie.

Can you meet me on 92nd and Tavern? Podcast material. Urgent.

He texted back he was on his way, though that intersection was in the city's north end, twenty minutes away even without traffic. No time to take a shower. He sniffed himself, detecting only Gisella's trace scent, and decided he wasn't offensive. He'd just go to the bathroom and put on a little deodorant and–

Mark froze before his reflection in the vanity. The stretch mark at his Adam's Apple had grown overnight and forked into separate paths that ran across his throat like a gash. He groped the garish purple line with both hands, his breath reduced to a choked sob.

Mark pounded his fists on the edge of the sink until each blow felt like a sledgehammer on the cabinet. Meanwhile, his phone buzzed a second and third time.

Then a fourth.

Mark hung his head and shuffled back to the bedroom. He took the phone off the mattress and started to throw it on the ground and stomp it. All the new messages came from Charlie.

Hurry.
This is big.
Sinister.

Mark pulled at his hair. He touched his throat again and started typing.

Hey. I'm sick. Just hit me. Can't come.

He could smell the bullshit even as he typed it and Charlie's near immediate response was scathing.

This is beyond the podcast now. Get the fuck here.

Mark zeroed in on the curse word. He almost couldn't believe Charlie had written it. Had he ever heard Charlie say something like that in anger? Or even telling a joke?

Keeping his left hand cupped across his throat as he moved, Mark went to his dresser and opened the bottom drawer on the right. He rummaged through a few layers of clothes and found a shirt he'd never worn. He'd bought it off Amazon months earlier, convinced that if he did the worst-case scenario wouldn't happen. But here it was and he needed this shirt, this *In Case of Emergency, Break Glass* piece of clothing.

He smoothed out the brown turtleneck and put it on. The neck sleeve hugged his throat like a dog collar. Why couldn't it at least be winter? He knew it'd be 80 degrees by noon.

But to hell with it. He'd rather get stares for a fashion choice than—

Being a freak show in the flesh.

Too shaken to drive, Mark summoned a Lyft. He arrived to find a heavy police presence and a few hundred people massed across the street behind a barricade. As Mark wormed and pressed his way toward the front, he felt less insecure about his turtleneck with each step. No one was scrutinizing anyone in this crowd.

Charlie messaged again.

I see you. Make your way to the left street corner. I'll fetch you.

Charlie was there by the time Mark muscled to the spot. "Here," he said, holding out a press badge on a lanyard. It looked like something he'd brought off the Internet. As Mark slipped it over his head, he saw Charlie's eyebrows rise.

"It's that damn rash. Looks pretty gross."

"Not more unpleasant than what we're about to see," Charlie said, leading him forward. They crossed the street to the police line. A group of officers gave them sour looks, but Detective Warren waved them through. This floored Mark, and he leaned a little closer expecting to catch a heavy whiff of alcohol on her breath.

"Wait," Mark said. "What's going on here?"

"That's what we're going to help the good detective determine."

Mark leaned in closer and whispered in Charlie's right ear. "What the hell are you talking about? She can't be letting us enter an active crime scene."

"Mark, you're about to discover that the entire place is an active crime scene."

He looked up the length of the building. It was four stories, originally designed for offices but developers had repurposed the spaces into trendy lofts over a decade ago. They entered the lobby and encountered the first of many harried forensic teams.

"Where do you want us, Adele?"

"The first couple of floors have too much activity. Let's go up to five. We've got the elevators locked down, so we'll take the stairs."

It took a few minutes to reach the top floor. By the third flight, Charlie had to stop, doubled over and wheezing. Mark started to attend to him but Charlie waved him off.

"I'm fine. Just fat and old. Adele, take him up the rest of the way. Take care of him. The youngster might not be able to handle the shock."

"What in the name of *God* am I about to see?"

The question went ignored. Detective Warren motioned for him to follow her. They climbed the remaining flights in a couple of minutes and exited the stairwell into a hallway. There were five doors on the right and four on the left. All the doors were open. The stink hit him a moment later, and he stretched the top of the shirt up over his nose like a neck gaiter.

"Charles is right when he says the entire building is a crime scene."

"You know neither of us have any special skills or abilities, right? We're just two guys running a podcast–"

Detective Warren shrugged. "At this point I'll consult anyone. No one knows where to start. You and Charles are used to talking about the weird and terrible. Here it is."

She gestured to the nearest door. Mark found he didn't want to go in but knew he had little choice. He pressed his right hand over the cloth covering his mouth and nose and proceeded forward. He didn't have to go far into the new room to discover the most brutal thing he'd ever encountered.

There were one or two bodies present. The sheer jumble of jigsaw pieces of bone, flesh and viscera made it hard to tell. A pair of legs stood in the middle of the room. Part of a torso, hewn clean, rested nearby, skin blackened, eyes boiled from their sockets. Bits of toe and finger joints were scattered across the carpet like dropped kernels of popcorn. The air was heavy with a sickening odor. He remembered the Teaneck cannibal couple episode when Charlie got Detective Tumlock to describe the odor of cooked flesh. *A bit like beef, a bit like pork fat.* That mix of odor filled his nostrils even through the protection of the fabric. It seemed to be everywhere.

He backpedaled into the hall. Charlie had rejoined them now.

"The next unit is much worse," he said. "Family of four."

Mark shook his head. The top of the turtleneck fell back down his face.

"And then the elderly man in the third unit, and the gay couple in the fourth, and—"

Mark turned and fled down the stairs.

Ninety minutes later, Charlie had Mark crammed into the booth of a breakfast joint over protests that he wasn't hungry and might not ever eat again. Charlie meanwhile ordered like he was eating for both of them. A big stack of pancakes, bacon, hash browns, two sausage patties, and a pitcher of orange juice. Mark's gorge rose at the thought of it, and he almost puked when Charlie smeared the pancakes with a chunky strawberry jam.

The booth was big enough for six and Charlie wasn't shy about taking up table space. The waiter had to arrange the plates around a spread of notes and a city street map. The pitcher occupied a precarious spot at the edge of the table that drew Mark's attention every time Charlie jostled it.

"This is profound," Charlie said after working down his first mouthful of pancake. "Beyond all belief. Beyond all scope—and it's happening in *our* city."

He kept chewing but exchanged the fork for a pen and made a few circles on the map.

"The Pennington incident was here, and the Sweetwater garage drowning is there. Remember when three deaths excited us?"

"I don't remember being excited by any death."

"You know what I mean. Now we're looking at 162 more—and all at the same time! Impossibilities atop impossibilities."

Charlie took up the fork again and stabbed at the pancakes and the sausage. Bread and flesh went into his mouth together.

"Glad it hasn't turned you off your appetite."

"I've spent my entire life in search of a moment like this. From the moment I picked up my first John Keel book. I knew my life would be dedicated to investigating the strange. What's it got me, really? I'm on a first name basis with more frauds than I can count. It's so tiring talking about werewolves and vampires and urban legends again and again like I'm hearing about it for the first time.

SAVING FACE

Like I *believe*. That's the worst part, Mark. Some time ago, I quit believing any of it. I'd become a fraud myself. This," he said, marveling at the papers, "is like rediscovering God."

He looked up at Mark, showing the shy smile of an unburdened confessor. Mark found himself wanting to respond in a single way. Didn't honesty require honesty? Wasn't this a moment for reciprocal trust and revelation?

His right hand moved to the top of the turtleneck. Mark saw Charlie's interest at once. It may have been the one thing that could divert his attention from the map. He paused, on the verge of pulling down the fabric. Instead, he just rubbed his skin through the cloth before bringing his hand back to his lap.

"That rash still bothering you?"

"It's nothing," Mark said. He'd never spoken two words faster.

Charlie grunted and then started tapping the map again, his excitement resuming. Mark leaned forward. An immediate queasiness overtook him. The map was disgusting. It was vile. He had an unaccountable and overwhelming desire to snatch it up and wad it into a ball or rip it to shreds. In the ensuing moments, as the nausea built, Mark had to look away. He focused his attention on the untouched glass of ice water to his right. A heavy condensation had built on the surface and one large bead near the lip began to slide down, etching a trail.

Mark whimpered in his throat, grabbed a handful of Charlie's napkins, and wiped the glass dry.

"Are you okay?"

"No, I'm not okay!"

Charlie reached over to grip Mark's forearm. "I understand. I've been very callous in my reaction. I know the bottom line is the people. We're going to discover what killed them and give them justice."

Mark bit his lip and nodded. He tried another glance at the map. Impossible. It looked like a mass of wet, entangled entrails on the table.

"Justice?"

"Special crimes require special talents. Solti is coming."

"He'll just bail again."

"Not this time," Charlie said, his lips pressed tight as he flashed a look of rebuke. "He's already en route. I'm picking him up at the airport this afternoon."

Mark tried to do remote IT work the rest of the day, keeping the turtleneck on and purchasing a few more for same-day delivery. He only got up 20 times over the next five hours to stand before the bathroom mirror with the neck pulled down, watching his index finger trace the garish purple scar across his throat.

Around 3 PM, Charlie texted to say Solti had arrived.

My apartment at 6. We're doing a ritual.

Mark raised his eyebrows.

Not sure I can make it. Work.

Charlie wasn't having it.

This is an all-hands-on-deck situation. This is about saving lives. 6 sharp.

Right, Mark thought, sighing. Mustn't miss the *ritual*.

He went back to the bathroom, pulled the cloth down and started applying another round of lotions. "Saving lives," he muttered. "More like saving the goddamn podcast. Anything for ratings, right Charlie?"

Mark closed his eyes and bowed his head.

Who was he kidding?

In that moment, he'd have traded a few hundred more lives if it could make the stretch marks go away.

Charlie lived on the west side of town and Mark arrived at his place at 5:55 PM. Charlie welcomed him into a room that was almost pitch black except for a few flickering candles on the coffee table and bookshelves.

"Forget to pay your electric bill?"

"Solti's orders. Candlelight only for now."

"Ah. For the ritual. Where is Solti, anyway?"

"Meditating in my bedroom."

"Masturbating in your bedroom. Got it."

Charlie grabbed his arm. "I need you to be serious."

SAVING FACE

Mark raised a hand in compliance and moved through the dark to the sofa. Charlie stood in front of the coffee table. The candlelight revealed he was wearing some kind of robe. Or was it a gown? It went down to mid-thigh level. His legs were bare, and Mark squirmed from the uncomfortable notion that Charlie might not be wearing underwear. The fabric had a dull sheen like silk, the sort of thing Mark imagined wearing for a Japanese tea ceremony.

"Sorry, I can't help myself. Is that your leisure kimono?"

"Don't laugh. Solti has one for you, too."

Charlie tossed the garment into Mark's lap.

Mark flinched and re-examined Charlie's outfit. It had a plunging neckline that exposed all of his throat and much of his chest down to the sternum. His pasty, unblemished skin could have belonged to a mannequin.

"I can't—I won't."

He threw the clothing back, aiming more at one of the candles on the coffee table than Charlie, who nevertheless snagged it.

"What the hell's gotten into you?"

"It's insulting. It's demeaning."

"It's *ritual*, and that's important. Everything has to be just right."

"Just right for *what*?"

"Solti's going to contact the dead and compel answers from them."

Mark laughed. He tried to make it sound as aggressive as possible and did his best to return Charlie's stare in the lengthening silence.

"If this is about the rash, neither of us care."

"No, it's not about the goddamn rash!"

"Then what's going on with you?"

"Nothing."

"Your erratic behavior this morning was understandable. It even made me feel ashamed of myself for not being bothered. But I thought there must be something else and now I'm sure of it."

"Just tired. Some of us have other jobs besides the podcast."

"That's got nothing to do with wearing this robe."

"I'm not wearing the robe because it looks fucking ridiculous!"

"You are being deceitful."

The soft, ethereal voice came from the darkened hallway, recognizable to anyone who'd heard Solti speak. He cooed his words, elongating and rarifying every vowel. Solti might be the one man alive who could make German sound like French, and his appearance was every bit as rounded as his pronunciation. He was not fat, but he had no edge to him anywhere. His bald head and oval face were smooth, and his chin so weak he resembled a marble bust who'd had that feature chipped away.

"Solti, I hope our argument did not interrupt—"

"There was no disruption," he said, coming to stand next to Charlie. Then Solti dropped to his knees, angling his face above a particular candle. He aimed a shadowy stare at Mark and said, "There is much anguish here. Much anguish and corruption."

"Anguish?" Charlie said, then pivoted to Mark. "*Corruption?*"

"I'm—I'm fine—"

"Much illness. Much abuse."

Anxiety touched Charlie's voice. "Who's abusing you, Mark? Come on and tell me what's going on!"

"Nothing—"

"I hear voices," Solti said, his head now lolling from side to side. "Oh, so many voices, so many breaths. They call to me from—"

Solti leaned forward, right arm extended to try and touch Mark's stomach. Mark flinched away and his leg struck the table and knocked over two of the candles. One fell onto the carpet.

The room became a jumble of noise. "Intersections, roads, paths, fates," Solti chanted as Charlie moved back and forth picking up the candles and tamping out a small fire on the floor. The singed carpet gave off a harsh odor.

"Mark—"

"Roads, paths, the damaged skin, the ruined psyche—"

"I'm leaving," Mark said.

"The engraved design, the hideous intent—"

"*Mark!*"

His phone buzzed. Gisella was calling, not texting, something she'd never done before. Mark answered at once.

"You okay?" she asked.

"No," he said. "I'm not."

"I knew it. I just had a feeling."

Mark almost couldn't hear her over Solti's rising voice. "The pathways, the damage, the hatred!"

"*Mark?*" she said.

SAVING FACE

"Here!"
"The intersection! Flesh and road! Flesh and flesh! Flesh and fate!"
"Where in the world are you?"
"Just at a friend's house," Mark said. "I'm heading home *right now*."
"I'll meet you there."
Charlie pursued him to the door. "You have to stay. Solti's never heard a reaction like this–"
Mark pocketed the phone. "Sorry, I've got a girl waiting on me. I'm done with all of this bullshit. I just want to live my life with her and make it as ordinary as possible."
Charlie grabbed at him and Mark shoved him in the chest. This action seemed to shock them both. They regarded each other in the dark like two strangers. Then Mark opened the door and sprinted to his car.

⸺⚷⸺

Gisella was waiting for him when he arrived. As soon as they were in his apartment, he fell into her embrace and started sobbing.
"Please stay with me. Let's be–*normal*."
She cupped the back of his head. "I don't think I could ever be that, or want it if I could."
"Then let me be the freak in your life."
"You're not a freak."
Mark stepped back and pulled down the top of the turtleneck and lifted his chin. He just stood there like that for a long moment, letting her look.
"Tell me how ugly it is."
"I won't do that because I don't believe it."
"C'mon, Gisella. There's no way you think it's not disgusting."
She looked down, rubbing his right forearm. "Let me make you another drink. Something to relax your mind."
He nodded. Gisella gave his crotch a little squeeze.
"I'll relax this part in other ways," she said.
"Hot damn," he whispered.
"Just one thing. Turtlenecks are a really bad look on you. I never want to see you in one again. There's no reason to hide any part of you from me. In fact, from now on when we're together I'd prefer it if you just walk around naked. You're gorgeous."

"And you're something else," Mark said, pulling the shirt off. "I'm so grateful to have you in my life."

They kissed again. She directed him toward the bedroom and told him to get ready. He stripped and got into bed and listened to her working in the kitchen. She was singing again and the song itself aroused him, though he didn't understand a thing she was saying.

The stretch mark on his neck began to itch.

"No," he whispered, getting up. He went to the bathroom and watched himself rubbing the itch.

A new stretch mark had appeared branching up from the middle. He watched it grow in front of him, slinking toward his chin.

"No, no, no!"

He took what he could find and threw it at the mirror, wanting to shatter it. But what he had on hand were soft plastic bottles of creams and lotions, tubes of expensive futility that shattered hope far better than glass. Maybe his hopes were just more brittle.

"Mark?"

Gisella stood in the bathroom doorway with a steaming coffee cup. She was naked and glistening like she'd anointed herself with some oil. Her earthy, herbal fragrance was stronger than before, almost overwhelming. Mark couldn't tell if it was the drink or the oil. Just then he didn't care.

"Here," she said, offering the drink.

He shook his head and lifted his chin. "It's happening again. Why? Why am I like this? What did I do to—"

"Just drink. You'll feel better."

"It's itching and moving! It's going to get my face!"

"Baby, you're imagining things. You're okay. You're beautiful. Just sip a little, okay? It'll calm you down."

Mark's breath came in hyperventilating hitches but he tried to do as she asked. A lot of the drink dribbled off his chin, but he swallowed a little and found it soothing. Even the itch subsided.

She had him drink some more. He did with growing assurance, looking into her eyes as he swallowed. Gisella put the mug on the sink and led him back to the bed.

"I'm in a kinky mood tonight. You don't mind, do you?"

Mark swayed on his feet. "No."

"I want you to be all mine."

"I am yours."

SAVING FACE

"Prove it?"

"What . . . what do you want . . . me to . . . "

He teetered. She laughed and pushed him onto the mattress, flat on his back. The ceiling spun like a Ferris wheel. The light fixture seemed to dance around from corner to corner and Gisella went with it. He had the vague sense she was moving all around him, taking his left wrist and then his right, pulling them so much his arms didn't quite feel connected to his body. He couldn't move either of them anymore. Now she was at the foot of the bed, splaying his legs, securing them far apart.

He was so very exposed and helpless. She kissed up his right leg to his crotch and then mounted him, taking control with two powerful pelvic grinds that threatened to make him go then and there. Then Gisella stopped and leaned forward, running her fingertips all over his chest.

"Mine," she said. "I've waited so long, but now you're all mine."

"That's right," Mark said, panting the words. "I'm all yours."

She laughed and bent forward, her nose hovering over his chest as she surveyed his torso. "No escape now. I see you. I hear you. All of you. No roof can shield you, no basement can shelter you."

Gisella traced her finger up the initial stretch mark to his sternum and followed a secondary onto a spot near Mark's left nipple. "There you are, Jonathan. Who's the whore you've got with you? I'm sorry for her. Guilt and punishment by association."

She bit him. The pain was so sudden and shocking that it made a temporary cut through his brain fog. He felt the absolute authority of his bindings and looked down his body at Gisella's face. Her lips were very red and wet. She gyrated on his cock again, just once, and then went back to inspecting another part of his chest. "Randy, where are you? Out of town? Too bad. Next time. But there's Melanie. You should have taken her with you."

She bit again, causing another bright burst of pain. Mark writhed and shouted, "Stop it! That hurts!"

"Hush now," she said. "Just be quiet so I can listen."

"To what?"

Gisella broke into a big grin. "*Them.* Everyone. The whole city—moving, sleeping, eating, fucking. Babies being born. There— a car crash on 9th Avenue. It looks very bad. I think someone died. And here we are," she said, tracing her fingers down to his right flank, near the hip. "Your apartment building. I'm looking at us through your window."

Mark squirmed against his bindings. "This—this is crazy—"

"Is it?"

She pursed her lips and blew on his skin. As she did, a fierce wind gusted through the window and the building's stressed beams creaked and complained. Mark gasped. Even without the bindings he couldn't have budged an inch in that moment. The only movement came from his diaphragm—rapid, shallow, desperate.

"But what's this?" Gisella said, cocking her head a little to the right. "Two people coming into the building. They're talking about you. Oh, Mark, you have friends! I'm so proud of you! Want to see?"

She put her left hand over his eyes, and in that instant, he saw Charlie and Solti hurrying up a familiar flight of stairs. It was like he was a ghost following alongside them.

Charlie had a pistol and Solti a knife.

"You're sure he's in there?"

"Yes, and the peril is tremendous."

Solti's voice was more fluttering and delicate than ever.

Mark watched them exit onto his hallway. His unit was just two doors down on the right, so close they had to hear him if he shouted.

"Help! Help!"

Gisella slapped him hard on the mouth. "Now, now. None of that. Your job is to watch."

Charlie and Solti started down the hallway, weapons ready. Gisella made a clearing noise in the base of her throat and spat onto Mark's skin. As it landed, a tidal wave of mucous appeared at the far end of the hallway and surged toward them. The two men stopped in astonishment, then turned to flee. The river of spit was too fast and overtook them, throwing them back against the stairwell.

"*Cutis magicae!*" Solti cried, only just holding on. "The skin witch is here!"

Charlie struggled to clean his face as the sudden flood abated. "Can you fight her?"

"I can try."

Solti closed his eyes. A few seconds later, Gisella grunted. Mark felt no movement from her at all.

SAVING FACE

"Yes, I'm in her mind. A dark, vengeful place. But industrious. Curious. Insatiable."

"Can you incapacitate her long enough for me to kill her?"

"I think so." Solti's eyes narrowed. He stayed in place, concentrating while Charlie waded his way toward Mark's door, the hallway still filled with spit up to his knees.

Mark saw him reach the door. He had no idea what Gisella was doing, but her body was unmoving and heavy atop him. He had the sense that she was paralyzed. Keep at it, Solti, he thought. Keep her frozen long enough for Charlie to put a bullet in her head.

As Charlie turned the knob, Mark shouted for him to be careful. Gisella stirred. Mark heard her moan, and then—a growl of rage.

"I know how to get you out of my head," she said. In the next instant, Mark shrieked from the sharp bite of her front teeth and then the merciless, relentless chewing of his flesh.

Solti screamed. Enormous bite marks appeared all over his visible skin. Blood leaked from his eyes and nostrils as the meat of his body began to dimple and degrade. He clawed at himself for impossible relief. Charlie looked back and started running to him, but he only got a few steps before Solti's right arm fell off, followed by his left. Solti's bloody sockets looked down the hallway—seemed to look into Mark's own eyes. There was a moment of pure terror, and then—

Mark heard a crunch from deep inside Solti, as sharp as the crack of an ice cube, as blunt as the breaking of a walnut shell before it surrendered its precious meat. A jagged, diagonal gash appeared on Solti's body and his torso slid along the line, bit clean through the skin, guts and bones.

Charlie turned, making a struggling coughing noise as he clutched his chest. He got the door open only to stumble and fall into the apartment hallway. Then Gisella took her hand away and he saw only her face wet with blood and spit and the bleeding bite marks on his torso. She pulled away from him and left the room. Mark heard her say, "I guess it's too late to tell you I was always a big fan of *Sinister Cities*."

Mark thrashed against his restraints as Gisella returned, dragging Charlie's body with her.

"This has gotten a lot hotter, a lot faster than I planned, baby," she said. She sat by the side of the bed and traced her fingers all over his stomach and chest, gliding from stretch mark to stretch mark, licking her lips. "I'm going to have to leave you here for now. Have a little work to do. Some finishing touches. You're going to be a good boy for me and not make a peep, right?"

Mark shouted and she laughed. "It doesn't really matter. I'm pretty sure I've killed everyone in the building. Collateral damage since I didn't have time to be precise when I started chewing. If there is anyone alive to hear you, they're in a lot worse shape. Still, you can't stay here too long. I've got a nice base of operations set up and a table where you'll spend the rest of your days. Just a matter of getting you transported over."

"You did this to me, Gisella? How? *Why?*"

"The psychic freak called me a skin witch. I guess that name's as good as any. Skin magic is the most intimate and personal form of power you can imagine. With ancient roots in tattooing, branding, and bloodletting. Decorating, disfiguring. I started by trying it on myself."

She caressed the scars on her breasts and began to dress.

"It works better on another. Intention is an important part of the process, and it's more difficult to be intentional with yourself. At least, I've always found that to be true. You weren't the first. I chose a very fat man, someone with plenty of stretch marks as it was. I had half the city engraved on him when he died of a heart attack. After that I decided to go for the fit and active. Finding someone really vain about their body was ideal. An added benefit to help the *intention*. Someone who made it easier for me to feel good about marking up, and easier for me to insinuate myself into their life by propping up their broken self-esteem."

Mark tried his bindings one more time and gritted his teeth. Gisella stared at him as she finished dressing.

"I created so many fake dating profiles and used them to bait potential targets. You sent multiple torso pics to every single one of them. I knew I'd found my guy. It was just a matter of tracking you down, and that wasn't hard. Getting a skin sample was more difficult. I had to painstakingly pick through your garbage more times than I can count. Now here we are."

"You mutilated me!"

Her brows furrowed. "You *are* a thing of beauty. I mean that in all sincerity. You're my perfect, gorgeous instrument, and I'm going to wield you whenever I want. Just have to finish completing you, and I can take care of that tonight. Then I'll get you secured

SAVING FACE

in your proper place and begin exploring your potential. Goodbye for now, Mark. I'll be back for you soon."

He struggled against the bindings for about ten minutes after she left before his energy flagged and the drink's narcotic effects began to reclaim his mind. Even Gisella's dire talk about tables and his *proper place* was losing its weight and importance as dull acceptance etched itself into his mind. He saw himself tied down on a board under a single light, with Gisella gloating over him. Whatever she'd done to him, whatever she wanted, her victory was inevitable.

Then Mark saw Charlie standing beside the bed, working to free his right wrist.

He gave a low, disgraced chuckle at the hallucination.

"Stay with me, Mark."

"You're not real."

Charlie slapped him.

"I'm as real as it gets. When I saw Solti's destruction, I knew my own was coming fast. Faking a heart attack was the only play I had. At least we know she can be fooled. Her powers don't extend to telepathy, and she's arrogant enough not to bother checking on small details like a pulse."

When Mark's right hand came free, a jolt of adrenaline defeated the drink's effects. Charlie *was* real. Then he realized he was naked and exposed and his liberated hand started pulling the top sheet over his body as best he could.

"Stop it!" Charlie said. "Let me see."

"Finish untying me!"

Charlie grunted, moving around to the other side of the bed. Mark saw him staring at his torso as he worked.

"Please quit looking. I'm hideous."

"How long have you been like this?"

"It started on my 25th birthday."

"Why didn't you tell me?"

"It's *humiliating*!"

"You've done enough podcasts with me to know the fear of ridicule is the biggest ally sinister forces have. It's what lets them operate with impunity! You should have trusted me."

"With what? It's a fucking random skin condition."

"Oh no," Charlie said, his voice hoarse. "It's not random at all. Solti didn't explain every cryptic remark he made, but some of the words make sense now."

He stopped working on Mark's left wrist long enough to take the city map out of his pocket. It unfolded like a picnic blanket and he held it up. "I've stared at this so much I bet I could draw it freestyle. I know all of its patterns. Don't you see the similarities?"

Mark shook his head.

"The Jonesport Expressway," Charlie said, tracing the heavy line in the middle of the map. Then he pointed at the stretch mark that ran from Mark's belly button to his sternum.

"And here's Highway 12, and the railway lines, and–"

Charlie went on juxtaposing the map with the stretch marks until Mark couldn't stand it. "Stop! Please stop!" It all had to be coincidental, a horrible happenstance. But he touched the stretch mark running across his throat and knew it was 92nd Avenue. The intersection at Tavern would be right where the laser struck.

Oh God.

Mark reached for the map, trying to tear it from Charlie's hand. The paper tore in their brief tug-of-war.

"Are you crazy? We have to document this."

"I'm not going to be the subject of a podcast episode."

"I'm talking about bringing the witch to justice!"

"Fine. Go call Adele."

"It has to be us. We're not official. Bring in the police and you bring in *process*. Red tape. Court orders. Endless delays."

"Are you a podcaster, or are you a vigilante?"

Charlie frowned. He dropped his fragment of map and finished freeing Mark's left hand. Then he started working on the ankle bindings.

"If we call Adele, there's a chance we end up spending time in jail as suspects. Who knows what will happen then. If anything, we need to get you mobile and moving as far away from here as possible. Make sure the witch can't get to you."

Mark was about to agree to that when he felt the itch. It went from one ant to thirty in a few seconds and he made no pretense of holding back. He scratched and dug at his neck. The ants were moving back and forth across his throat and spreading up his chin.

"She's getting to me now," he said as Charlie stood there red-

SAVING FACE

faced and helpless. "The itching must happen whenever she's attacking me."

"Let me see."

Mark lifted his chin. He felt the fibers of his skin breaking apart like fissures in an earthquake. Charlie stared at him with his mouth agape.

"Show me the top of the map," Mark said. "How much is left to go?"

"About fifteen blocks."

"Gisella's going to complete the map tonight. She's going to take my face, and there's not a goddamn thing I can do to stop her."

"Don't you know where she lives?"

"No," Mark said, closing his eyes tight in despair. But in the closing of his eyes, he found himself standing naked in the middle of the Jonesport Expressway. Headlights bore down on him. He screamed as cars pounded past him–and through him.

"Mark? Mark?"

Charlie's voice came from the sky.

"Where am I?"

"What do you mean? You're in your bedroom."

He opened his eyes and looked at his torso. His right index finger was touching a spot below his sternum. Keeping it there, he closed his eyes again–

The flow of traffic roared toward him.

He opened his eyes to the bedroom again.

"What is it?" Charlie said.

Mark was too fascinated and uncertain about this new discovery to answer. He moved his index finger to a stretch mark on his side and closed his eyes. He found himself in someone's living room where a couple was having a fight.

Keeping his eye shut, Mark brought his finger up toward his left nipple. His surroundings blurred and resolved into a new environment. He now stood in a movie theater in front of a man who went on eating popcorn and staring straight at him as if Mark were the entertainment. Mark reached for the popcorn but his hand passed through the bag.

Charlie pressed his question on Mark again.

"It seems like Gisella isn't the only person who can use me as a map. Maybe it's because of the drink she gave me."

Mark let his finger go from stretch mark to stretch mark, and he jumped across miles in an instant, roving through streets and houses, eavesdropping on conversations, spying on people having sex, watching a solitary man sobbing alone in his living room. He saw kids vandalizing their school, a woman proposing to her girlfriend, a man climbing the fence of a closed cemetery to leave a flower on a grave. He witnessed scenes joyful and sad, mundane and thoughtful. The city and its people were his to visit at will.

Mark touched the stretch mark at the top of his left hip.

The woman he saw had her wrists bound with a belt. She kicked and screamed at a man who just laughed as he groped her and made heated, whispered threats. Mark stood beside them unnoticed.

"You're gonna love it when I'm through."

"No!" Mark shouted.

Charlie's voice boomed from the ceiling. *"What is it? What are you seeing?"*

"Call 911. A woman's about to be raped."

"Where are you?"

"I don't know."

Charlie was silent. Mark heard a vague rustling sound, also from the ceiling.

"Based on the map and where your finger's at you're somewhere in the 300 block of South Edison. But that won't do any good to a police dispatcher, Mark. I don't know what to do!"

The woman screamed. The man was on top of her now. Mark's body shook with rage. This was on him. He alone could stop it. How had Gisella manipulated matter? How had she–

Killed?

The itching along his throat flared again. It threatened his concentration and for one horrific moment the scene was gone and he saw only Charlie in a heavy sweat as he studied the map and his cell phone trying to determine a concrete address. Mark dug at his skin but the itch was becoming as bad as it had been in Mortelli's office. He thought of the laser and its consequences for everyone inside the lofts on 92nd and Tavern. He thought of Gisella's bites and poor Solti.

"I have it," he said.

"You do?"

"I think so," Mark said. "Something I have to at least try."

He closed his eyes and returned to the bound woman. He fixed the rapist with a cold, hard stare until the man occupied all of his thoughts.

Then he pinched and twisted the stretch mark.

The rapist howled, falling off the bed and writhing. He sprawled across the floor like he'd been kicked in the gut. A grinding, thudding noise came from within, alternating between the crunch of bones and the sound of meat being tenderized.

Mark pinched harder.

The rapist shrieked. His body spasmed from head to toe as a final breath came gurgling out of him. His wide, sightless eyes retained a final expression of terror, and Mark looked to the woman wishing he could personally assure her of her safety.

Her back was to him, but her body was curled up and shaking. Mark leaned over and saw her face was bloody and broken.

And he knew the rapist wasn't the man who'd done it.

"You're sure about this?"

"Yes," Mark said.

"But why do you have to physically find her? Why not use—yourself? Destroy her from afar?"

Mark shook his head. "If I knew I could find Gisella alone and isolated, that might work. But what if she's in an apartment complex like mine? I don't have the skill to avoid—collateral damage."

"Then why can't I come with you?"

"*No.* Leave the city. Drive at least beyond the boundaries of the map. It's the only way to guarantee your safety."

"But I want to stay with you," Charlie said. "You'll need help."

"There's no help you can give me on this one."

Charlie held up his gun. "You're telling me this is useless?"

"We don't know one way or the other. Let's say the worst happens and it isn't. She'll know you're alive after all. Her revenge on you will make what she did to Solti seem like mercy. No, Charlie. Get off the map and hide yourself. You're going to be the backup plan if I fail. You're the new resistance."

Charlie pressed the gun into his grip and said, "Might as well have it on you as a last resort." Then they shook hands and Charlie got into his car and headed east, the quickest way out of town.

Mark slipped the gun into the pocket of his black trench coat. He wore no shirt beneath it and put his finger on the corresponding stretch mark, allowing himself to occupy Charlie's passenger seat until he was sure Charlie wasn't trying to trick him. The instant the car passed the map boundary Mark found himself jerked back into his body.

He took a deep, measured breath. "I'm coming for you, Gisella."

Letting his right index finger stray to another part of his torso, Mark set off on foot, eyes half-shut, the city before him and the city under his finger occupying equal measure in his sight. He was getting used to skipping from stretch mark to stretch mark now, the way a practiced pianist can occupy an entire keyboard without looking at the keys. He heard traffic at the intersection ahead and a sweep of voices like a wind moving through the trees, the rapid sampling of a thousand conversations as his index finger scoured the city.

He'd walked a few miles when he caught Gisella's familiar earthy scent. Mark wasn't sure just where he was sensing it. The odor was in his nose but not in the air. Was he closing in on her?

Another twenty minutes passed with him following any path that made the odor grow stronger. His physical location and the position of his index finger on his torso began to synchronize until both came together on a single spot before a mundane brick home.

There was a maple tree in the small front yard and he leaned against it and pressed down a little on the stretch mark. This placed his consciousness inside the living room. Gisella's scent almost overpowered him. The room itself was full of dead candles and figurines made of crystal. The coffee table had a strange pattern on it, like a labyrinth.

A noise from the hallway drew his attention. He walked through the darkness, guided by the faintest bit of light from an open door that led down to a basement. Gisella's scent rushed up at him from below, potent, concentrated.

She was down there.

He descended into a room that almost defied his comprehension. It was about 300 square feet, but where most would have turned the finished space into a family room, Gisella had made a peculiar dungeon. Torture implements hung on the wall, but Mark's gaze focused on a full-sized pool table that had

SAVING FACE

been modified with a series of restraints and straps. A tapering black candle arose from each pocket.

That's where she means to keep me, he thought. I'm to live out the rest of my life on that table as the instrument of her will.

The walls were covered in pictures, interspersed with painted symbols—unrecognizable glyphs mixed with clear renditions of body parts, eyes and hands, mouth, nose, feet and penis. The pictures were photos printed on paper. Mark recognized all of them as selfies he'd sent to various girls when he was 19 and 20. How many of those profiles had belonged to Gisella?

Coming closer, Mark saw many of the photos were drawn on with a black Sharpie. One had a deep line going from his belly button to his sternum. Another photo, a profile shot taken in a mirror, showed several dark lines etched up his side. Mark got the sense he was looking at failed attempts, early stabs at inflicting the dark fate she'd decided for him.

He heard the sudden, soft coo of an infant, followed by a gentle "Hush" from Gisella. Both sounds came from his right, where Mark noticed a freestanding room partition. He found Gisella standing alongside a table that hosted a male mannequin. The plastic torso was covered from waist to neck in a collage of map scraps interspersed with pieces of his selfie photos, placed on the plastic surface and then brushed in place with a clear liquid that turned the finished product into a hardened shell. He watched her applying these scraps along the base of his left jaw now.

There was a crib behind her. The child inside it couldn't have been more than a few months. It kicked a little, staring up at the mobile hanging over its head. The mobile was a miniature globe. Mark looked from infant to globe and back again as the child gave another sigh.

"Hush, now. You'll eat just as soon as I'm—"

Gisella went rigid. For a long moment she didn't move at all. Then she turned and seemed to look right at him.

"Mark? You're here, aren't you?"

Gisella held out her hands and he flinched away as if she could touch him. She rushed forward and for a moment she was standing inside him like someone passing through a hologram. She shuddered, clutched her head and fell to the ground. But she was laughing.

"Isn't it amazing, the power I've given you? The whole city at our disposal? And all it cost you was your pretty body."

She moved to the main room and the pool table, her splayed fingers massaging its green velvet surface. Mark stood to her right, but Gisella addressed him as if they were facing off across the table.

"Take a good look at your new bed. Think of the fun we'll have together. Go anywhere in the city. Given enough time and experimentation—and flesh—even the world . . . "

The infant started to cry. Gisella smiled.

She reached into one of the table pockets and took out a lighter. She lit the first black candle and moved toward the next one in the upper right corner.

"We can punish anyone for their crimes at any time. That's what got me on this path in the first place. This is about righteousness, Mark. This is about justice."

She was speaking faster and faster, moving about the table, lighting each candle and looking all around as she talked.

"Imagine the things we'll do. Imagine how fulfilled you'll be, how easy you'll have it? All you have to do is lie down. You'll be well-rewarded. I'll keep you very happy. More sex than you've had in your life."

Gisella lit the final candle and took it from its holder at the bottom of the pocket. She wrapped her right hand around the base and gave it a suggestive stroke as she looked about the room.

"You know how good I am at pleasing you. All you have to do is be mine. I'll keep your candlestick burning—unless you want me to blow on it instead."

She jerked the candle close to her lips and spat out a breath to extinguish it. A tremendous amount of smoke came from the wick and Gisella turned, waving the candle like a wand, sending the smoke in all directions. As soon as the first tendrils reached him, Mark experienced something like a bodily shock, and coughed as if he had lungs. Gisella spun in the direction of the sound, her eyes bright and gleaming.

"*There* you are!"

Mark coughed harder, stumbling back. Gisella took another candle and extinguished it right in his face. The smoke's earthy scent suffocated him and drove him to his knees.

"Little far from home, aren't you, sweetie?" she said. "Feeling a little disembodied? Here's the thing, Mark. All I need is your shell. Your mind can atrophy as far as I care. I was just going to be nice and give you a good time in exchange for your sacrifice. But you'll be a lot easier to manage under the new plan."

Mark found the smoke wrapping around him, binding his arms against his sides. Gisella stood over him with the third candle in hand.

"The only real problem is going back to your apartment and getting your body over here. That was always going to be an issue, but I figured I'd drug you into a state of compliance. That option won't be available now."

Mark tried jumping back into his body. For a second, he seemed to occupy both places. The brief taste of fresh air through his actual lungs was a jolt of strength. But the smoke held him fast in the basement. His first instinct was to pinch hard and bring down the whole roof.

But the baby . . .

"I figure you're good for one, possibly two more candles, Mark. Then your thoughts will just dissolve away into nothingness."

He made a second effort at leaping back. This time he was able to open his eyes and lurch his body forward a few steps toward the front door before the smoke pulled him back to the basement. He saw Gisella getting ready to blow the candle out in his face.

"Wait," he whispered. "You might . . . might need . . . "

She laughed. "I assure you, I don't–"

He leapt back. Got his body moving forward. Then the cruel return.

"–You're just someone fate dealt a bad hand, if you believe in that sort of thing."

Back into his body. Pumping the muscles. Reaching the front door. Trying the knob.

Locked.

"Damn," he said, coughing just as Gisella blew out the candle. It struck his face like acid. She was right. He felt like he was dissolving.

Door's locked. What can I do? What can I–

Back into his body. How many more chances would he get? How much time was left? *The baby. Save the baby.* He struggled to raise his right arm. It was like trying to curl a 25lb dumbbell with his pinkie. But he lifted it. He jabbed at the doorbell.

Mark heard the doorbell ring in the basement. Gisella looked at the ceiling.

Got to make her—make her—go—
Another leap into his body. He pushed and pushed.

In the basement, the chiming doorbell made it sound like a crazy person was at the front door. Gisella had a look of confusion and a little worry. She started up the stairs.

Just a few more rings.

Pushed a fifth time. A sixth. Mark swayed on his feet like a man on stilts. If he lost this final balance, if he fell, there'd be no standing.

Mark heard Gisella approaching. He rang a seventh time and pitched himself right, back flat against the brick. Just a little bit more, he thought. Open the door. Step out. Step out.

He got his right hand into the pocket of the trench coat. He couldn't pull the gun free.

Step out.

The door was opening.

Couldn't pull the gun. But he could raise his hand, gun and all. The right side of the trench coat rose.

Save the baby.

Gisella poked her head out. Not all the way but just enough. Her mouth opened when she caught sight of him just standing off to the side, posed almost like a mannequin himself. He saw total incomprehension in her expression. Then something passed through her mind. Maybe it was the realization that she wouldn't have to do nearly as much work as she'd planned in order to get him onto the table. Maybe it was renewed confidence that whatever god or power she worshiped was delivering for her in ways she'd never expected, making everything go her way. Maybe all of this and more were passing through her thoughts just before something else passed through her brain.

Mark fired.

Joshua Viola *is a Colorado Book Award winner and Splatterpunk Award nominee. He co-authored* Legacy of Kain: Soul Reaver—The Dead Shall Rise, *an official prequel to the beloved video game series, which became the 4th most funded graphic novel of all time on Kickstarter, raising over $1.4 million. He edited the* Denver Post *#1 bestselling horror anthology* Nightmares Unhinged *and co-edited* Cyber World, *named one of the best science fiction anthologies of 2016 by Barnes & Noble. He co-*

SAVING FACE

authored the comic book slasher series True Believers *with Stephen Graham Jones, featuring official cameos from icons like Jamie Lee Curtis, R.L. Stine, Jeffrey Combs, and Barbara Crampton. As a producer, he has contributed to films such as* Aliens Expanded, The Thing Expanded, TerrorBytes, Shelby Oaks, Shrine of Abominations, Deathgasm II: Goremageddon, *and the recent* Deathstalker *reboot directed by Steven Kostanski (*The Void, Psycho Goreman*), starring Daniel Bernhardt (*The Matrix, John Wick*) and produced with Slash from Guns N' Roses. In 2024, he founded Bit Bot Media with musician Klayton (Celldweller), a multimedia company focused on original and licensed IP, including* The Terminator, Legacy of Kain, Evil Dead 2, *and more. Bit Bot also collaborates with Canadian film studio Raven Banner Entertainment on film productions, merchandise, and distribution, including titles like* The Autopsy of Jane Doe *and the documentary* Hate to Love: Nickelback. *Joshua's video game development includes work on titles such as* The Rocky Horror Show, Pirates of the Caribbean: Call of the Kraken, Unioverse, The Smurfs, TARGET: Terror, *and others. He is the owner and chief editor of Hex Publishers and resides in Denver, CO, with his husband and son.*

Sean Eads *is a writer and librarian living in Denver, Colorado. He is originally from Kentucky and has a Masters degree in literature from the University of Kentucky and a Masters degree in library science from the University of Illinois. His first novel,* The Survivors, *was a finalist for the Lambda Literary Award. His third novel,* Lord Byron's Prophecy *was a finalist for the Shirley Jackson Award and the Colorado Book Award. His fifth novel,* Confessions, *was also a finalist for the Colorado Book Award. His favorite writers are Ray Bradbury, Herman Melville, Cormac McCarthy and Ernest Hemingway.*

VULTURES

Naching T. Kassa

They slip into my room,
Their beaks like razors,
Ready to peck and rend,
Before my body grows cold.

The breath rattles in my breast,
As they lay about the floor,
Bundles of black feathers,
Stirred by my gasps,

How could I have birthed,
Such beasts as these,
These monsters whose faux smiles,
Hide the hate they hold.

In the throes of death,
Their thoughts I witness,
To them I am nothing more,
Than a soulless lump of gold.

Their shadows loom above me,
Moments ticking slowly by,
Like the beats of my shattered,
And throbbing heart,

VULTURES

Soon they fall upon me,
Hastening the death desired,
I grin for they cannot know,
I changed the will long ago.

Naching T. Kassa *is a wife, mother, and writer. She's created short stories, novellas, poems, and co-created three children. She resides in Eastern Washington State with her husband, Dan Kassa.*

Naching is a member of the Horror Writers Association, Mystery Writers of America, The Science Fiction and Fantasy Writers Association, and various Sherlock Holmes Scions. She serves as the Talent Relations Manager at Crystal Lake Publishing and was a recipient of the 2022 HWA Diversity Grant.

A CLOWN AT MIDNIGHT

Mia Dalia

THERE WAS SOMETHING about the air here. Every time the circus crossed the Mason-Dixon line, he felt it in his bones—the barometric pressure pushing him down, closer to the earth.

Maybe it was just age. He wasn't getting any younger. Staying ageless under the thick clown makeup might trick the audience, but he felt every one of his years like tree rings around his heart.

Every night after a performance the clown sat in his wagon in front of an old patinated mirror and slowly took off his garish makeup. He ate an apple while doing it; he was never really hungry after the show—too amped up to eat—so an apple proved to be a perfect balance of nourishing and refreshing. A perfect midnight treat.

The face revealed beneath the bright colors was old and tired. Wrinkles around the eyes, jowls beginning to sag, a long nose that drooped, arrow-like, toward a downturned-in-perpetual-disappointment mouth. But mostly it was in the eyes—the sheer exhaustion of year after year of forced jollity.

Sad clowns were a cliché. He didn't want to be a cliché. He only got into this racket because once upon a time running away with the circus seemed like the most exciting and romantic of ideas. Sure, he chased a skirt there, young and foolish as he was, but she left, and he stayed. Stayed and discovered he didn't have much by the way of circus skills. He was neither flexible enough nor small enough nor odd-looking enough, but he could make people laugh. That always came easily to him, he was always clowning around. And so, he turned a natural skill that got him cuffed behind the ear

A CLOWN AT MIDNIGHT

one too many times by his pa into a profession. Became a clown by trade.

A decent enough of a gig, a decent enough of a life. Then the days began to blur into one another; years passed by like calendar pages flipped too fast, and, somehow, he got old.

There was no one in his life to notice, no one to care. The other performers formed cliques, but he was never really a joiner. Some of the newer circus folk probably wouldn't even recognize him out of his clown costume, and the anonymity was nice. Sometimes lonely, but mostly nice.

Made him feel like he could just disappear, and no one would notice.

The clown fantasized about it some days. Puff and gone, like a magic trick. Nothing left behind but an empty wagon with too few earthly possessions to speak of a man's life, a wet condensation ring on the bar counter, a pair of oversized bright red shoes with no feet in them.

Who'd know? Who'd care? Show must go on. He knew just how quickly he'd be replaced.

Another bite of an apple. Red Delicious tried too hard. A name like that . . . He preferred the tartness of a Granny Smith or the juicy sweetness of Galas, but he wasn't too picky.

He wiped some of the makeup off with a clean but permanently stained towel. Prepared to meet the familiar stranger in the mirror.

Only this time there was no stranger; there was no one at all. With makeup gone, there was only a space where a cheek should have been.

It looked like something out of a trick mirror, but his mirror, though old, held no tricks that he knew of. He wiped at his face some more. The result was the same. The only thing the makeup removal revealed was emptiness.

Soon it was all gone. In the mirror image, he ended above the oversized frilly clown collar. No neck, no head. He took a bite of an apple and watched it disappear.

Peeled off his white gloves and realized he couldn't see his hands either. An invisible hand held up the red apple to the invisible mouth as he took another bite. It was surreal.

MIA DALIA

His heart squeezed tightly in panic, and he took a deep breath waiting for it to let go. He quietly reveled in the terrifying strangeness of what was happening. It seemed oddly appropriate somehow—reality manifesting his thoughts and feelings.

If this was a trick, the best he'd ever seen. And he'd seen plenty.

Apple eaten to the core, he discarded the rest into the bin. Then he took off his entire costume and his underthings. Beheld the invisible man in the mirror. Ageless once more, but through different means.

He lay down on his narrow bed and thought of the meaning of this. Then of all the possibilities this altered future might hold for him. Then of all the limitations.

What would you do if you could go unseen? Spy on people if you're so inclined. Rob banks, maybe, but surely that took more than invisibility. He imagined every possible practical application, and nothing stood out. The only thing, he supposed, was magic. But he had never had any aptitude for it, and the circus already had a magician.

In a way, being invisible was sort of like freedom, but not the good kind. No, this was the one where there was nothing left to lose. He had only ever had his face, his body—a pliable appearance, readily made into a joke, easily marketable as entertainment. The only way to bring it back would be with layer upon layer of makeup.

He'd never be seen as anything other than a clown now, but then again, that has long been the case anyway. And so what? That's life for you. A mystery with a sense of humor. He shrugged, pulled up a tattered old blanket over his invisible form, and fell into a dreamless sleep.

Mia Dalia *is an internationally published, CWA-nominated author of all things fantastic, thrilling, scary, and strange. Her short stories of horror, noir, science fiction, mystery, crime, humor, and more have been featured in a variety of anthologies, magazines, literary journals, online, and adapted for narrative podcasts.*

Her stories have been voted top ten of Tales to Terrify 2023 and shortlisted for the CWA's Daggers Awards 2024.

She is the author of the novels Estate Sale *and* Haven, *novellas* Tell Me a Story, Discordant, *and* Arrokoth, *and the collection* Smile So Red and Other Tales of Madness.

https://daliaverse.wixsite.com/author
https://linktr.ee/daliaverse

SUSPENSION

Brandon Wills

THE CARS BESIDE my home never move. Nothing does anymore. I am the only living thing on this planet that isn't permanently frozen in place, stuck as if the film has been paused. Strangely, everything else still functions normally—the wind blows, the weather changes, the trees and foliage still shift with the previous two, but all types of animals are stuck just like humans. There are perhaps millions of birds that have plummeted to the ground during mid-flight, same as how our airplanes did. I still don't know what happened, but this is how it has been for seven lonely years.

The first day was like any other—I woke up at 8 AM for work, had my morning routine, and hopped into my car for work. The first thing that gave away the problem was the completely immovable traffic. Going through town was normal enough but I didn't encounter another vehicle until I tried to merge onto the interstate. Not a single car, truck, or semi was proceeding.

At first, I thought there had been an accident, which does happen occasionally. After about an hour, my patience had worn thin. No one had pulled in behind me, so I angrily threw the car into reverse and tried an alternative route. That attempt had the same results, jammed traffic again. Frustrated, I went home and decided to work from home that day.

I tried to call my boss to tell them, but he didn't answer. Then I tried several of my co-workers, who also didn't answer. That was when the alarm bells started ringing loudly inside my agitated brain. I remember thinking, *'What in the hell is going on? Am I still asleep?'*

BRANDON WILLS

When I tried my girlfriend, Sandra, who also didn't respond, that was when the panic began. I tried every person in my family, even those that I hadn't spoken to in years and none of them answered either. I checked all my social media and not a single post went beyond 7:59 AM, not even from major corporate news sites who normally post something at least every five minutes. What was going on?

My rattled brain gave up after several hours, deciding to just lay on my bed and watch television. The feed for all the news channels was constantly playing commercials, no live feeds whatsoever. Other channels that didn't have live shows were running as usual.

Once I felt somewhat rested, my desire to find out what was going on returned and I decided to venture outside. Carefully, I looked around to make sure that something dangerous hadn't happened, and after concluding that it was safe, I wandered about town.

My realization at the truth came when, a block from my apartment, I walked past a restaurant with a large front window. In it, I could see patrons having their breakfast, but they resembled mannequins more than humans. All of them were stuck in various awkward positions while they had been eating, drinking coffee, or as one person was, purchasing.

Curious, I went inside to find answers. I walked very slowly around the place, terrified that they might do something horrifying, like all spring to life suddenly. The older gentleman at the counter purchasing was the first one that I approached. I tugged on his polo sleeve and said, "Excuse me, sir. Excuse me?" Nothing, not even a twitch of the head to indicate he had heard me. His mouth and face were frozen as if he were able to say something to the cashier, who was smiling and holding a bag of food toward him. I walked around the place, waving my hands in front of people, yelling directly into their ears, breaking things and banging pots and pans, none of which produced any results.

Frustrated and confused, I left. On my trek back to the apartment, I ate food from the restaurant and decided that I would hop into my car and head over to Sandra's place. She was off that day, and as far as I knew, she didn't have any plans. Once I had made it to her townhouse, I found the spare key and let myself in. Her home sat quiet and dark. My watch said it was now 1:17 PM

SUSPENSION

and that would normally be unlike her to still be asleep, or maybe she was gone.
    In her bedroom though, I found a heartbreaking scene. She was sleeping soundly in her bed, nude as always, but beside her was another man. I had no idea who this was. In a fit of primal rage, I dragged him out of the bed and beat him until my fists and wrists throbbed in pain. He didn't react whatsoever to my rage-fueled pummeling, but he still bled and bruised. Sandra lay in the same position, appearing as if stuck in a deep sleep. I said some choice words to her, gathered numerous things I had bought for her, and went back to my apartment.
    I spent the next few hours sulking and nursing a bottle of liquor. After deleting all the pictures of her and I from social media, I realized how pointless that seemed to be. Every website from across the planet seemed to show the same halt in time. I even found traffic cameras in Japan that showed stalled traffic with glimpses of people inside, all frozen in place. By that point, I was confident that I wasn't having a nightmare.
    The next day, after what happened with Sandra the day before, I wanted to explore other places. I packed a few bags of essentials, loaded them into my car, and set my destination for a random place by the Pacific coast in Oregon. Navigating my way out of the Eastern time zone was difficult, and the interstate had to be avoided completely. It took me much longer than it should have, but once I was in the Midwest, traffic had thinned significantly.
    I only needed to occasionally move around paused vehicles on the interstate after I was in Colorado. The rest was smooth sailing. The town in Oregon also had the same strange case of paused people and I soon found an empty little cottage that I claimed as my own. After all, who was going to stop me? This is where I lived for the next year.
    I utilized my time wisely. With no need for a job or a social life, I decided to travel. I've been to almost every state in America, including Alaska. I did teach myself how to sail with some internet videos that I found, and I decided I was going to use those skills to head to Europe. I waited until summer and sailed first to Iceland, then sailed east toward Ireland.
    Oh, let me tell you, Ireland is breathtaking in person. If you can read this, you should go. It's well worth learning how to sail. Soon, I found myself traveling all over Europe, exploring castles,

breaking into high-security places such as Buckingham Palace and the Vatican. No one was going to stop me, so why not?

On occasion, I will find people in some rather, shall we say, vulnerable, circumstances. I have seen lots of people on the toilet or in the throes of coitus. But there are also people who are permanently frozen in horrific situations. I once found a man stuck bleeding to death from a gunshot wound to the chest, his face stuck in a look of agonizing pain, and his eyes wide stretched open in absolute terror. I'll never forget it. I have found car crashes with people bleeding behind the steering wheel, people dangling from ropes in their homes, and people frozen in the middle of beating someone else senseless. Sometimes it doesn't pay to be nosy.

Right now, though, I'm traveling the left coast of Italy heading toward Pompeii. If somehow, anyone is out there and they can read this, please reply. It's been a very lonely seven years. I cry myself to sleep on many nights, and on others, I suffer from the throes of anxiety and cannot sleep.

Television stopped working years ago. The internet somehow still does. Places that derived their electricity from renewable sources still have power. All over the world there are plane crashes, ships that have crashed into harbors, massive fires that wiped out towns because no one was there to put them out. I keep traveling, to constantly run away from the fact that I am truly alone in this world, and yet, it's always there to remind me.

I haven't mentioned the strangest part of all, and this is the part that causes me to have rough nights. Once the sun begins to set, I can see what appear to be shadows of people going about their daily lives. They walk down the street, get into vehicles, wave at each other—all the normal things in life. I've even tried to respond to them with my own shadow, but they never react.

I think I'll go to bed now. When I wake up, I hope this will all be over.

Brandon Wills *was born and raised in West Virginia. He has been reading, writing, and telling stories since he was old enough to do so. He writes for* Paranormality Magazine, *is a member of the Horror*

SUSPENSION

Writers Association, the WV Writers, Inc., and is part of the Wild & Weird Radio podcast. He still lives in West Virginia with his wife, Emily, and three children, Paisley, Brody, and Bryce, along with their plethora of cats, dogs, and chickens.

HELLO

Karen Bayly

"LAST STOP!"
The guard strode to the front of the carriage and turned to face its occupants, his clipped moustache bristling with officious glee. None of my fellow passengers, currently slumped in their seats, were keen to sit up, let alone leave.

It had been an arduous journey. Forbidden to speak and crammed into a space furnished with narrow benches and no air conditioning, we understood our place. The food was barely edible—leathery meat and stale bread washed down with tea so weak it was indistinguishable from dirty water. I suppose selection for the Outlands meant you forever relinquished any dreams of simple pleasures.

"Come on, you lazy good-for-nothings!" he shouted, smirking. "Time to leave. Or will I introduce you to my friends?"

He smiled and nodded to outside, where six masked soldiers stood, guns at the ready.

The woman next to me leaned closer and whispered, "I expect we'll be 'introduced' soon enough."

She was a lovely creature with glossy black hair and luminous skin, but her eyes were hollow with fear.

Squeezing my arm she asked, "Promise you'll say hello when you see me?"

I hesitated for a split second. We were strangers plucked from our ordinary existence to serve the State. Our future was with the working men of the toxic Outlands, bringing sexual relief to their short, brutal lives. I wished I could reassure her, but what was the point?

HELLO

"Please. I'm afraid of losing myself, of not being me anymore. If you say hello, I'll remember who I am. It's important if I'm to survive this."

The guard leaned over us, a mean dog itching to bite.

"Well, aren't you the Chatty Cathy?" he snarled at my companion. She shrank back into her spot.

I realised the other women were spilling out on to the platform. As the first woman passed by the soldiers, they reached out, fondled her breasts and buttocks. She didn't utter a single word. The second woman followed, head high, and the men pawed at her body but to no effect. Then came the third and the fourth and so on—all with heads held proudly. Not one of them flinched. None showed any emotion. Brave women, braver than me.

A scuffle behind me caught my attention. Our tormenter had grabbed my companion's wrists and was wrenching her from her seat.

"You." He looked straight at me. "Get out."

I stumbled down the aisle. There was no sense fighting. This was our life now. The gains we'd made, the fight for equality, the #MeToo movement, all for nothing. One devastating world war and it had all come undone.

I heard my friend cry out in dismay as he pushed her to the ground and forced himself into her. I wanted to scream like a banshee, rip his throat out, and cut the heart from his chest. Instead, I drowned in powerlessness.

At the door, I turned, desperate to do something. He was on top of her, bare bottom rising and falling with each invasive thrust. Her gaze drifted upward to meet mine.

"Hello," I whispered. How painfully desperate and inadequate that one word sounded.

Her face glimmered with hope as she mouthed "Hello" back at me.

Shaken, I walked out into the blazing heat and toward the waiting women, ignoring the soldiers and their filthy, probing fingers.

"Hello," I said, wondering if one word really could have power.

The eyes that met mine brimmed with sisterhood.

"Move on," yelled a soldier.

Heads bowed, we shuffled off, silently swearing revenge.

We would find a way.

KAREN BAYLY

Karen Bayly *is the author of three books—*Tesato's Code, *a dystopian cyber-thriller, and the steampunk adventure novels* Fortitude *and* Courage. *Her short stories have appeared in anthologies from Crystal Lake Publishing, Black Beacon Press, Black Hare Press, and Specul8.*

Her writing is a mix of speculative fiction, horror, noir and mystery, though she also writes the occasional story for younger folk. Karen lives in the outer suburbs of Sydney, Australia, with two indoor cats, two guitars, and two ukuleles. You can discover where she lurks on social media here: https://linktr.ee/karenbayly

PHILLY'S LITTLE BOY

Linda D. Addison

(inspired by Alessandro Manzetti's *Kolkata's Little Girl*)

Chestnut Street, at midday.
Tommy is counting the yellow cabs
go back and forth, full of tourists
with their faces framed in windows.
He's waiting, in front of the manicured
park for someone to tell his story;
it's only one dollar.
—fifty-two, fifty-three.

He's only eight,
a thick leather collar around his golden
brown neck; a frayed rope hanging from
a loop at his throat; a strange rosary
for a thin boy. He's still waiting,
with eyes unblinking, so ancient, a
brand unhealed on his shoulder.
—seventy-five, seventy-six

A dark brown girl, with a toothy smile
and flowered yellow dress
stops near him; she seems to see him.
Maybe she notices me? thinks Tommy.
Or did she catch his shadow?
But the girl raises her hand and
waves to a man near him, who rushes

LINDA D. ADDISON

to lift her in his arms and run across
the busy street, without a glance at him.
—eighty-five, eighty-six

It's only one dollar, Ma'am
whispers the little boy, stretching his hand
towards a tall pale woman wearing a long
blue striped dress, a style at least a century older,
her blond hair piled high on her head, walking
past his piece of sidewalk,
this wicked place.
But she doesn't answer him, opens a lace parasol,
like it will deliver savory hope, and continues
on her way, skipping like a little girl.
Maybe she's a ghost too, thinks Tommy.
—one, two.

Linda D. Addison is the award-winning author of five collections, including How To Recognize A Demon Has Become Your Friend. *She has been honored with the Horror Writers Association's Lifetime Achievement Award, Mentor of the Year and the Science Fiction & Fantasy Poetry Association's Grand Master of Fantastic Poetry. Find her work in:* Blood Games: A Vampire Anthology, Playlist of the Damned, Enter Boogeyman, *and* Bestiary of Blood: Modern Fables & Dark Tales. *Her site: www.LindaAddisonWriter.com.*

ASHES IN WOOD

Jonathan Winn

THROUGH THE KEYHOLE, he stood in the center of the room digging in the front pocket of his well-worn khakis. And, buzzing cell now in hand, brought it to his ear.

"You in?" her voice, familiar and frantic, said on the other end.

"Yepperoo, just got here."

He put down his scuffed and faded duffle bag before running a hand through hair the color of rain-soaked earth. Face pleasant and forgetful, spots of pale pink blushing his round cheeks, he was neither thin nor fat, tall nor short.

"And?"

"It's a room," he said. "Bed, pillows, blanket—sorry, duvet—side tables, desk, a few lamps. Big window. Curtains. Oh."

"Oh? Oh what?"

"There's a chair. In the corner." A pause. "Guess I got upgraded to a VIP suite."

"Ha ha."

A shared laugh.

"And, oh wow, check it out. I even have a bathroom with a shower. Whoa, and a toilet?"

He could hear her smile. "Living large, buddy."

"Now," he said, sitting on the edge of the bed, "Is there a reason you insisted on this room in this hotel?' He glanced toward the closet. "You're not gonna, like, jump out of the closet in some sexy bear costume with a can of whipped cream or something, are you?"

"A sexy what?" She laughed. "What the hell? I think the flight attendant slipped you one too many bags of peanuts."

"Not for three bucks a pop, she didn't."
"You drinking your water?"
"Yes, ma'am." He reached in the end pocket of his bag, took out a plastic bottle, unscrewed the cap, and took a long sip.
"Good."
Another sip as she talked. Something about the weather feeling like rain, and Tipsy, the neighbor's dog, bounding up the driveway and getting slobber on her Manolos, and then something about what that insufferable bitch Marjorie said in yoga class this morning.

The stream-of-conscious rambling a predictable, well-worn path that had become a calming constant in the six months since they'd first exchanged numbers. The sharp ping of his first text as they still stood chatting, followed by the sound of her happy tapping as she texted back, the both of them sharing the first of many laughs. This surprise love upending his predictable days in unexpected, delightful ways.

And then—

"I'm familiar with that hotel, you know," she said.

"This one,"

"Yeah, Great-Grandpa Theo, from the Old Country, my dad's dad's dad—yeah, that's right, dad's dad's dad—he stayed there when he first came to the States."

"Really."

"I think Great-Grandma, before she was Great-Grandma, a very smart woman, one of the few who could read and write back then, and beautifully, by the way, was working at the front desk when they met."

"Ah, so that's why you wanted me to stay here."

"Call it tradition."

"I call it sneaky." He grinned. Cleared his throat. Took another sip of water as she stumbled through a story told to her too many years ago by an aunt or a friend of her mother's or maybe it was someone her uncle knew or something about something-something-something to do with an annual whatever around the holidays, or a holiday. An Old Country thing, she wasn't sure, but all the family would meet and celebrate with tons of food and whispered prayer and something, something, something, she couldn't quite—

He coughed.

ASHES IN WOOD

"You drinking your water?" she said.

"What, you some kind of majority shareholder in—" He glanced at the bottle. "Unlabeled generic plastic bottled water company or something?"

"Yes, and Unlabeled Generic Plastic Bottled Water Company is good for you, so—"

Another cough. Loud and long.

"Drink your water," she said.

"Jesus." A sip. "I'm sorry. Damn."

"That sounded rough. You good?"

"Yeah." Another sip. "Listen, sweetie, I think I might be fighting something. Gonna rest for a sec, if that's okay."

"Of course it's okay. More than okay. Lay down, keep drinking your water, and do nothing."

"We'll catch up later, yeah?" he said with a nod, and then felt stupid because how the hell is she going to see him nod?

The bottle was sitting on the floor at his feet. He didn't remember putting it there. And she was taking forever to say goodbye but, goddamn, he had no idea what she was talking about.

It was like she was speaking another language, none of the words sounding familiar or fitting into sentences he could make sense of. And he really should say something but his head was starting to thump-thump-thump and there was now silence on the other end.

Had she hung up?

He wondered how long he'd sat there, cell to his ear, listening to nothing.

Setting the phone aside, he took a breath.

The room was standard. The oversized bed firm, but still sinking soundless under his slight weight. Two deceptively plump pillows feeling much too Clorox-bright snuggled the wood headboard, the heavy duvet a dark green field spread wide, draped head to foot, its skirt running off the smooth edges to not quite graze the ground.

Across the small room waited the door and an over-large wooden desk, its corners scuffed, with a budget-friendly chair, a landline phone, a flat-screen TV, and a boxy remote perched in all its dust-covered glory along the edge.

If he had to guess, in the front drawer would be well-thumbed menus for bland Chinese, cardboard pizza, passable Thai, greasy

Italian, and an outdated phone book no one needed next to a hotel directory that everyone, himself included, ignored.

To his right waited a bathroom, to his left, standing sentinel on either side of the bright white and running green, two matching side tables with two matching lamps.

Heavy curtains, floor to ceiling, were pulled half-closed, the late afternoon sun shining through the limp sheet of thin white linen or whatever it was covering the center of the large modern single-pane window.

The oatmeal-colored carpet beneath his feet looked rough and scratchy and the walls were painted a pale shade he imagined Corporate called "Who Cares, It's Cheap."

Between the door and the bathroom, an amateur painting of a chaotic carousel of garish dancing horses hung awkwardly.

He exhaled, long and slow, his head thick and tight and spinning and still thump-thump-thumping. The throbbing between his eyes now a constant keening ache that spread over his jaw in a threatening fog of impending agony.

His eyes closed, he found himself wondering if the rough and scratchy oatmeal beneath his feet would be cool against his cheek.

He stood, the room spinning before he calmed it quickly with a cleansing breath, and then made his way to the bathroom, his steps halting and careful.

The lights above the mirror too bright, he ducked his head to the sink, an unsurprising rectangle of thick porcelain, his hand fumbling for the faucet. A moment later, palms cupped beneath a steady stream of clear water, he quieted, for the moment, the burn on his cheeks, forehead, neck, lips. His wet hands safe and soothing.

The marble on the walls, faux or no, surprised him. As did the wall-to-wall mirror crowning the sink and the marble countertop. Where the main room felt basic, this felt more . . . Like someone dipped into their own pocket to augment Corporate's Dollar Store budget and at least try. Or something.

His stocking feet felt cool against the large tile on the floor.

When did I take my shoes off? he wondered, his knuckles white as he found himself gripping the countertop, the room lurching to the left, and then the right, his stomach following suit, the bile burning and sour as it flooded the back of his throat.

He swallowed.

ASHES IN WOOD

He needed to sit down.

The hardwood floor felt cool against his cheek. He'd come into the other room, he realized. The main room. The basic room. The room where no one tried.

He was lying down.

Whatever was hitting him was pummeling him like a prizefighter, his aching muscles spasming so hard he was afraid they'd rip through his skin. The chills racking his body made his teeth chatter like Siberian winter. His cheeks were hot, his hands cold. His vision, his fucking vision, was blurring. Which never happened.

What the hell?

This wasn't the flu. Too fast. Too severe. And it wasn't COVID. He'd done that and this was worse. Food poisoning? He hadn't eaten anything but bran cereal with vanilla yogurt and that was hours ago. If it was food poisoning, he would've blown chunks on the plane.

No, this was hell. Torture. Confusion.

Fear.

And the light streaming through the bare window was killing his eyes. He had to close the curtains.

He lifted to his elbows, slow. And then, rising to his knees, he pivoted, the metal springs in the slender bed squeaking as he rested his chest against the thin mattress. Clutching fistfuls of patchwork quilt, he raised his head and stopped.

The window faced him, but it looked different. And there was a too-small desk, a chair with an ornate rounded back before it. The curtains not heavy, but light and gathered in their billowing middles with a tasseled cord. He blinked. Looked again.

A large window. Two horizontal panes separated by what appeared to be a thick slab of wood frame. A crank on the side to open them. Tiny desk. Lamp overwhelming one corner, the lampshade reminding him of those vintage faux Tiffany ones cluttering the second-hand furniture shops downtown. Chair with a rounded back, yes. Light curtains with a tasseled cord hooked to the wall. No thin white linen or whatever between them to mute the sun.

He turned and sat, collapsing, his legs stretched before him, back resting against the mattress, palms splayed flat against the wood floor. Steadied his breath. Focused on the wallpaper near the dark wooden door and a slender standing coat rack. Wondered where the plastic bottle of water was. Felt too awful to look.

Hadn't there been scratchy oatmeal against his cheek? He thought so, but when? Another place? Another time? Where did this standing coat rack come from?

He couldn't remember, moments ago feeling like months, minutes like years.

And who the hell used wallpaper anymore?

Pausing, he looked again at the heavy wooden door and then the coat rack, a large, rounded knob on top to hold a hat, he imagined. A fedora or a straw hat, maybe. And, above, what looked like a gas lamp capped with a dome of frosted glass. The kind he'd seen in old black and white movies, it jutted from the wall between the door and the desk.

And the wallpaper. Rising from waist-high wainscoting—large panels of scratched and scuffed wood set end-to-end—it lay, puckered and wrinkling in the middle, the edges peeling at the corners.

A muted collision of dusty flowers and faded-green grass, it was, the long sheets a continuous tale of a chubby-cheeked girl picking flowers, bonnet tied in a too-big bow under her double chin wearing a blue dress sun-bleached pale and white bloomers over thick, pale knees, and a boy golden blond with a sailor hat and eyes that shone too-bright and tiny feral teeth smiling too-white with faded navy-shorts capping bony knees and slender, pale calves forever frozen in mid-leap as he ran pushing a tiny paper boat with a tiny scrap of a sail with a small stick in a sudden pond with a duck that had been yellow many suns ago but was now—

He heard himself shout. Or cry. The noise odd and wrong. His hand flattened to his lips to strangle the sound.

His heart raced, his throat closing. He fought to steady his breath. To recapture reason. The bottle in his hand was empty. He didn't recall searching for it, or finding it, or lifting it, or holding it. He dropped it to the floor, the sound of flimsy plastic rolling on wood sounding far too far away and somehow not real.

Needing water, every swallow an agony of razor wire slicing slow, carving deep, gauging clean to bone, he fell forward, crawling on elbows and knees to the bathroom.

Where there had once been large squares of cool tile, more hardwood waited. The sink was no longer a modern rectangle but,

ASHES IN WOOD

instead, a dainty porcelain oval. After a squeak, rumble, sputter, the antiquated faucet, darkened with age, spurted a thin, hesitant stream of lukewarm water. The mirror above wasn't the corner-to-corner span of perfect clear, but a small circle of clouded glass hanging in a polished wooden frame.

Palms cupped, he brought the murky pool to his lips.

The toilet had a tank sitting above it with a cord.

Another gas lamp sat on the wall.

He needed a doctor.

A woman sat in the chair with the rounded back in front of the window.

"Can you call a doctor?" he heard himself say. He was back in the main room, standing, his legs feeling heavy, his knees threatening to buckle. His voice was faint. Too faint to be heard. He swallowed. Grimaced. Almost wept. Realized he was now kneeling. Crawling, slow and careful, his elbows coming again to rest on the bed, the springs squeaking as the thin mattress gave way.

"Can you—" he started to say and then stopped. His eyes felt heavy. He wanted to rest his head, close his eyes. Stop. His throat burned. He swallowed again. A metallic tang lingered on his tongue, wetting the roof of his mouth, coating his cheeks, slipping over, between, around his teeth.

Blood.

The stranger at the window was writing. Her quill pen dipping into ink drawn from a squat glass jar of viscous black, the words staining the page in what felt, even from a distance, like careful, ladylike cursive, only to return to the inkwell—yes, that's what it's called; an inkwell—dip, and begin again.

She was small. Her silver hair pulled into a bun that sat on the top of her head. Her high-collared dress buttoned in the back, ending in a ruffle at the neck. They looked like pearls, he thought, the buttons on the back, though everything was more blur than not by now except for those brief moments when a blink brought clarity, and clarity more panic and confusion.

A thick skirt fell to ankle boots which looked like the kind that buttoned in the front. But her back was to him so he wasn't sure. And she was sitting so he couldn't actually see where the skirt fell so he was just imagining old-timey boots that buttoned in the front.

For some reason, he felt certain she smelled of bright lemons and sweet mint. Was there even a perfume that smelled of lemons and mint? He didn't know.

He took a deep breath and cleared his throat. Regretted it.

She stopped, the pen pausing, her cursive halted in mid-memory. Her head lifting, she turned toward him, slow, the pen coming to rest on the small square of paper.

Another spasm gripped his muscles. The keening ache between his eyes made him gasp. He steadied his breath though Siberian winter had returned to chatter and click his teeth.

Facing him now, her eyes met his and then looked past him, beyond him, to the door. She started to rise, the silk of her dress rustling, her skeletal hand gripping the rounded back of the ornate chair, the knuckles reddening as she pushed herself up slow and careful.

He blinked, her face blurring, and she was gone.

The chair sat empty, the desk clear.

"Help," he said, the whisper sounding so unlike him he wondered if he'd even spoken at all.

He turned and slid to sit on the floor, his back against the bed. And for a moment, it looked like a face in the wall was watching him. Across the room. The forehead, cheeks, nose, chin, a neck pushing from the wallpaper as two eyes found him and stared.

This is crazy, he said to himself as a long stream of red slipped from his mouth to slide down his chin and land in his lap.

The wood felt cold against his back. He was lying down. His muscles cramped. He could, in his mind's eye, almost see them unwinding, his muscles. Detaching. Letting go. Ligaments and veins and nerves slithering, disengaging, unwrapping, untangling. Leaving the familiar safety of solid bone and glistening flesh. Hanging loose to dangle, their exposed ends tender and raw. Vulnerable.

"Are you lying down?" her voice, familiar and frantic, said on the other end of the phone.

He didn't remember calling her. Or answering the phone. Or finding the phone to hold to his ear. *Was* he holding it to his ear?

He didn't think so.

His tongue swollen, his teeth chattering, blood coating his throat with every swallow, he answered without words, Yes, yes, I am, I'm laying down, I am, laying down, yes.

"They're coming," she said.

ASHES IN WOOD

Thank you, he tried to say. This is bad. So bad. So fast. Out of nowhere. I think I'm dying. He started to cry.

"Do you see them?"

Who? he wanted to ask. The doctor? An ambulance? Please let it be an ambulance. Someone with a shot to make it all go away.

There was a woman here, though, he thought of telling her. An older woman in olden times clothes. With grey hair. A bun on top. And a quill pen she dipped in black ink from a thick, heavy inkwell. A real inkwell. She wrote cursive. Fancy cursive.

Did she get help?

He lifted his head. His hands were at his side. He stared at them for a long moment, blinking his vision clear, establishing that, yes, they were at his side and he wasn't holding a phone. But he was hearing her and she was saying

"You need to drink your water,"

but he couldn't. It was empty, the bottle, the cloudy memory of plastic rolling along wood feeling like lifetimes ago.

He was going to sleep now. Exhausted, no doubt, from the shivers and the spasms and the pain and the fucking razor wire mauling his throat with each bloody swallow.

Someone was kneeling next to him. He caught the smell of an old heavy suit rancid with sweat. And powder. Talcum? And there was something else, too, like hair gel, or dye, or pomade. He didn't even know what pomade was.

Funny word, that: pomade.

Whatever it was had the pungent stink of oil, thick and heavy. The kind that speckles your brow on a hot sunny day. Or runs over your ears and down your neck, staining your collar before sliding in slender streams of dark along your spine.

An arm, thin and wiry and strong, was around his shoulders lifting him. A bottle was at his lips, water splashing his chin, running down his neck. The one, two, three swallows lava hot and tasting of crimson.

He heard the silk swoosh of long skirts nearby. The light tapping of heels on wood. In his mind's eye, she sat, pen in hand, ink dipped and ready. Her silver hair gathered into a neat bun.

"Theo," came the whisper.

"Hush," the stranger cradling him said.

Cold fingers were unbuttoning his shirt, pushing aside the

striped cotton so an even colder palm could lay flat against his chest over his heart.

It felt nice. Soothing. Calming the burn, quieting the fever.

He lifted his head to say thank you, blinked, and saw that face, in the wall, pushing free.

A small boy, it was, his nose and chin made of wallpaper as he emerged, his slender shoulders agile wood pushing from the waist-high wainscoting, the wall pliant like chewing gum sticking to him in long ribbons. Almost desperate, it seemed, the wall, in its reluctance to release him as first one leg, and then the other stepped free, it all settling back into solidity as the boy stopped, turned, and looked at him.

Impossible, he tried to say, and then laughed. The cold palm on his chest shushed him as the laugh turned to bone-rattling coughs, the coughs to the feel of razor-wire gouging his throat, the swallowing of the inevitable blood bringing yet more stinging waves of incendiary pain.

He could feel his socks being rolled down his calves and tugged over his heels. Then the sound of someone approaching. New footsteps. Not the boy, who he imagined was the one now placing small hands on his bare feet, ankles, shins. And not the silk swoosh of skirts. Or not the same skirts, at least.

But light and limber. Small, he imagined, but not young. Not a child. Someone kneeling next to his waist, though, someone new, her dress rustling, yes, followed by the sounds of jars.

Jars?

Glass, sturdy and thick, jostling in a crate, perhaps. Like milkmen, back in the day, announcing themselves by that distinctive clink-clink-clink as they strode up the flower-lined path to the back door or up one-two-three stairs onto the porch before rapping three-two-one on the front door.

These are paramedics, he found himself thinking. Yes, as his shirt was removed and what felt like balm being massaged into his shoulders, his chest, his biceps. The hollow of his neck. The bottles are medicine and the arm cradling him was a a doctor and the sudden burn of a knife slicing along his collar bone, tracing shoulder to shoulder, in one long, deep, merciless cut—

"See us," a voice whispered in a pleasant cloud of lemon and mint, the breath hot against his eyelids, the lips as near as a mother's kiss.

ASHES IN WOOD

A night many decades ago. This room, new. Night outside the window. He saw it. The gas lamps glowed bright, the wallpaper fresh and smooth, the corners resting perfectly. The desk at the window and the coat stand by the door, a fedora resting on the bulb on top. A wiry man, older, sat smoking a pipe, his long arms cradling a small newspaper on his lap. Across from him, the lady in ruffled silk-stained thick paper with careful thoughts. A young boy lay on the wood floor nearby, feet up, ankles crossed, propped on his elbows, a small book laid before him.

Then, a fist pounding, the door shaking.

"See what they did," the voice whispered again.

A wet tongue licked his eyelid and then, fingertips drawing them open, traced, wet and rough, around his eyeball. The tongue was soon followed by the lingering kiss of soft lips and the delicate gnawing of small teeth.

Smoke filled the air. In this impossible time in this still-new room decades ago. Thick black smoke billowed from a wall of fire slicing the room. In a corner, there, they huddled, coughing, gagging, retching.

Faceless, in silhouette, strangers stood beyond the flames, thick-shouldered and broad, blocking the door, guns in hand.

One lifted a pistol, finger on the trigger.

"Gotta let 'em burn," a gruff voice said, lowering the gun, the sneer unseen but heard.

The silk skirts caught fire first.

"Turned lies into enemies," another whisper said much too close to his ear as the first whisper suckled the sight from the delicate globe of gelatinous blue.

One eyeball was gone, he knew that now. There was no pain. Odd. Not even when, stiff ruffles covering the small bosom of the familiar stranger smelling of lemon and mint pressed to his forehead, fingers pinched open the second eye and, blessing with a kiss, bit the defenseless orb with her teeth to gnaw anew.

"Trapped us," the whisper said as in living memory coughs became screams, hair exploded in great towers of unruly flame, tender skin blackened and bubbled and peeled, and bodies exhausted by agony, their lungs smothered in blankets of acrid smoke, collapsed to lay silent. Lifeless arms still raising as muscles contracted. Torsos sitting only to drop again. Legs, though dead, bending and kicking slow.

JONATHAN WINN

The arm cradling him lowered him to the ground, the cold palm still resting on his chest as the hungry stranger followed, her teeth sawing muscle, her tongue coaxing nerves, his remaining eye no longer his own as it wiggled free in a gulp to burst against her tongue.

Cleaved shoulder to shoulder, he lay, a lone finger dipping again and again into the cut. His blood the ink for what felt like letters, or maybe numbers, traced on his naked flesh. A careful underline here, the pointed period of a full stop there. A red prayer, he imagined, spanning wide from deep collarbone cut to the bottom of his rib cage.

The finger stopped. Words were being whispered before jars jostled and clinked as skirts rustled and a heavy hem scraped wood, the thin sound of a small woman on heels soon a fading chorus of click-clack to a corner.

The palm, cold and smelling of thick pomade and a sweat-stained suit, rested below his ribs.

"Ashes beneath wood," came the whisper. "Charred bone in corners long forgotten."

I don't understand, he wanted to say. What do I—?

His stomach was wet. He could feel it, warm, almost hot, pooling on his skin. Spilling in rivulets down his sides and curving along his back as he breathed.

There was an odd feeling, then. A shifting in his guts. Like fingers, careful and slow, had parted the flesh to burrow deep, moving aside intestines, liver, pancreas, kidneys. And then the soft caress of knuckles grazing the underside of his ribs.

A door opened. Manolos tip-tapped across wood.

"Thank you," her voice, familiar and frantic, said from somewhere near but somehow still too far.

He could feel her kneeling next to him.

"This feast, it goes back and back and back with my family. Beyond memory. It simply is. Inescapable and always." He heard her sigh. "And you were so easy. So trusting and warm. Eager. For love, to belong, to please" He imagined her smile, then. "And desperate hunger knows nothing better than an innocent heart eager to please."

Those gentle fingers deep in his guts paused on the thump-thump of his heart.

"In the end," he felt her words warm on his cheek. "Your kindness killed you."

ASHES IN WOOD

Then they pounced, those fingers, clawing blood-pumping muscle, tearing free thick pumping red in a greedy fistful.

And somewhere, too near but still too far, the sharp ping of a text came through, the tap-tap-tapping of her response to this new kind soul, this new love, this new trust, growing faint as those ashes in wood, his still-beating heart in hand, enjoyed their feast.

Jonathan Winn *is the award-winning author of* Eidolon Avenue: The First Feast *("a great read . . . powerful and jarring," Cemetery Dance) and* Eidolon Avenue: The Second Feast *("Makes Elm Street look like Sesame Street."—Rex Hurst, author of What Hell May Come),* Martuk . . . the Holy *(A Highlight of the Year, 2012 Papyrus Independent Fiction Awards) and* Martuk . . . the Holy: Proseuche *(Top Twenty Horror Novels of 2014, Preditors & Editors Readers Poll) as well as* The Realtor: an Eidolon Avenue Short Story, *part of a series of free reads from Crystal Lake Publishing, and* The Martuk Series, *an ongoing collection of short fiction inspired by Martuk . . .*

His work can also be found in Horror 201: The Silver Scream, Writers on Writing, Vol. 2, Tales from the Lake, Vol. 2 *with his award-winning short story* "Forever Dark," *various editions of* Shallow Waters, *and* "Ashes in Wood" *in* Hotel Macabre, Vol. 1, *all from Crystal Lake Publishing.*

A VIDEO READING OF "TAKING THE PISS"

JASPER BARK

Enter if you dare!

SCAN ME

ALL WE ENDURE

Grant Longstaff

YOU DON'T KNOW how long you have been driving, but the bones in your fingers ache and the skin stretched over them has turned a bloodless white from gripping the wheel so tightly. The deserted road ahead, which you have come to think of as your own, snakes through a starless night. The sky above is wearing all the colours of hurt. You know these colours deeply, intimately.

But now you are running.

Now, you are free.

You are alone in this world and there is nothing but black road in the headlights until—a thumb, a fist, an arm—a woman by the side of the road. You do not know her, but you know the fear on her face.

You have worn fear, too. And too often.

You stop, watch the girl bathed in the bloody red of brake lights stagger into the road behind the car. She stops at the passenger window and you see some part of yourself, in another body, from another time and place, looking back. You see the tears, still fresh on the girl's bruised cheek, and know they will sting the split in her lip should they reach it. You open the window to warn her, to tell her that even when she thinks the pain has stopped it will keep coming, but instead say, "Where are you going?"

"Wherever you are going, I guess."

The girl is beside you. It is not a cold night, but she is shivering in the passenger seat so you turn on the heater, knowing there will be no comfort in it. You offer her a crumpled paper handkerchief, still damp, made thin with your own tears, and the girl presses it to her lips without hesitating.

You drive.

"Who did this?" you ask some time before dawn.

"An old flame. You?"

How does she know?

You glance at the girl; she is holding the wad of tissue in her open palms. Watered with your collective grief it has blossomed into an ugly, grey flower.

"Someone who swore to love me." You swallow old agonies.

"How often they say that. How often they use it to make us stay." The girl sighs. "All we endure."

The pale circle of flesh which haunts one finger, the ghost of a ring you left behind, is the only visible relic from a life of torment you can't ever forget. Your heart will forever be a coiled knot of scar tissue.

"Keep running," the girl says, "keep running for those of us who no longer can."

The girl places the handkerchief onto the dashboard and then she is gone and you are alone again.

You weep for the girl as the light of a new day chases away the wounds of the night.

You drive on, and on, and on.

You will survive.

No.

You will live.

Grant Longstaff *is from Gateshead; a small, suitably dismal town in the North of England where nothing much happens. He had no choice but to write fiction. Though he now lives in Glasgow, his heart remains in the North East.*

His debut novelette, Between the Teeth of Charon, *was released in June 2022.*

His short fiction has appeared in the Bram Stoker Nominated Arterial Bloom *and on* The Other Stories *and* Tales to Terrify *podcasts.*

You can find him on Twitter/X @GrantLongstaff and Instagram at @grantlongstaffwrites.

ON A SWING

Patrick Malka

THE SWING FACES a rusty chain link fence, train tracks, and some sparse woods beyond that. The sky is a vibrant blue, dotted with tall white clouds. I can feel the heat on my skin and the steam rising from the damp overgrown grass. The park is isolated, built between a strip mall and train tracks. The equipment was never moved or reappropriated. My father is behind me pushing the swing, singing a few lines of Iron and Wine's "Passing afternoon." But the singing starts to slow and slur. Then the pushing stops. I hear my father breathing hard, groaning. Then the thud of his body hitting the ground. Looking down, all I see in my available field of vision is his hand on the ground, reaching out, displacing the tall grass. I look ahead and there is nothing and no one. I am entirely alone. Two years old, alone is not a feeling I know at all. I am a twelve-minute walk from the nearest person, but I may as well be an astronaut making his way around to the dark side of the moon. All sounds have condensed to a windy white noise and the sizzle of insect wings. It's getting hotter, and the thick, black vulcanized rubber the swing is made from is getting uncomfortable to touch. With the swing chain screeching a regular rhythm and my feet dangling from the little leg holes four feet off the ground, I don't know anything is wrong yet. The empty world lulls me to sleep. And there's darkness for a while.

PATRICK MALKA

My father died of a heart attack at the age of 36. What made his death so spectacular, other than his young age, was the fact that he died while pushing me on a swing in an isolated, essentially abandoned playground he favored exactly because it was a quiet space that could just be ours. He collapsed with me still swinging above him, propelled by the momentum of his final push. My father was a high school math teacher; he had a few weeks off in summer and he and my mother agreed he would look after me during that time to save a bit of money on daycare costs. My mother was a pediatric nurse and it happened to be her turn in the rotation to work the night shift. She needed to sleep as much as possible during the day. Not that having a two-year-old helped much. She'd often said she woke up that afternoon and couldn't understand how she had slept so well for so long. Then she realized, we hadn't been home all day.

When I, the two-year-old me, wakes, I immediately feel pain. My skin feels tight and is uniformly red under my thin white T-shirt with a baseball-playing bear on the front. My stomach hurts and my lips are cracked. My diaper is wet but as it dries, the cotton sticks to my irritated skin. At some point, my baseball cap fell off my head. I can feel the thin skin of my scalp tightening and cracking under the beating sun. I try to shift but burn myself on the exposed seat and metallic nuts and bolts of the swing. I'm stuck and begin to realize the extent of my isolation and the fact that my father is no longer there to help me. I don't cry and I don't cry out for help throughout this memory, which is odd. It feels like something any kid would have done. Instead, I sit and struggle and feel pain in silence. Pain I don't know will ever end.

Then I feel a presence. A shadow falls over me. My eyes sting and tear from the relentless sun so I can't immediately see but I like the feeling of being hidden behind whatever, whoever just stepped up in front of me. I look down; my father's hand is no longer in the grass. I look up. He is standing a foot away from the swing. He looks so disappointed. He looks like he's about to cry. His eyes are so bloodshot, anything dripping from his eyes would surely also run red. He's mouthing, very softly whispering the final

ON A SWIG

line of that Iron and Wine song over and over. I reach up my arms for him to pick me up, feeling safe now that I see him, but instead of reaching for me, he throws his hands up to his face and screams. A loud, rasping sob of a scream that is drowned by the simultaneous passage of a train in the distance. I feel it like a smack. I close my eyes and scream too, but the only thing my exhausted, sunburned, dehydrated little body can muster is easily drowned out by the hurricane of regret produced by my father.

That's the moment I open my eyes, lying on the floor in my son's bedroom, arm painfully numb from holding his hand. This memory only seems to come to me when I am comforting my son at night. After some time spent singing and holding him, he sleeps, and I feel as far from him as my father probably felt from me while standing in front of that fucking swing. I've already had more time with my son than my father ever had with me. I'd like to believe I have more to come. But my father probably thought he would have more time, too.

We were discovered that evening. I was unresponsive and barely recognizable, but I survived. When I open my eyes, lying on my son's bedroom floor, I don't know that I ever left that swing.

Patrick Malka *(he/him) is a high school science teacher from Montreal, Quebec, where he lives with his partner and two kids. His recent fiction can be found in* Black Glass Pages, 34 Orchard *and* Brave New Weird Volume 2 *among others. He can be found online on X @PatrickMalka*

HELL COME HOME

Amanda M. Blake

dear Satan I want a bike and a place to stor it were I can hide to.

Not all letters addressed in his name come to him. Christmas magic reads intention. If the kid writes 'Satan' by accident, it goes right up to the big man at the North Pole. But sometimes . . . sometimes the letters flutter over his weary hooves.

The first letter from Gracie is clearly a misspelling, but it ends up in his hands anyway, which means she's too ambivalent about Kris Kringle for the letter to reach the right recipient.

Satan doesn't mind. It's something to entertain himself with during a season when most attention is on the birth of a savior and the antics of his cartoonish sidekick.

Hundreds of years—and traveling all the time, as Dickens once wrote. Without chains, though, such wandering is freedom. During Christmas is even better. People have expectations of what the Devil is supposed to do in pale winter moonlight, but he enjoys the lights as much as anyone else, even if he loves darkness, too.

He is an adversary, not an enemy; he can dance as he wills, good or ill. Those who invoke him are usually angry, jaded, cynical, ironic, selfish, too clever by half. The children are best, their desires simple, his magic on the same shelf as God and Santa Claus. Their love, too, is clean and pairs well with cookies and milk.

Dear Satan, How has your year been? I've been good and don't want much. I know my parents are struging but

HELL COME HOME

could I have one of the dolls that closes her eyes and doesnt cry?

Even when she should know how to spell Santa Claus correctly, she continues addressing the letters to him, maybe because she receives what she asks for and doesn't want to ruin a good thing.

As a point of personal pride, he is an excellent gift giver.

It is a pleasure to come to her house on Christmas Eve, although it isn't fancy. It doesn't have lights, just mistletoe strangling the trees around it, and the only cookies are off-brand vanilla wafers. A droopy tree showers needles on the carpet, but it's decorated in whatever could be scrounged together with trash plastic, macaroni pasta, construction paper, and Elmer's glue. The only clue that Gracie anticipated him rather than his jollier counterpart is ram's horns drawn into the dust around the radiator. He leaves hoofprints there for her to find in the morning.

Sometimes what her brother puts under the tree for her doesn't stay there, while Mommy or Daddy refill the cabinet under the sink with things that smell like juniper instead of bleach. Satan leaves gifts at the foot of her bed instead: a bike, a doll, a handheld console, a board game. One year, a blanket, to fold over her until she no longer shivered.

Dear Satan, I don't think I've been good this year. The tree in back is bare of switches, but I swear I try. Is hell at least warm where you are? I'm so cold I don't think I'll ever be warm again.

He usually keeps some of his less human aspects when he isn't planning to mingle. However, a nice red suit the color of drying blood and a Santa hat seem festive while he makes his own rounds on Christmas. There's no reason not to enjoy a little whimsy at work.

He enters Gracie's room through her door, locked from the outside. Under strands of multi-colored Christmas lights strung through her room, she's propped up on her pillows with her arms around her knees, sobbing into her flannel pajama pants. Hungry. Alone.

At the foot of the bed, he makes no attempt to conceal himself or quiet his hooves. He can walk the circumference of the world and never be seen, either as what he imagines himself to be or what he is when the costumes fall away. He's accustomed to observing and not being observed; they feel his presence sometimes, but he doesn't occupy his entire existence with manipulation and corruption. Sometimes he just *is* and walks as close as death without them ever knowing.

Most people don't recognize evil when they see it, much less the Devil when he passes them by.

But as he lets his sack slide down his arm to thump onto the floor, Gracie raises her tear-streaked face. Her red eyes widen.

He pauses. Is she reacting to something behind him? Or perhaps to a terrible, terrible thought he accidentally gives her, from what simmers behind his brimstone irises.

She stretches out her legs under her blanket, the same one he gave her the previous year, and wipes her face with the edge. Lip still quivering, she seems to take in the cut of his suit, then looks back up at his face, into his eyes. Somehow, he *knows* she can see him as clearly as he sees her.

A small handful of people can see him when he doesn't reveal himself; not prophets, saints, or clairvoyants, just regular people. He doesn't know why. The only thing in common between them is that they're so desperate to see *someone*—and for someone to see them.

He always sees them.

Neither speaks a word. He knows she isn't sleeping, but being awake doesn't break *his* rules. He simply stores the knowledge she can see him on the shelf of his long memory and pulls out her gift: a stack of second-hand pulp novels.

Her face lights up. They're the ones she asked her Aunt Janice to buy her at a garage sale, but her aunt insisted they were the devil's handiwork.

And now they are.

He sets the stack on her nightstand. Then he reaches into the sack and presents a dinner tray with a bowl of steaming chicken pot pie, a packet of plastic utensils, and a Dr Pepper—not off-brand, and not sugar-free.

He sits at the foot of the bed while she eats something warm and comforting, something that fills her stomach almost to its brink. Then he hands her a crinkly package of Hostess Cupcakes.

He stays with her until her eyelids droop in exhaustion and

absolute trust, her face flushed with contentment instead of crying. Then, putting his finger to his lips in shared secret, he steps back through her door.

Dear Satan, Aunt Janice says the Devil lives in Mom and Dad, that I need to pray for them, even when my knees are bruised. I think you're just a convenient excuse, because I have to forgive them if the Devil made them do it. All I really want for Christmas is a little peace, just for once.

A duet that isn't Christmas carols welcomes him inside her home. The Christmas tree leans drunkenly against the wall, empty beneath except for broken ornaments and glasses.

The bedrooms down the hall are closed. They haven't padlocked her in for a few years, but she bought a slide lock with some money she made babysitting.

Locks have never kept him out before.

As he steps through, he's awash in her colors once more. She has her own Christmas tree now, two feet tall and artificial. Lying on her side on top of her blanket, she stares at its cheap silver decorations with blinding white fury in her bruised eyes. The yelling from the kitchen and living room competes with her radio, but she can't turn it up without inviting further wrath.

Gracie knows better and wishes for more. She's done crying for the night. She's done with everything.

Satan slides her Christmas gift over her head, placing thick, cushioned headphones over her ears. She smiles as he plugs it into her radio, so that she no longer hears anything but gentle Christmas music that slowly unwinds the tension in her shoulders.

Before he can leave, she reaches out.

When he's not trying, he doesn't touch. No one wants to, if they know what he is. But she wraps her fingers around his wrist, then slides them down to his hand.

He follows her direction and crawls onto her bed behind her, his hooves heavy at the foot. She draws his arm around her, hugs it like a stuffed animal; all of hers have been eviscerated and eliminated by the man of the house, with his big knife and smile of too many teeth, even though he's missing one.

All she wants is to not be afraid, to be held as well as seen. So rarely is he a comfort that he burns in lieu of the inadequate heater. She draws him closer and closes her eyes. Her breathing slows, deepens.

When the shouts outside her door turn to screams and wet choking, then abrupt silence, she hears none of it, only "Silent Night."

A mass of tentacles and rose vines masquerading as a person, **Amanda M. Blake** *is the author of such horror titles as* Question Not My Salt, Deep Down, *and* Out of Curiosity and Hunger, *the dark poetry collection* Dead Ends, *and the Thorns fairy tale mash-up series. For more, visit amandamblake.com.*

NOTHING FUNNY ABOUT A CLOWN AFTER MIDNIGHT

Mark Allan Gunnells

I WASN'T SURE at first what had awakened me. I lay in bed for a moment, staring at the shadows that crowded around the bedroom. I glanced toward the door, and though I couldn't exactly make out the shape in the dark, I knew it was still closed.

Not that a closed door had ever kept out any monsters. My dad always told me that monsters didn't exist, but I knew better. Adults couldn't always see them, but kids could. And at eleven, I already knew the truth that sometimes adults couldn't see the monsters because they were the monsters.

A sound caught my attention. A squeak, sort of a honk, coming from somewhere outside. After a few seconds, the sound repeated.

I crawled out of bed and went over to my bedroom window, which looked down into the backyard. A security light provided a frosty glow that stretched from the patio halfway to the fence at the edge of the property. And yet the security light activated on a motion-detector, only coming on if movement triggered the sensor.

I heard the squeak/honk again, and this drew my attention to the very edge of the lighted area. I saw a shape hovering there, and then it stepped forward, as if into the spotlight.

I gasped and then giggled at such a ridiculous sight. There was a clown in my backyard, an honest-to-God bonafide clown. White face paint, exaggerated red lips, tufts of green hair above each ear, colorful jumpsuit, floppy shoes. The whole nine yards.

As I watched, the clown held up one of those little squeeze horns with the rubber bulb on one end. He squeezed the bulb, eliciting another of those high-pitched honks. Then he did a silly little dance where he flailed his arms and legs as if his limbs were made of rubber. He looked right up at my window, waved with one hand, then motioned for me to come down.

I felt myself chilled at the sight. I thought of John Wayne Gacy, who I'd heard about on some documentary my father watched once, and that killer clown from the Stephen King movie I saw on late night cable. It was common knowledge that clowns weren't cute and silly, but scary and dangerous.

Especially when one showed up in your backyard in the dead of night.

The clown reached into an oversized pocket and brought out a small cup of popcorn, then reached in again for a stick of cotton candy. He capered around in a circle, did a wobbly pirouette, then motioned for me to come down again.

I thought about the newspaper my father had left on the coffee table yesterday. The story about the disappearances of two local kids, vanished without a trace. The police didn't know if they were linked or not.

But watching the clown, I suspected they were.

I knew I should yell for my father, who might call the police or more likely grab the baseball bat out of his closet and go after the clown himself. And yet I kept quiet.

I knew both the kids who had gone missing, and they had it almost as rough at home as me.

The clown did a headstand then flipped back onto his feet. From his pocket he pulled a handful of candies and tossed them into the air like confetti. He motioned once more.

I glanced back at the closed door. Somewhere on the other side was my father. With his temper and his shouting and his fists and his baseball bat. Every bruise on my battered body burned.

I glanced back at the clown, who leaped into the air and clicked his heels together. He might take me away to some eternal carnival with rides and snacks and funhouses; he might take me into the woods and do unspeakable things to me. Fifty/fifty either way.

Still, I liked those chances better than if I stayed here. I knew what awaited me here.

Decision made, I opened the window and climbed out, making my way down the trellis.

NOTHING FUNNY ABOUT A CLOWN

Mark Allan Gunnells *loves to tell stories. He has since he was a kid, penning one-page tales that were Twilight Zone knockoffs. He likes to think he has gotten a little better since then. He loves reader feedback, and above all he loves telling stories. He lives in Greer, SC, with his husband Craig A. Metcalf.*

GROWING GARDENS

NICK ROBERTS AND CHRISSY WINTERS

"It really is hard to say what my favorite thing is about this place."

Gladys Miller pushed her walker across the lobby of Growing Gardens Rest and Retirement Home, guiding prospective residents, Ed and Jane Bresnick, on their tour.

The couple's son, Brandon, and the Director of Growing Gardens, Elaine, had gone to Elaine's office to discuss pricing and availability, leaving Gladys, Growing Garden's unofficial ambassador/greeter, and the Bresnicks to finish the tour on their own.

"Oh, it seems so lovely, Ed," Jane said. Her soft face was hopeful, as if a solution to a nagging problem would finally be solved. "I think we could be really happy here."

Ed poked Gladys lightly in the back with his cane. Gladys turned her head, eyes widening in surprise.

"Cut the bullshit lady. What's in this for you?"

"Ed!" Jane's face reddened.

"She's like a used car salesman. And I can tell she's trying to sell me a lemon!" Ed detoured around Jane and Gladys. "I'm leaving. Tell your son I'll be in the car!"

Jane looked on the verge of tears. Gladys smiled that beaming smile, showing off a row of teeth that were all her own—a rarity at the age of eighty-five. Having had a few years' experience working through moments exactly like this one, she knew what to do. She reached over and patted her shoulder, and Jane returned a grateful look.

GROWING GARDENS

"Oh, that man! Gladys, you ignore him. We are so appreciative of your help today. We really are."

"Oh, please don't fret. Ed is expressing his concern. This is such a difficult season of life. Change isn't easy. And believe you me, after I lost my Barry, I was beside myself. But once I got settled in, The Garden—that's just what I call it—well, it became my home. I've met so many wonderful people here! Friends I know who will be with me to the end."

"I'm so sorry about your husband. Look at me feeling sorry for myself. How long were you all married?"

"Twenty-five years. He was my second husband, and it was the best twenty-five years of my life. Now, you go to your husband. He'll come around. These things take time."

Jane smiled politely, leaving Gladys behind to meet her son and Elaine as they came out of the office. Gladys just watched, knowing what was coming next. The woman shook her head, and her son rolled his eyes.

"How did that go?" Dolores, Gladys' best friend at The Garden, asked from a plush leather armchair.

"They just need some time to adjust to the idea," Gladys said as she eased into the matching chair beside her best friend.

The two women sat positioned across from the front desk where Trudy, the bleach blonde receptionist, watched videos on her phone and chewed gum under a disposable face mask. She looked up at the ladies through plastic, tortoise-shell glasses that swooped up into the shape of a cat eye. The lenses fogged as she spoke.

"Say, Dolores, your little gal still comin' to see ya today?"

"Bet your bottom dollar on it," Dolores said without a shred of doubt.

"How long's it been since she's been here?"

Gladys picked up on the snarky receptionist's tone even if Dolores didn't. She knew Trudy didn't think Dolores' granddaughter would show up. It had been over six months since Ruby had visited.

"Now, now, Trudy. You know Ruby is a world traveler," Gladys' well-rehearsed, placid voice, answered for her friend. "She's out there living her best life and still makes time to come see her grandmama. That's what any grandmother wants, right Dolores?"

Dolores nodded, gratefully.

"That's right."

Trudy only shook her head and dove back into her cell phone. Gladys sensed the smug smirk behind her mask, but she kept her real thoughts about Trudy to herself. She turned to Dolores.

"Where's Ruby coming back from this time, again?"

"Indonesia! She just finished studying abroad and took a little vacation. Even sent me photos on the phone. Did I show you those?"

"No, I don't believe so."

"I thought I did. Hell, I have to get one of the nurses to help me open the damn thing." She held up her shaking hand, typical of Parkinson's. "I can't press buttons or swipe this way and that half the time. Remind me to show you when we go back to the rooms."

"Okay." Gladys gave her friend a bemused smile. "What was she doing in Indonesia?"

"Island hopping. One of the pictures was of the Borobudur temples. I think that's how it's pronounced. She said she's bringing me back a souvenir." Dolores smiled.

"Ohhh, that sounds exotic."

Trudy looked up from her phone again.

"Well, Ruby has about four hours to get here from Indonesia before visitin' hours end."

"We're aware of the time," Gladys shot back.

Trudy raised her eyebrows. Gladys looked at her with kind eyes and a slight grin at the corner of her mouth. She still had the dexterity to flawlessly apply makeup. Her lashes perfectly stretched and framed her round blue eyes. She batted them innocently but the tension that was always present in her jaw radiated down Gladys' neck and she clenched her manicured fingers into her palm.

"Thank you, Trudy. I think we'll take a few laps around the grounds," she said, standing back up.

"That sounds like a fine idea," Dolores said and got to her feet a bit slower than her friend.

As the two women walked toward the recreation room, Gladys half-looked over her shoulder and said, "Do call for us when young Ruby arrives."

"Yes, ma'am," Trudy said in a slightly more respectful manner.

They made their way across the large dining room, nodding

politely to their fellow residents as they pushed their way out to the courtyard patio, one of their regular spots. The late afternoon sun glowed, and the women moved to sit at an umbrellaed table.

The patio was Gladys' favorite part of The Garden. Elaine was notorious for being a penny pincher, but the outside sitting area was opulent with bright potted flowers.

Gladys was happy to volunteer her services free of charge to come up with and pick different arrangements. She'd always had an excellent green thumb.

"I love the color of your nails." Dolores smiled as she observed Gladys' hands.

"Thank you, darling. Barry always liked it when I had a fresh manicure." She looked at the freshly coated nails and did her best to ignore the wrinkles and veins on the hands that housed them. "That's the only reason I still do it. It's not like I'm trying to impress anyone here."

Dolores chuckled and looked down at her shaking hands that looked neglected compared to her friend's.

"Charles didn't care much for the glitz and the glam," she began.

Gladys had heard the story of how Dolores' husband, Charles, had died from a heart attack two decades ago, leaving her with her son, Dylan, who she claimed was such a lovely man but so busy running his wealth management company. She knew exactly where this conversation was headed because they'd been down this road too many times in the last few months. It only added to Gladys' concern for her friend's inevitable mental deterioration on top of the Parkinson's.

"I do wish I could see him more, but he's got his own family to take care of. He reminds me of how hard-working Charles was before he passed. Oh, the heart is a fragile thing, especially when you have a diet like he did." Dolores sighed. "Yes, seeing Ruby will have to suffice. I do wonder what it would be like to still be married, though . . . to still have a man around, you know?" She shrugged and exaggeratedly threw her hands in the air. "It just wasn't meant to be."

"Hon, this again? You've lived a good life, Dolores. And it sounds like you had good years with Charles, even though they were cut short. Let me tell you, marriage isn't always what it's cracked up to be. Barry was a saint, but my first husband . . . Let's just say, I'm glad he couldn't reproduce because no one needed another Rick running around. And kids were never in the cards with Barry, either. At least you got to experience motherhood." Her stomach fluttered, and a familiar tinge of agitated regret regurgitated up her throat. She gulped, swallowing it deep down, back to where it belonged.

"Gladys, are you alright? You look like you've seen a ghost." Dolores tilted her head, and curiosity loomed on her sagging, tired face, which always reminded Gladys of an old hound dog.

"Yes. It's just sometimes when I look back and think about Rick, I wonder what I was thinking marrying that cad. He couldn't keep his dick in his pants if his life depended on it," she deadpanned.

"Gladys!" Dolores whooped. "You always know how to make me laugh when I'm feeling down."

"That's what I'm here for," she said with a smile, glad to be off the topic.

Dolores' attention turned to the patio door, and she eagerly clapped her shaking hands together.

"Ruby!"

Gladys turned and eyed-up Dolores' granddaughter. The young woman wore black leggings, a faded T-shirt that featured a sunglassed skeleton gripping a guitar with red roses propped on its head. Her arms were adorned with tattoos, and her purple hair was piled up sloppily in a bun. Aviator shades covered half of her face.

She could have at least dressed up to see her grandmother for the first time in six months.

Gladys brooded underneath the inviting smile as the young woman dragged a chair over and joined them on the patio.

"Nana!" Ruby bent over and kissed the trembling woman on the cheek. "I've missed you so much."

"I know you did, dear. And I missed you, too! You remember my friend Gladys, don't you?"

Ruby pushed her glasses off her face, sitting them on top of her head, and flashed Gladys a smile.

"Yes, of course I do. I hope you and Nana have been staying out of trouble while I've been gone."

"Of course, we have, dear. We could say the same about you." Gladys served back at Ruby, whose mouth fell open in mild surprise before focusing her attention back on Dolores.

GROWING GARDENS

"I'll give you two some time to catch up. Dolores, I'll see you at supper."

Dolores nodded but didn't take her eyes off her granddaughter.

"It was nice to see you, Gladys," Ruby said as Gladys stood to leave.

"M'hmm."

Ruby side-eyed her, but Dolores didn't appear to notice.

"I want to hear everything about your trip, Ruby! Absolutely everything! But first things first. Did you meet anyone?"

She's so happy. That girl better have gotten her a gift. Dolores will live off this visit for weeks.

Gladys shook her head and pushed her way back inside. As she walked through the building, she nodded polite hellos and friendly waves to whomever she encountered, doing her best to spread a little positivity when needed. Like clockwork, her body started to ache. More than anything, she just wanted to get back to her room. Her evening block of network TV started at four. She only took a break from it during the news hour to go down to the dining room to eat with Dolores. The daily regurgitation of worldly atrocities didn't agree with her. It had been that way ever since Barry had died.

"I guess Dolores's granddaughter did show up," Trudy said from behind the desk as Gladys approached.

"Of course, she did, Trudy."

"Well, I shouldn't have given her a hard time about it. I realize that now. Please don't tell Elaine. I'm on thin ice already. I really need this job to work out."

Gladys looked the middle-aged receptionist up and down. The white button up shirt she wore as part of her uniform wasn't done up high enough in her opinion; it showed too much cleavage. She knew Trudy was a single mother and she'd heard from some of the other residents that her ex regularly skipped out on child support payments. A small flash of sympathy fluttered in her chest.

"I won't say anything. Just remember to be more respectful next time."

"I will."

Gladys turned from the desk to head in the direction of her hallway, her natural grin emerged as soon as she rounded the corner.

NICK ROBERTS AND CHRISSY WINTERS

Later that evening, Gladys, Dolores, and a visibly ready-to-leave Ruby all sat around a small, white-clothed table. A Dollar Tree candle with no scent burned in the middle of the three dinner trays. Gladys eyeballed her fried chicken and scrunched up her face, thinking of how much Rick used to praise her fried chicken during his grooming period.

Barry was genuine with his compliments. You really lucked out the second time around.

She wondered if she would've been so good to Barry if she didn't endure the years with Rick.

Everything happens for a reason. You know that.

"What do you think, Gladys?"

Gladys looked up from the burning flame at Dolores who was wearing a necklace that looked like it was made from polished white stones. A bizarre metal clasp, shaped like a clawed hand, gripped a violet stone which hung down the center of Dolores' chest. She opened her mouth to respond, but an image flashed through her mind: a garden enclosed with decorative stones. Her stomach went hollow.

Barry's garden? I haven't thought about that since . . .

"You don't like it?" Dolores asked.

Gladys blinked away her bewildered expression and flashed her diamond smile.

"It's lovely, Dolores."

"I picked it up from a vendor outside the Borobudur temples in Indonesia. Oh, my God, if you ever get the opportunity, you must go."

"Sounds exotic," Gladys said, repressing an eyeroll but still smiling. She knew her world-traveling days were over. "And it truly does look lovely on you, Dolores."

"The best part is the story behind it," Ruby said and took a bite of mashed potatoes mixed with peas.

Gladys watched her, waiting to see if she would begin this story with a mouthful of food or if she'd make them wait for her to chew and swallow; she honestly didn't know which would be more impolite.

GROWING GARDENS

"So, I saw it, and I guess the guy could tell I was interested, so he said that the stone came from the actual rock from inside the temples. There were Buddhist monks who made pilgrimages to the temples a long time ago until they just stopped one day. And this is the real morbid part..."

Both women leaned in as Ruby continued.

"One day, they just stopped, and the vendor told me it's because a bunch of them were slaughtered... like in some sort of ritual sacrifice or something. Ever since, many of the Buddhist locals consider the place cursed, especially now that it's basically just a tourist attraction. I mean, I bought a bottle of Dasani on my way out."

"Oh, my, my," Dolores said as she clutched the rock from between her breasts and gave it a second glance.

"It's okay, Nana," she said with a chuckle. "That was a long time ago."

Gladys found it difficult to remove her eyes from the stone that Dolores rolled between her thumb and index finger. Dolores lifted it to her eyes.

"The color is so pretty, Ruby." She gave her granddaughter a one-armed hug and a kiss on the cheek. "I love it, and I love you."

"I love you, too, Nana."

Groups of other residents began standing from their tables, cluster by cluster.

"Dinner's over," Gladys said.

"I guess this means visiting hours are over," Ruby said.

"Sure does, unfortunately." Dolores sighed.

"It's okay, Nana. I booked a room at the Hampton Inn for two more nights. I'll come back and see you again before I leave. There's a tattoo parlor in downtown Atlanta that everyone on TikTok is raving about. I have to check it out."

They all stood from the table at various speeds, Dolores being the slowest.

"Oh, Ruby. You're gorgeous just the way you are."

"Thanks, Nana. But you're not talking me out of it."

"Oh, I know you better than that, hon."

The ladies all said their goodbyes, and Gladys stood back and watched as Dolores escorted Ruby to the front of the building. Their arms were interlocked the way Rick used to do before he let his drinking get the better of him.

No. I will not entertain thoughts of Rick. Keep your mind on Barry.

But even as she thought that, she pictured the stone necklace with its torrid backstory, gleaming like it held some terrible secret, and the hollow feeling returned to her gut.

It's Barry you need to remember . . . and the garden.

That hollow feeling returned. She stood there baffled as to why her treasured memories of her Barry were making her feel ill. She stiffened her back as much as she could and waited for her best friend to return.

As expected, Dolores had tears in her eyes when she returned. Gladys placed her hand on Dolores' lower back, and the two of them trekked to their hallway where their rooms were situated directly across from each other. Gladys could sit up in bed and see into Dolores' room if both women kept their doors open, which they never did.

Eventually, they made it back, and just as the two women split to go to their respective dwellings, Gladys found herself staring at Dolores' necklace again.

"You really like it, don't you?" Dolores asked.

"Huh? Oh, yes, dear. Better take it off before bed, though. It can't be comfortable. Looks cumbersome."

"Oh, Gladys. I'm never taking it off. It's a constant reminder of Ruby. They'll have to pry it off my dead body."

Blood-stained clothes.

Gladys gasped at the intrusive thought, and then downplayed it when she saw Dolores' concerned reaction.

"Well, that could be tomorrow morning, the way *you've* been moving around today." She recovered with a friendly joust.

Dolores let out a belly laugh so hard that she cried. Gladys couldn't help but chuckle, too, despite the confusion brought on by the necklace's arrival. She just needed to rest.

"See you in the morning, dear," Gladys said, turning to her door. "And take off that damn necklace."

"Nope," Dolores said as she unlocked her door. "I'll meet you at our table bright and early." She shut the door and began a coughing fit so violent that Gladys paused and waited for it to subside. When it finally stopped, she went into her own room to prepare for a bath before bed.

GROWING GARDENS

After tossing and turning for an hour, Gladys had finally fallen asleep. Somehow, she'd gone from curled up with her favorite body pillow to lying in the fetal position on damp earth. It took her a second to realize that this wasn't regular dirt; it was freshly tilled gardening soil. She opened her eyes and peeled her face from the ground, feeling bits and flakes of soil falling from her face. The moon illuminated her immediate surroundings like some dreamlike spotlight. She recognized this place. It was her garden at the dream home Barry had bought for her. The thought of Barry made her feel giddy, until she felt the loose soil underneath her move. A smell like copper seeped up through the dirt, and that's when she heard what sounded like a dog lapping up water on a hot summer day.

And just as quickly as she'd entered dreamland, she was back in the warmth of her bed. She opened her eyes and realized that something had woken her up. She listened to wet slurps—the same as from her dream—coming from inside her room.

Gladys slowly lifted her head and looked into the dark corner near the door. What she saw chilled her to her core. A pale figured sat on top of her glass table, holding something in its hand, licking it in a deliberately profane manner. She gasped when she realized it was Dolores crouched on the tabletop, wearing a dingy yellow terry cloth robe. Her wig was off and thin strands of hair were hung over her shiny scalp. In her hand she held an ice cream cone that was nearly gone. She slurped at it while the necklace Ruby had gifted her glimmered in the dim light of the apartment.

"Dolores!" she finally managed to say, placing her hand over her heart.

"Hello, Gladys," Dolores said and then shakily turned the cone and licked it all the way around, staring at her the entire time.

"How did you get in here? I locked my door. I didn't see you come in." A cold panic overcame her. Something was terribly wrong.

"Just wanted to visit with you. You're my closest friend, my only friend. Did you know that, Gladys?"

A drop of vanilla ice cream rolled down Dolores' chin and into her lap.

"Well, yes. We have become close, but, but you can't just come in here. You should go. I'll see you at breakfast." She did her best to remain calm despite the fear metastasizing throughout her being.

"Do you remember these ice cream cones, Gladys?"

Gladys' eyes found the cone with its crinkly yellow paper wrapped around the bottom. There was indeed something familiar about that cone. The glimmering necklace seemed to implant word by insidious word into her mind.

Bloody clothes. Ice cream cone. A child. The garden. Barry.

"You were always kind to me. I hope you're rewarded for that."

Gladys looked up from the yellow paper on the cone and back to her disturbed friend.

"Rewarded?"

The corners of Dolores' thin cracked lips turned upward as her eyes blurred and darkened.

"Dolores! Dear Lord! I'm calling the nurse."

Blood pounded in Gladys' ears. She picked up the phone that sat next to her bed—there was no dial tone, only a loud static. She pounded her finger on the button labelled 'Medical' to call the night duty nurse. The static intensified.

Dolores stood and smiled ear to ear; her gummy mouth was a tar pit in the dark corner. She winked and turned the cone around as she lifted it to her mouth. With one violent jab, she shoved it down her throat, wedging it sideways so a bulge protruded from her aged esophagus. She coughed and gagged as ice cream and drool ran down her chin.

Gladys shrunk back as her friend stood on top of the table and used her index fingers to pull back the corners of her mouth like some kind of children's game. She barked, and a phlegmy wad of bloody cream and cone plopped on Gladys' tile floor.

"Stop, Dolores! Stop it right now!" Gladys begged, putting her hands to her ears. "I'm going for help." She disregarded her walker and dashed to the front door.

"Don't forget the wrapper," Dolores teased.

Gladys stopped and looked at the balled-up wrapper on the floor. The Happy Boy Cones' logo gave her the assurance she needed: Barry always kept a box of them in their freezer. She

GROWING GARDENS

looked from the wrapper to the necklace swinging from Dolores' neck like a hypnotist's pocket watch.

Barry was a good man. Rick was the scumbag. Barry was . . .

Dolores leaned in close and whispered, "Poor, perfect Gladys. Everyone's favorite resident at Growing Gardens. Look at you now, thinking about your own garden, aren't you, Gladysssssss?"

Gladys gasped and stumbled as her world spun. She reached for the knob but fell on her side. She rolled to her back to see her slowly spinning ceiling fan and then Dolores' head come into view. Her friend smiled as Gladys' vision swirled to unconsciousness.

The floating sensation told her that she had returned to a dream state. She floated down a dark hallway toward the light of a living room. Nostalgia filled her being. This was once her living room, but not the one she shared with Barry. No, this was the home she'd lived in with Rick. And, as if on cue, she noticed the recliner in the corner of the room, and her first husband casually rocking himself with his tiptoes.

"Rick?" she asked, barely above a whisper. "What the . . . what the hell are you doing here?"

Rick forced a smile.

"First of all, Gladdy, this isn't Hell, which is good news for us both; second, nice to see you, too."

Gladys couldn't help but roll her eyes at him. The surrealness of the situation made her instantly forget about Dolores. On top of that, Rick was young, in his late thirties, the age he'd been when they divorced, looking just as handsome in his jeans and white T-shirt with tattoos lining his arms and a scruffy beard on his face. He'd always been easy on the eyes, no matter how much of a bastard he became.

A pretty smile can blur the reddest of flags.

This was far from what he looked like when he passed away in his sixties from lung cancer. She only knew this because his brother had sent her a pity picture with a plea to help cover hospice care and possible funeral expenses.

Let the bastard rot, she remembered thinking. And now, standing mere feet from her in all his youthful glory, he'd taken her breath away yet again. She fought through the temptation, quelling feelings she hadn't had in years.

"Please tell me what is going on."

Rick smiled at her, but something was off about it. It just wasn't Rick's smile.

Oh no.

The same grin that had distorted Dolores' face moments ago was now plastered across this façade of her abusive former husband.

"Ah, Gladdy, still full of fire. I've missed you. But don't worry, I'm only here to give you some information."

Gladys scoffed. "What are you playing at, Rick? I don't need any information from you."

"Where is Barry? Why are *you* here? Why not him? *He* was a good man!"

"Really?" He laughed so hard it sounded like he'd hack up a lung.

"Am I dead?" she blurted out.

"Oh, no. Like I said, this isn't the afterlife, Gladdy. If it was, it might very well be Barry sitting here in front of you."

"Don't you even say his name."

Rick grinned.

"Saint Barry, that's right. You even referred to him that way earlier, but there was much about Barry that no one knew. Wasn't there, Gladys?"

"Stop it! I'm not going to fall for your games. I've been done with that for years."

"The human mind is a funny thing, Gladdy. It warps things for us, doesn't it? So we can stay comfortable with our choices. Say, do you want some ice cream? I think I have a cone in the freezer. Barry would approve."

"I don't know what you're talking about, and I don't want to be here anymore." Gladys put her hands to her ears, curling herself up and falling onto the couch that reeked of cigarettes that she'd always hated.

"It'll come to you, sweetie. The memory will sprout like one of the flowers in your prized garden."

Rick stood over her. The room behind him dissolved back into her apartment, and the vision of him was replaced with Dolores, naked and covered in shit, still wearing the damned necklace from Ruby. A foul stench filled her nostrils. Dolores' cold, clawed hand gripped her chin and turned her head to the left. Written on the

GROWING GARDENS

wall of Gladys' normally pristine apartment, was the word: 'Remember.'
Remember what?
"The children!" Dolores hissed through strained vocal cords. Before Gladys could scream, Dolores lifted her head just enough to slam it back on the floor, knocking her into a dreamless sleep for what remained of the night.

⚊⚊⚋

"Gladys, wake up," a familiar voice called.
She felt hands on her shoulders, gently shaking her. She opened her eyes and found herself on the floor of her brightly lit apartment, quickly trying to get up and find her bearings.
"It's okay, Gladys. Calm down. You're okay," the person kneeling beside her said.
It took her a few seconds to realize that she'd been screaming, wailing, and for quite some time if the soreness of her throat was any indication. She stopped and took quick, shallow breaths, relaxing when she noticed Manny, one of the more respectful workers at The Garden, coaxing her back into reality.
"Oh, Manny. Oh, my, my. Dolores. Dolores attacked me," she said, sitting all the way up.
"Say what, now?"
"In the middle of the night. She did. She came in my room wearing that damn necklace and eating ice cream. She's the one who slammed me on the floor and knocked me out. She even wrote that on the wall . . . " Her voice trailed off as she pointed to the pristine wall.
That evil bitch must've cleaned up after herself to make me look crazy!
"Manny, I swear, there was something written on that wall. I'm not losing it."
"No one said you were, Gladys. I think you just took a tumble in the middle of the night. It looks like there's some ice cream or something all over the floor."
So, it really did happen. It was no dream. Play it cool or they'll put you on the second floor with the poor residents on their way out.
"Oh my. I did. I had a cone in the middle of the night. I

remember dropping it and going to clean it up, then lights out! I'm so embarrassed."

"It's okay, Gladys. You gave me quite a startle, but you're okay," he said with a relieved smile forming. "Do you feel up for breakfast? You're a little late, but they'll make an exception. I noticed you weren't at the table with Dolores and came to check on you."

The image of her grinning, feces-covered friend shocked her senses and made her heart skip a beat. And then there was that cryptic message: 'Remember.'

What the hell does that mean?

Oh, deary, you know what that means.

Gladys blinked away the thought and focused on the young olive-skinned man before her.

"And how is Dolores this morning?" she asked. "Forget what I said about her coming in here. I must've been having a nightmare."

"Ha! Will do. I can't picture Dolores doing much damage to anyone in her current state. I didn't talk to her, but she did seem a bit distracted. Probably worried about you. Why don't you go ahead and get dressed and come see for yourself."

Gladys bristled at the thought, but thanked Manny, nonetheless, assuring him that she was okay, and proceeded with her morning routine.

The dining hall had already been cleared by the time Gladys made her way down. She knew she could pick up a plate from the kitchen if she wanted to, but she didn't have much of an appetite. She spotted Trudy at her desk, scrolling through her phone per usual. As soon as she approached the young woman, she looked up from her screen like she hadn't been lounging about on the clock.

"Can I help you, Gladys?"

"Have you seen Dolores this morning?"

"I'm pretty sure she went outside after breakfast. Are you just getting up?"

Gladys ignored her question and headed through the sliding double doors. She scanned the courtyard and gulped when she saw her friend with her back to her, sitting at their usual table. She took a deep breath and trudged onward.

GROWING GARDENS

"Dolores?" she asked, approaching the rigid woman who seemed to be staring off into space with a smile so fixed that it looked painted on.

"Dolores' wig was off kilter, and she was wearing her yellow robe over the clothes she'd worn last night when Gladys had said goodnight outside their doors.

She's still wearing that damn necklace.

"Hey, little boy! Would you like an ice cream cone?" Dolores said in a man's voice—a man that Gladys knew all too well. "Come on, son. Come get your ice cream!" Gladys turned and glanced behind her—there was no one there.

What the hell is Dolores playing at?

"Oh, it's too hot to eat on the side of the road. It'll melt. Come sit in the car with me. I'll even drive you home. How 'bout that?" Barry's voice said from the woman's mouth.

Dolores' odd smile disappeared and her face turned crestfallen. Tears brimmed her weak eyes.

"I'm so sorry, but I do have to do this. Please don't be mad at me. It won't hurt for very long."

Why is she talking like Barry? Who is this version of Barry talking to? What won't hurt for very long?

The message on the wall clicked in her brain: *Remember.*

No!

"Dolores! Get a hold of yourself!" Gladys glanced around again, hoping to see a nurse or another staff member that she could ask for help.

Dolores looked straight into her eyes, and Gladys felt Barry's stare upon her, the one from that day. The stone necklace seemed to glow in the sunlight.

"You have to help me, Gladys. I'm sick!" Barry's voice said, but it softened as it transitioned back into Dolores' speaking voice. "Help me, Gladys!" she shrieked.

Before Gladys could even process what was fully transpiring, the necklace glistened, and Dolores stood on her chair and lunged wildly at her. Gladys' walker toppled over and both women fell to the stone patio. The distinct smell of shit filled Gladys' nostrils. She wretched as she did her best to keep the snarling woman from hurting her.

And then she heard voices; it was Manny and Trudy.

"Stop her!" Trudy shrilled, but before either of them could do anything, Dolores dug her dentured teeth into Gladys' neck.

Gladys screamed as Manny pulled Dolores off her. Trudy rushed over, knelt, and put her cool hand on Gladys' forehead. A look of deep concern formed on her face.

"Oh my God! Gladys! Are you okay?" Gladys looked up, past Trudy.

Dolores was foaming at the mouth and trembling in Manny's arms. She had urine running down her pants and robe. The necklace continued glimmering gleefully in the sunlight.

"Keep her restrained, Manny. I'm calling 911!" a voice from behind them called out.

That was Elaine. Shit must've really hit the fan if the director is out here.

The morning sun beat down on Gladys' face, causing her eyes to squint shut. She felt ill. Her stomach rolled and the scene around her began to spin. The panicked voices blurred and quieted into the atmosphere.

"Gladys? Gladys! Stay with me!" Trudy's fading voice was surprisingly compassionate, but before Gladys could think any more about it, blackness fell over her again.

Gladys looked down, surprised to see that she was kneeling and wearing a pair of blue jeans. She hadn't worn denim in years. Her eyes widened at the sight of her old gardening gloves covering her hands.

I'm dreaming again.

No, you're remembering, a voice that sounded like Rick's said inside her head.

She stood in the middle of a lush, green garden she hadn't seen in years. The collection of stones bordering it made her heart content.

"My garden, my beautiful garden."

The sun beat down on her face, and she reached up and wiped a bead of sweat off her brow with the back of her elbow.

"How did I get here? How did I get back home?" Her voice was full of childish curiosity and wonder. This didn't feel like a nightmare.

The beautifully landscaped backyard sprawled out behind the large Tudor-style home that Barry had purchased when they got

GROWING GARDENS

married. Her dream home was situated in an affluent neighborhood with good schools and high property taxes.

"It's safe; respectable people live here," Barry had told her on the day he put down a cash offer. She'd protested at first, worrying that it was too much, but she was soon taken in by the built-in bookcases, quartz countertops, and gleaming wall to wall hardwood floors.

But it was the garden that stole her heart. She'd spent hours digging, planting, pruning and watering, triumphant every time she loved a new flower into a state of glorious bloom. She barely even noticed the long hours that Barry put in at work. She was perfectly content in her home. Comfortable and safe for the first time in years.

"What is it about this day that feels so familiar?" She wondered standing easily on her feet and surveying the green grass, the rod iron-fenced pool with the rich-looking gleaming white stamped concrete surrounding it.

A piece of dark hair fell into her face, and she blew it off easily before realizing.

"Oh, my stars! I'm young!" She did a happy little jig and pointed her face up at the sun. "I'm young!" She yelled into the forested bush that grew behind their generously sized yard.

Barry's truck pulled into the laneway that led to the back of the house, interrupting her glee. He drove slowly and parked in front of the matching Tudor-style detached garage that he kept meticulously tidy.

Barry stepped out of the truck. Her mouth fell open at the sight of him. His light blue pinstriped shirt was untucked and stained.

I just picked that up from the dry cleaner.

But it was the look on Barry's face that stopped her heart and sent it plummeting to the depths of her bowels.

"I need your help, Gladys. I've made a mistake." He calmly enunciated his words while approaching her, as if he was talking about the weather. The sun reflected off his bald head. He smelled like sweat, cologne, and something else.

What was it?

His eyes betrayed the smooth velvet in his voice. They were bloodshot and full of fear. She'd never seen Barry scared of anything before.

"What is it? What have you done?"

NICK ROBERTS AND CHRISSY WINTERS

He looked back at his truck. She spotted the red droplets on the passenger window.

No, it was all a bad dream. It never happened. I won't remember this. I don't want to remember . . .

Whatever you have to tell yourself to sleep at night, Gladdy, Rick's voice taunted her.

She trembled and tried to scream, but her throat closed, and no sound came out.

"Gladys! Gladys. It's okay, honey. We're looking after you."

She fluttered her eyes open, and Manny's warm brown ones met them. His smooth face furrowed at the brow.

"Shhh, now. You fainted outside and gave us a scare. Here, have a sip of water. It's been quite the day at The Garden."

"What—what happened?" Gladys said, slowly sitting up in her bed. She winced as a soreness pulsated in her neck.

"Well, this makes two times now that you've conked out today. Take it easy now. You're on the mend," he said, standing at her bedside.

"On the mend?" An image of Dolores lunging at her with her teeth bared like some feral animal sprang into her consciousness, and her eyes widened. "Dolores . . ."

Manny nodded with a solemn look on his face.

"Yeah, Dolores. She did that to your neck. Hey, do you remember when you said Dolores attacked you last night?"

"I told you that was just a nightmare. Today was real."

She raised her hand and felt the gauze bandage.

"I wouldn't go messing with that too much. Let it heal. It's superficial, but it's fresh."

Gladys just shook her head, unable to believe how much her life had changed in such a short amount of time.

And it all started with that damn necklace.

"Dolores is being treated for dementia, Gladys," Manny began. "I'm sure you've noticed the gradual decline in her memory, her personality."

She nodded along as he continued.

"And because of today's violent outburst, she'll have to be moved to the second floor for extra supervision. Right now, she's in her room, sedated and under supervision."

The lockdown ward.

GROWING GARDENS

Gladys shot him a glance.

"Oh no. She doesn't belong up there. Not yet."

"It's for her safety as well as the other residents'. You understand."

She sighed.

"Yes. Doesn't mean I like it one bit, though."

"I'm sorry, Gladys. I know you two are close," he said and touched the back of her hand.

Barry used to touch me like that.

She thought of the garden from their dream home and what was buried underneath it, and that forced smile spread across her face like a protective shield.

"Say, Manny, did I miss dinner?"

"No, ma'am. Casserole is about to be served within the hour. I can have a plate brought in here for you, though. I hope we're not going to make a habit of bringing you special meals every time you take a tumble."

"Ha! That would be lovely, dear. Thank you."

He smiled and nodded.

"You got it."

As he turned from the bed, he paused and picked up the TV remote from her nightstand, offering it to her.

"Do you want to watch something? No use sitting in here staring at the wall."

"Yes, thank you. It certainly has been a day."

She took it from him and turned on the news.

"That it has," he said and walked to the door.

As soon as she heard him turn the knob, she watched the opening widen until she could see Dolores' closed door directly across the hall. Her heart skipped a beat. She pictured a haggard version of her friend standing directly behind it, smiling that dead smile, and wearing that damn necklace.

"Gladys, you okay?"

She quickly broke from her trance.

"Yes, Barry."

He furrowed his brow, and she felt her face blush.

"Manny. I meant to say Manny. I don't know where that came from."

"I've been called worse," he said, waving it off. "Your dinner will be right up."

NICK ROBERTS AND CHRISSY WINTERS

The fake smile remained on her face until he left her room, and then she stared blankly at the TV and the images of the smiling children in the commercial.
The children . . .

As nightfall descended on Growing Gardens, Gladys scooted her walker to her bathroom. She'd never used it to get from her bed to the toilet, and when she caught a glimpse of herself in the mirror behind the TV, she suddenly felt like an old woman. This was different, though. She was injured, and she'd been in bed most of the day.

It's just a setback. Let's not make it a habit.

After she emptied her full bladder, she brushed her teeth and cleaned her face with a washcloth—careful not to get her wound dressing wet. She scooted over to the dresser and put on a nightgown. Her body ached, begging to go back to bed, but her mind raced like someone was flipping through channels in her mind.

Children—Barry—Dolores—the necklace—the garden—Barry covered in blood—Dolores grinning—the message on the wall—the necklace—secrets—secrets—SECRETS!

She let go of the walker and fell into her bed, breathing harder and faster than she had in years, wondering if this was what a heart attack felt like. After a few deep breaths, she somewhat regained her composure, scooting up the bed and leaning back against the stack of pillows. There was no way she'd be able to get any sleep. The constant ache in her neck had intensified as the pain meds from earlier wore off.

Something about the pain brought on a deep sick feeling that she couldn't put her finger on.

When was the last time I'd taken to bed feeling this way? Gladys searched her memory and her feeling of frustration emerged. *It's not like me not to be able to remember things.* Gladys' frustration grew.

"I'm not the damned one with dementia." She spit through gritted teeth gripping her blanket. A bead of sweat formed at her brow and her teeth clenched together like a vise grip.

Then a fragment of a memory. Her gardening gloves. The pale

GROWING GARDENS

green ones with the bright yellow daisies on them. Gladys' hands started to ache. Her finger joints throbbed, and her tensed arms trembled as she continued to grip her blankets. The pain screeched at her, relentlessly intensifying.

"It hurts so bad." She mouthed with parched lips and a dry thick tongue. There was something about the gloves that was different than she remembered. They weren't covered with rich blackened earth. The kind that's smell gave her comfort and made her feel connected to a God that she often forgot. No, it wasn't soil.

Blood.

Dry and darkened, and lots of it. Not a dainty yellow flower was spared. Splotches and patches of what could only be blood saturated her gloves. A thoughtful gift that Barry had given her when they'd purchased the house, and one that he'd ruined on that dreadful day.

That dreadful day . . . Yes, Gladdy, remember, Rick chided in her mind.

What did he do? What did I do?

Another memory, years later. Right before she'd moved to Growing Gardens after Barry died. She was driving away from her home for the last time, but it wasn't her home that held her gaze. It was the garden and what fertilized its tainted soil.

In a cold sweat she picked up the phone and, in a panic, pounded her finger on the medical button. The night nurse answered.

"It's Gladys. In room 302. The pain is too much. I need some relief. Yes, thank you. Please. hurry!" She slammed the phone down and closed her eyes, taking slow, calming breaths.

A few minutes later, the tired night nurse assessed Gladys, passed her two small white pills and a paper cup, and left. She eagerly chugged them down and felt her body ease and relax. Her eyelids grew heavy.

Sweet relief . . . A good night's rest and I'll be right as rain in the morning. All these jumbled thoughts will go back to wherever they came from.

I'll make sure they don't, Gladdy, Rick whispered from inside. *Remember.*

You just want me to remember something bad about Barry . . .

The meds took hold and began pulling her into oblivion, but

just before she could fall asleep, Rick said, *No, Gladdy, I want you to remember what YOU did.*

A tear rolled down her cheek as she passed out.

Gladys stood in her garden once again. It was the same day she'd dreamt of earlier. Barry stood in front of her with that pathetic look in his eyes. The blood spotted his truck window.

"What did you do?" she asked.

"Gladys, I can't stop. I have a problem. I'm a bad, bad man, and I won't ever stop."

"You . . . won't stop what?"

"There's a boy in the truck. Probably six or seven years old." A look of deep shame flashed on Barry's face. His voice broke while he shook his head. It was as if he couldn't believe his own words.

"Snap out of it, Barry! Is that his blood?"

He nodded. "Call the police."

"What?"

"Call the police or kill me, Gladys. It's the only way I'll stop, and if you don't do something now, I'm going to change my mind, so just please fucking do what I say." He dropped to his knees, crushing one of her daisies. "Please. I'm begging you."

Gladys stared at the broken daisy, the shattered dream. Another pathetic man who once again failed to live up to her standards. He was Rick all over again, just a different breed of beast.

I'm older now. I have experience. I can fix this.

"No," she said.

He looked up at her with shock behind his bloodshot, teary eyes.

"What?"

"I fucking said no, Barry. Stand up and get the shovel out of the shed. We're adding to the garden."

His eyes widened as he looked her up and down.

"We're burying this part of you. And you *will* stop. And we will never talk about this ever again. We won't think about it. Soon enough, we won't remember it. To remember is to die, and we're stronger than that. *You're* stronger than that. You gave me all this . . . and I will not let you take it away from me!" Fire burned in her

GROWING GARDENS

eyes, and for the first time since the confrontation, her heart steadied. There would be no turning back.

Barry got to his feet, peered into her eyes one final time, and marched off to get the shovel. Gladys made sure her prized gloves were pulled tightly up to her wrists, and she stormed the truck. She took a deep breath and jerked the passenger door open, looking up as the boy's body slid out of the seat and fell to the ground. She exhaled and looked down. It was the first time she'd seen a dead child. Her stomach begged to empty its contents, but she'd been through too much to let some minor little fuckup ruin her dream life. She'd endured Rick, found Barry, and would be struck dead before giving everything she had away.

Gladys bent over and gripped the battered boy by the ankles and dragged him across the yard to the garden just as Barry met her with the shovel. She looked at the man she fell in love with, the man who'd rescued her and swept her off her feet, and said, "This never happened."

A cold hand grabbed Gladys' wrist, jolting her from her slumber and immediately up into a sitting position. A familiar putrid stench assaulted her senses, and she knew where it came from.

Dolores and that damn necklace.

Now, do you understand, Gladdy? Now, do you remember? Rick's voice echoed.

I covered it up. He wanted to stop, and I covered it up. But what choice did I have? I loved him.

Ha! Then there's still one missing piece, Gladdy . . .

Gladys' eyes focused, and she gasped at the sight of what used to be her friend sitting at the end of her bed. Her wig was off, and drool and blood fell from her mouth onto her naked body. No clothes, no wig, no dentures—she only donned the necklace.

"Dolores! Oh, my God." Her fear turned to seething hatred as soon as she homed in on the necklace. "Take off that damn necklace."

Dolores or Rick or whatever sinister spirit inhabited that necklace just sat and stared.

"That god damn necklace!" Rage filled Gladys' soul, and she lunged for it, but Dolores easily grabbed her shoulders and threw her back on the mattress.

209

"You think I'm the monster?" She clicked her tongue and waved her finger. "Then we still have some things to discuss."

"Who are you? What the hell have you done with my friend?" Gladys lay still, but narrowed her eyes on the rabid old woman.

"I'm right here. We've always been such good friends, Gladys. I wonder why that is. What is it that we have in common?" Dolores had a maniacal look in her darkened eyes, and her mouth moved in a peculiar fashion. It didn't seem to quite line up with the words being uttered. Blood and saliva continued to dribble out of her mouth. "I mean, as far as you knew we were friends, but you always were so flippant with your good fortunes. You're the star of The Garden, our Golden Greeter, Elaine's little personal welcoming committee, always cheering everyone up while I just sat in my fucking chair, trying not to shake and hold onto what few memories I have left." Dolores began to creep toward her.

Gladys froze, hooked on Dolores' words. Dolores' head jerked to the side, and her big-lobed ear touched her shoulder. A smirk fell on her cracked lips.

"Your straight teeth, your manicured hair, your perfect personality, the husband who adored you. Or did he? Maybe all of this is just a pretty mask you put on?"

Gladys recoiled in shock, realizing what Dolores was getting at.

"Dolores," Gladys whispered. "You have it all wrong. I never meant to hurt you. I truly valued our friendship, and you have Ruby!"

Dolores threw her head back and cackled. Spit and blood shot out of her mouth and rained on Gladys' neck and face.

"Oh, you always know how to make me laugh, Gladys. It's one of the things I like most about you."

"What do you want from me? Why are you doing this? It's that damn necklace, isn't it? Dolores. Look what it's done to you!"

Dolores sat up and straddled Gladys, squeezing her wobbly legs together with a surprising strength. She reached her hand up to her chest and lovingly stroked the ornate piece of jewelry that hung from her wrinkled turkey neck. Gladys was grateful for the floral poplin pajamas that separated her groin from Dolores'.

"I think you're just jealous, Gladys. And to be honest, I used to be jealous of you. I thought you had it all. But then I became privy to some information."

Gladys squirmed, and her heart sank. She remembered the boy

GROWING GARDENS

in the garden, but then, just as Dolores smiled, a flood of more memories washed over her polluted mind.

She'd spent nights lying in bed wondering what had happened to the other ones—all the boys who'd disappear from the cities where Barry would "do business in." Anytime she had a doubt, she'd convince herself that it was just a coincidence, choosing instead to put her faith in her husband just like she said she would in her wedding vows. But some nights, she'd wake up to an empty bed, sweating and wondering how long it would be before they got a knock on the door from the police matching blood from a crime scene to Barry's DNA.

But she always managed to find solace in the garden. She could just walk out back and look at all the beauty growing from the decay beneath. And in essence, that was her, a blooming flower nourished by a lifetime of buried mistakes. She looked and Dolores and that fucking necklace and realized that the most beautiful flowers have thorns.

That a girl, Gladdy, Rick whispered.

Oh, fuck off. I don't need you either, you weak piece of trash.

And then Rick fell silent.

Gladys looked up at Dolores, careful how she would play this out. "That necklace is so beautiful Dolores. You're right. I'm envious of it. I'm envious of your relationship with your granddaughter. What a nice girl she is! How obvious it is, how much she loves and respects her grandmother. Just like everyone does around here. Manny and Trudy, they were talking about how much they loved you the other day. You have it all wrong. *I* was always the sidekick."

Dolores blinked and cocked her head. She looked like she wanted to believe Gladys, that a small piece of doubt had penetrated the evil that possessed her.

"That necklace you're wearing . . . It's stunning! It brings out your lovely eyes. Did I ever tell you how much I loved your eyes? They are the perfect shade of hazel."

Dolores took a shallow breath, and she absently raised her right hand to touch the necklace again with a whimsical off-putting smile on her toothless face.

Gladys took her chance and reached up, clawing her perfectly manicured nails into the folds of skin that made up Dolores' neck. She squeezed harder than she ever had, harder than she knew she had strength for.

A flash of that day came to her. She'd surprised herself on that day, too, digging a grave and throwing a lifeless body into it. Barry couldn't even bring himself to do it. It was all her.

Dolores shrieked and slammed her head into Gladys'. Both women wobbled. Dolores threw her head back to do it again, but as she did, Gladys took her opportunity. As her head throbbed, she wrapped her hand around the necklace and slid it off Dolores's bald head and onto her own. The weight of it felt good on her chest and, before Dolores could slam her head against hers, Gladys reached for the phone and slammed it against the frail old woman's skull. Blood and bone splattered Gladys' face, but she was unfazed.

She shoved Dolores' body off the side of the bed and it landed with a thud on the floor. Gladys stood without a thought and slammed her foot into Dolores' skull, finishing off the job.

"Code White. Code White," a crackling voice spoke over the intercom. "We are in lockdown. Code White."

They know Dolores isn't where she's supposed to be.

As soon as Gladys took a step off the bed and that necklace caressed her flesh, she realized that everything she'd ever been through in her life had led to this moment. A youthful, orgasmic wave of power and strength pulsating from every pressure point in her body. When she breathed, her chest expanded with pride, causing her to stand a bit taller, more upright. She looked down at her hands and saw not the wrinkled, gnarled hands to which she'd grown accustomed.

No, she wore her gardening gloves.

As more announcements came over the intercom, she listened to footsteps of the night shift making their way down the hall. She looked at the knife block on her pathetic excuse for a kitchen counter and pulled the two biggest blades out, holding them in front of her, crossing them like gardening shears.

Gladys thought of the night shift nurse who hated her job; she thought of Trudy, the rude receptionist; she thought of Elaine, the director who was only there for the paycheck; she thought of all the poor souls on the second floor who just needed to be put out of their misery; lastly, she thought of Ruby, the slutty granddaughter who ruined Dolores' life by giving her the necklace. They were all just weeds and eyesores to The Growing Garden Rest and Retirement Home.

She made a scissor motion with her makeshift blades as the

GROWING GARDENS

footsteps stopped in front of her door and started to unlock it. The necklace blazed against her heart. This was her garden, and as soon as the door opened, she went about pruning it.

Chrissy Winters *is a writer who lives surrounded by golden wheat fields and swaying soybeans in rural Ontario, Canada. A graduate of Simon Fraser University's The Writers Studio, Chrissy is a wife and mother of three. She loves creating characters, reviewing books and is fueled by exercise and coffee. Connect with her on Instagram @chrissyreadsandwrites.*

Nick Roberts *is a native West Virginian and a doctoral graduate of Marshall University. He is an active member of the Horror Writers Association and the Horror Authors Guild. His works include* Anathema, The Exorcist's House *Universe,* It Haunts the Mind & Other Stories, *and* Mean Spirited. *He currently resides in South Carolina with his family and is an advocate for people in recovery from substance use disorder.*

UNSOLICITED ADVICE FROM A WITCH WHO'S BEEN THERE

Diana Olney

Dear White Knight,
or Aspiring Hero,
I'm not sure which title you prefer,
I hope this letter finds you well,
or that it finds you at all.
Avian correspondence is so fickle these days,
punctuated by staccato shrieks and
rapacious talons more interested in roadkill
than doing my bidding.
But if these words make it to your doorstep,
pay no mind to the dissonance of the messengers.
They're only vagrants,
supporting players
scavenging for happy endings.

You fell for a fantasy like that,
once upon a time.
In the introduction,
she was a perfect heroine:
Doe-eyed, strait-laced,
a one-of-a-kind archetype.
Until the sinuous second act swept her away
—she came back, of course,
but she was never
quite the same after the coma.

UNSOLICITED ADVICE FROM A WITCH

It's a hard truth, my dearest Prince,
but sometimes, when a spell breaks,
it leaves a stain:
A darkness that deepens like shadow,
like memory,
like smoke from starving flames.
You thought you could outrun it,
when you whisked your sweetheart into the sunset,
but shadows never stray far from the sun, do they?

Your maiden wasn't perfect,
wasn't pure,
and yet, she didn't seem like damaged goods.
You loved the way she moved, felt, tasted—
the way her kiss sugared your breath,
and left your mouth bloody,
a venomous shade of red
that looked more like murder than romance.
Loved the way her alchemy sparked,
incandescent,
fevers spreading like
arson in every room she entered.
The way the heads turned,
knife-point profiles drawn in envy,
while the hourglass on your arm
slid right through your fingers.

But even the wildest spirits
can be tamed with a witch on your team.
My first recommendation:
Make the damsel face her demon.
Who knows, perhaps she'll acquiesce
once the smoke is back in the mirror,
glass shattered,
cursed lifted,
and you'll be right by her side
eagerly waiting
to pick up the pieces.

DIANA OLNEY

And if reflection fails, there are other means,
paths laid for desperate measures:
Towers, hollows, alcoves,
woods wound tight as labyrinths.
In those places, you can give a bride away,
let a forest grow around the heart
she wouldn't let you keep,
barbellate branches pricking
sharp as spindles
while ancient roots undulate,
snaking, forging
a cage,
not gilded with gems like the last,
just dreams and dirt—
a fallen angel's oubliette.

But you are not callous, not cruel,
even as your beloved starts to slip,
all you want to do is save her,
offer your hand,
your kiss,
your ultimatum.
It's up to her
how she wants to wear her halo:
As a noose or a tiara.

If she chooses wrong, I'll take the blame,
that's what wicked witches are for.
Though in an epilogue this dark,
you may not need a villain.

Once the curtain drops,
no one will hear her pleas—
no one but you,
her Has-been Hero,
you can bear witness,
safe, secure,
at the edge of Ever After,
as night enfolds your old flame,
starless sheets eclipsing smoke and shadow

UNSOLICITED ADVICE FROM A WITCH

in pools of permanent ink,
a pillar of salt and cinders
too weak to hold a shape.

That's when you'll see the twist
entangled in the fine print
of your fairy tale:
Just because it's magic,
doesn't mean it's meant to be.
But you're lucky, my Charming friend,
for you, the world is an open book,
and no matter what happens,
you can turn the page.

Diana Olney is a Seattle based author, but she is most at home in the shadows, exploring the dark paths between dreams and nightmares. Her stories and poems have appeared in publications by Small Wonders Magazine, Crystal Lake Publishing, Worldstone Publishing, Critical Blast, and more. She is also a columnist at Memento Mori Ink Magazine, as well as the creator of Siren's Song, an original comic series that will debut this winter. Her influences include Gwendolyn Kiste, Cassandra Khaw, Richard Kadrey, Jack Skillingstead, and her furry assistants, black cats Dolce and Gabbana. Visit her website dianaolney.com or her Instagram @dianaolneyauthor for updates on her latest tales.

BATSQUATCH LIVES!

Larry Hinkle

"ON APRIL 19TH, 1994, Brian Caldwell was driving in Pierce County, Washington, near the foothills of Mount Rainier when his truck sputtered and died. As he sat in the cab wondering what to do, a creature descended from the heavens and landed on the road thirty feet ahead of him.

"This creature, however, was no angel.

"Nine feet tall, humanoid, with yellow eyes, a canine muzzle, blue fur, sharp teeth, talons on its hands and feet, and leathery batlike wings nearly as wide as the road when outstretched, it stared at Brian as if it were challenging him to exit the truck. Then, as quickly as it landed, it took to the sky. A few minutes later, the engine restarted on its own. Brian raced into town and told his story.

"And thus was born the legend of Batsquatch."

"Cut." Lisa turned the camera off.

"Seriously? I thought that was great," I said. "What was wrong with it?"

"'And thus was born . . . ?'" Lisa rolled her eyes. "That's *Destination America* level crap and you know it."

"Maybe. But you can't tell me you'd turn down basic cable money."

"Probably not. But you're better than that. *We're* better than that."

"Are we?" I leaned against our van, which was also our studio, office, and, lately, living space. "I mean, look at us. We can't afford a crew. Your camera's held together with duct tape. We're shooting, editing, and practically living in our van." I took a deep breath. "What are we trying to prove?"

"Right now, we're trying to prove that Batsquatch is real," she

BATSQUATCH LIVES!

said. "That's why I want you to pick up after 'told his story.' But this time without that 'And thus was born' crap."

I didn't want to fight, so I ran my hands through my hair and smiled at the camera. "Okay, let's take it from the top."

If only I hadn't given up, Lisa might still be alive.

⚷

We did line pickups until the sun got too low. Lisa liked to shoot in natural light or under a spot. Dusk didn't fit with her artistic "vision" for the show.

While we waited for full dark, I pulled out our Coleman stove and opened a can of beef stew.

"What's the occasion?" Lisa threw a couple of Styrofoam bowls on the folding table.

"This is the 50th episode of *Tales of the Cryptid*. I think we deserve something better than another baloney sandwich."

"But baloney's good for our budget."

I wasn't in the mood to talk about dwindling cash, so I changed the subject as I stirred the stew.

"What's our latest numbers? Any new subscribers?"

Lisa opened her laptop and waited for her phone to hotspot. "Seventeen new subscribers. Not too bad."

"Nice. Maybe someday we'll have enough to get an actual sponsor for the show."

"I have a good feeling about this Batsquatch story. It has everything. Part bat, part Sasquatch, part canine. If we can get your narration nailed down, this could be our Mothman."

"Part bat, 'squatch, part dog, huh? Three things, just like ManBearPig." I filled our bowls with stew and sat down.

"Yeah, except ManBearPig's a cartoon. Batsquatch is real."

"Speaking of, how's the animation coming?"

"Not too bad, actually. My skills have finally progressed beyond MS Paint."

After dinner, I cleaned up our dishes while Lisa worked on the graphics.

By the time she finished, the woods had gone full dark. The moon would be up soon.

"Do you want to start a fire while we wait," I asked, "or shoot some wilds with the spot?"

"I have a better idea," she said. "Let's drive a little farther up, then hike up to the ridge. I'd like to get some footage in the woods as we go. We can camp above the tree line overnight and get some great shots at dawn."

It took us about thirty minutes to reach the trailhead. Normally we wouldn't hike through the woods in the dark, but the path was well-marked and the full moon lit our way. We shot B-roll and some ad-libs to pass the time as we hiked.

We finally reached the ridge and found a nice flat space to camp. I pulled our tent from my backpack and set it up. It was summer, but we were above the tree line so there was still a little nip in the air. But between our light blankets, body heat, and some extracurricular activities, we stayed plenty warm. After, we fell asleep in each other's arms.

I don't know how long we'd been out before a tremendous burst of wind woke me. As I rubbed sleep from my eyes, I heard something circling our tent. Shuffling footsteps and wet, heavy breathing. Its shadow was significantly taller than the walls of our tent. I reached over to wake Lisa, but she was already up, camera in hand.

We sat, frozen, as the thing circled the tent again, panting as it walked. Then it just . . . stopped.

After a few minutes, we decided to go out and look around.

I grabbed the zipper of our tent just as something pushed up against the flap. It was cold and hard and *big*. I'm not embarrassed to admit I screamed. Lisa pulled me back. I turned on my flashlight and the thing shuffled away from the tent.

It ran around our tent and tried to push through the back wall. Something sliced through the tent fabric. A talon. A *huge* talon, sharp and hooked and lethal. It was Lisa's turn to scream. I threw my light at the wall and the creature retreated.

We huddled together in the middle of the tent.

The footsteps started again. First here, now there. Always circling. Loud, angry breathing and low, guttural growls surrounded us. And then everything went quiet. Even the insects seemed to hold their breath.

Lisa turned on the camera. We used the flashlight for ambient light and she started shooting.

I tried to put on a brave face. "We were sleeping up here on the ridge," I said. "A few minutes ago, a powerful gust blew through

BATSQUATCH LIVES!

camp and woke us. Was it the wind, or had Batsquatch paid us a visit?"

Lisa turned the camera to the tear in the tent as I continued. "It circled our tent several times and tried to rip through the fabric. Then it just . . . stopped."

We sat in silence as Lisa panned the camera around the interior of our tent.

"Of course, it all died down as soon as we started shoot—"

A sudden burst of wind buffeted the tent. Something grabbed the poles where they crossed at the top of the tent. Whatever was out there was trying to lift us off the ground.

Lisa swung the camera up just in time to see a giant claw rip through the tent fabric. A dog face with blue fur, yellow eyes, and straight, sharp teeth leered down at us.

"Holy shit, Batsquatch is real!" I yelled as I lunged for the flap and ripped at the zipper. I finally got it open and looked back. Lisa was still sitting in the middle of the tent, filming.

"Lisa, we have to go!" I reached for her. Batsquatch was faster. He grabbed her by the hair and yanked her through the roof of the tent. The creature flapped its massive wings and rose into the air.

I jumped up and grabbed Lisa's legs. Its wings beat faster, but it couldn't lift both of us. It landed and ran toward the cliff, dragging us behind it.

And all the while, Lisa kept filming.

We were almost at the cliff. I screamed at Lisa to drop the camera and fight, but she wouldn't stop shooting. I don't know if she could at that point. Ten feet from the cliff's edge, we hit a large boulder. I lost my grip on Lisa's legs. Without my extra weight, Batsquatch quickly took to the sky. It shifted its grip as it flew and carried Lisa by the waist.

The last I saw of her, she was silhouetted against the full moon, a hundred, maybe two hundred feet above me.

Still filming.

"I don't know what happened to her, if she's alive or dead," I say. "But I know Batsquatch is real."

The interviewer turns to her cameraman. "Do you think we got it?"

LARRY HINKLE

"Yeah, that was great." He packs up his equipment.

They thank me for talking to them. The episode should air on *Destination America* in early fall. They're going up to the ridge tomorrow night to film a "recreation" of mine and Lisa's last night together.

I wish them good luck and wait for the guard to take me back to my cell. They seem like nice kids. If they're unlucky enough to find Batsquatch, I pray it doesn't take the cameraman.

New footage is the only chance to have my conviction for Lisa's murder overturned.

Larry Hinkle *is the least famous writer you've never heard of. A copywriter living with his wife and two doggos in Rockville, Maryland, when he's not writing stories that scare people into peeing their pants, he writes ads that scare people into buying adult diapers, so they're not caught peeing their pants. His debut collection,* The Space Between, *was published in February 2024 by Trepidatio Publishing. Fingers crossed, his new novella,* The Eris Ridge Trail, *will be released in March 2025. Additionally, his work has appeared in* The Rack: Stories Inspired by Vintage Horror Paperbacks; October Screams: A Halloween Anthology; *and* The NoSleep Podcast, *among others. He's an active member of the HWA (his short stories made the preliminary Stoker ballot in 2020 and 2022); a graduate of Fright Club and Crystal Lake's Author's Journey short story and novella programs; an HWA mentee; and a survivor of the Borderlands Writers Bootcamp. Stop by and visit him at thatscarylarry.com or stalk him on the socials at @thatscarylarry.*

ALL THE CHILDREN ARE INSIDE

Jamal Hodge

JOY WANDERED THE city's veins, her shrill cries piercing false light, high into the darkness above, as New York screamed bitter chill beyond layered flesh, into shaking bones. She was a young woman, barely in her early twenties, pale as pain, haggard as sorrows. Dressed too thinly for the unforgiving cold; it bit into her skin like teeth. Her voice, raw and cracked, echoed with the same desperate mantra.

"My baby . . . My baby . . . My baby . . . "

She screamed it at the buildings with their illuminated eyes, she screamed it at the cars as they trampled through the last remnants of the December snow, she screamed it alone where no one cared to hear, into the night, her pleas filling the empty spaces between shadows.

Grief had stripped her of all beauty, leaving only the hollow shell of hysteria, and she stumbled through the streets beneath an incalculable weight, her tears freezing on her cheeks, eyes wide and searching with a frenzied hope.

"They took my baby!" she shouted, her voice breaking.

The few people who passed by quickened their pace.

"My baby! AHHHH! AHHH!! My baby!!!"

She stopped at every dark corner, every empty alley, looking for a sign, any sign, of her missing child.

Finally, someone stopped. A middle-aged black man with the rugged look of a city worker, and his companion, a caramel-skinned woman in her mid-thirties, dressed fancy enough to seem out of the man's league.

"Let's not do this again," Amy snapped.
"What's wrong with you?" he asked, glancing at Amy.
"I'm serious, Richard. Not right now. I'm cold,"
Richard hesitated, "Let me just see if she's alright,"
Amy rolled her eyes, "Come on! You want to be a hero to everyone all the fucking time! Look, take me home, Richard. Save *me* from the cold."

With a reluctant sigh, Richard let Amy pull him away, his gaze lingering on Joy as she continued her lonely search.

Joy wandered deeper into the city's neglected corners, finding herself outside an old, derelict Hotel. The structure loomed, red-bricked, dark and unwelcoming, its façade crumbling with age and neglect. The title, in dimly lit letters, gave its name: *HOME*.

The Doorman seemed of identical condition, too wrinkled, too slender, African-black with a 1920s disposition, dressed in a uniform that seemed too pristine for the filth around him. His hand, one degree from bones, creaked toward Joy in welcome, his deep black eyes aglow with a horrid acceptance.

"A good night for a stroll, ma'am," the Doorman said.

Joy stopped, "My baby . . . "

With a slow, deliberate motion, the Doorman opened the door, revealing the black maw of the building. His eyes never left hers, unblinking, patient. "All the children are inside," he said.

Joy hesitated. She could see faces inside—faces twisted with pain, mirrors of her own suffering. They did not smile, but their hands curved, waved, reached out, beckoning.

Lily danced alone, her movements fluid and seductive, her olive skin aglow under the faint light of the moon. The music from the streets below played a haunting melody, flowing through muscle and bone. Suddenly, it stopped, the notes fading. Lily's dance halted, her violet eyes opening, glistening with tears.

"The music . . . " she sighed.

The moonlight flickered, casting her shadow in strange, unnatural ways. She closed her eyes again, her chin lowering as the

ALL THE CHILDREN ARE INSIDE

silence was replaced by a painful hum, a high-pitched tinnitus that clawed at her mind. Lily winced, clutching her ears.

She stepped out of her apartment into a derelict hallway, where figures slumped against the peeling walls. Half-deads, wearing tattered clothes that clung to their emaciated bodies. Huddled together in corners like piles of dirty clothes, whispering their whispers, speaking in tongues foreign to sanity.

In contrast, Lily seemed to carry an inner light, too bright and much too clean in the dimness of the dilapidated hall. A high-definition image in a black and white world, she radiated the color and the immaculate demure of a Disney princess come to life.

"Momma . . . Momma . . . " A man reached out. "Momma . . . Momma . . . " he cried, his voice echoing through the desolate space. Lily moved past him, her hands slowly dropping from her ears as the ringing transformed into a chaotic cacophony of sorrow. Seeing her, those that could stand stood, those that could reach, reached, each hand played a different note, creating a dissonant melody in her ears.

Lily sighed, the music soothing her. As she swayed, with the familiar rhythm of the suffering all around her, she glimpsed from the corner of her eye one of the figures speeding toward her in the slow sluggish way of human beings, Shaun . . . it was her Shaun.

"LET US GO!!" Shaun lunged forward, bringing the knife down.

Lily glanced to see the blade's point protruding from her chest. She coughed delicately, blood staining her lips.

Shaun yanked the knife out and raised it again, his eyes wild.

Lily turned to face him, her expression calm, motherly. She wiped the blood from her mouth and then her chest.

There was no wound.

The knife clattered to the floor as Shaun fell to his knees, gnashing his teeth, his breath ragged, as he pulled at his hair.

"Let you go? Child . . . sweet Shaun . . . I did not come to you. You, came here . . . to me."

Shaun bolted for an EXIT door, but his feet grew heavier with each step. Lily lifted her head, raising her hands toward the ceiling. The hallway fell silent, the murmurs ceasing as everyone turned to watch Shaun's struggle in unison. His steps slowed. He fell back to his knees, gasping for breath as he moaned.

"They came deeper into the forest . . . " Her voice resonated with the cadence of a story told a thousand times, " . . . and if help did not come soon, they must die of hunger and weariness."

Shaun's movements grew sluggish, his body sinking lower with each word. He struggled against the invisible force holding him down, but it was no use, he was a fly in an unseen web, his labored breaths echoing through the silence as Lily continued her recitation, her voice slow, serene, melodic.

"Alas, they reached relief," she continued. "And when they approached the little house, they saw that it was built of blood and covered with sin, and that the windows were of a clear sorrow."

Memory crashed into Shaun like a wave.

Shaun's black-gloved hand gripped the butcher's knife, the blade gleaming in the dim light of the quiet living room. He moved stealthily, his footsteps silent as he approached the bedroom door, blood was leaving other parts of him, flowing now to one central point in his pants. The anticipation threatened to blind him—the arousal, the passion, the excitement. Inside, a couple lay asleep, gift-wrapped by fate, their bodies close together, in the comforts of love.

Shaun loved them too, as the wolf loves the sheep, as the knife loves flesh. Made to sever it cuts, splits the bonding of cells, of tissues, to reveal the truth of bone. The secret of spirit.

The swelling in his pants threatened to burst. Throbbing, seemingly in synch with each rise and fall of their chests. Loving their love. Loving them for this opportunity, to feel, to have, to be. Shaun's knife hovered above the husband's neck, the veins pulsing gently with each breath. He hesitated for a moment, the still perfection of the scene almost lulling him to tears, then Shaun slid the blade in without a sound. Blood gushed, warm and dark, the life draining from the man's eyes before he could even comprehend.

Half asleep, the wife stirred, her hand instinctively reaching for her husband. Her fingers brushed against the wetness, recoiling. Her eyes snapped open, wide, confused, and blue, as Shaun loomed over her, the knife poised for another strike. She didn't have time to scream.

The pressure in his pants released, as Shaun gave a long-lived

ALL THE CHILDREN ARE INSIDE

moan, the knife fell, savage and unrelenting, over and over, turning the bed into a battlefield of gore and bouncing springs.

Lily stood behind Shaun as he wept, his body wracked with the weight of his sins. She looked down at him, her violet eyes glowing softly in the dim light. "My path is easy, my burdens are light," her voice was a soothing lullaby. "And what you have brought me, we shall make right."

Shaun turned toward her, his face wet with tears. "I'm sorry, Mom. I did it again. I tried not to. I'm sorry!"

"I know."

Shaun took her outstretched hand, rising slowly to his feet. Lily's gaze pierced the trappings of flesh, her eyes delving deeper, finding every note of sorrow.

"You've been very bad," she said.

"Yes, Mom,"

"I need you to do better, Shaun. I need you to be redeemed."

Shaun slapped the sides of his head violently, "Be redeemed! Be redeemed!" he chanted, his voice growing louder with each repetition. "Be redeemed! Be redeemed! Be redeemed! Be redeemed!"

Lily placed a hand on his cheek, "Now, now, hush child. Do not be afraid. I'll always be here. Something to stab, something to bleed, something to love..."

Shaun's sobs subsided as he leaned his head against her shoulder, seeking comfort in her arms. "Thank you, Momma. Thank you so much!" he mumbled; his voice muffled against her as Lily gently stroked his hair, her eyes scanning the phantoms that littered the floor—men and women whom life had forgotten, and death did not want.

Joy sat in the corner of HOME's crumbling stairwell, her thin body swaying in silent agony. Blood dripped from her mouth, thick globs pooling beside her. On the ground lay half her tongue. Nearby, a pair of heroin addicts sat on the stairs, watching Joy bleed. One of the junkies, his arms already riddled with needle marks, set a tourniquet around his forearm. Unable to find a vein, he pulled down his pants, searching for a place to inject. His companion, lost in his own high, barely noticed, the two of them swayed like two malformed trees rooted to carpet and brick, while Joy bled out beneath the shade of their apathy.

Lily descended the stairs, her presence almost ethereal in a flowing dress and tight leggings. One of the junkies, his voice weak and trembling, mumbled, "Mommy..." as she passed.

Lily glanced at him briefly, before her gaze fell on Joy. The young woman's eyes were wide and terrified, her voice a garbled mess as she tried to speak.

"Child, what have you done to yourself?" Lily asked.

Joy's words were barely coherent, each syllable drowned in blood. *I want to die, I want to die, I want to die!*

Lily placed Joy's head on her shoulder, cradling her as a mother would.

"I don't know why I'm here! Why am I here!"

Lily's expression remained calm, almost tender. "Because your soul is filth."

Joy tried to rise, but her body was too weak, her strength drained by her own self-inflicted wound.

"Do not be afraid," Lily soothed, her hand gently caressing Joy's blood-covered cheek. She turned the girl's face towards her, her violet eyes locking onto Joy's. "Look and see."

Joy gazed into Lily's eyes, finding her own reflection in those violet depths, and something else, too old, much too old—Antediluvian, before the flood. Eyes older than terror from before, before, before... peering into the abyss of her soul.

"My baby... they took... my baby..."

Alone in the small, suffocating room, Joy sang a lullaby to the crying baby in her arms. Her baby, the child she should love. But Joy's eyes were sunken, dark circles etched beneath them, evidence of countless sleepless nights. She rocked the baby with a mechanical gentleness, as if the weight of the world had pressed her down into this tiny, endless, cage.

The baby's cries were relentless needles, piercing Joy's fragile composure. She shushed it desperately, her voice cracking. "Stop.

ALL THE CHILDREN ARE INSIDE

I don't know what to do. Please stop . . . STOP IT!! STOP!!" But there had been no stopping, not during the nights when *He* crept into her room and made her do things she'd wanted to save for a boy she loved. "But don't you love me too?" *He* had said. She had, but not like that, not like that at all, but *he* wouldn't listen, *he* wouldn't stop. Not until the swelling told. His sins given life. She'd confessed only to be slapped. Money given too late for a termination. She wouldn't do it. Not even after he was locked up. Not even after mother learned to despise the sight of her.

"Please stop . . . Please . . . . Stop . . . "

Her family's shame all over the internet. Blood given seed by blood to raise blood.

Disgrace. Whore.

Why had she waited so long to tell?

Horrid, cruel accusations.

Run away. Alone. With the mewling sin.

The breathing sin.

Son or brother?

Abomination. Nasty. Forever scarred.

"STOP IT!! STOP IT!!"

Her eyes darted around the room, searching for an escape, any respite from the constant noise. Joy noticed the window, slightly open, just a crack. *Enough.*

She carried the crying baby to the window, her hands trembling.

The wailing drifted further and further away, fading, like a ship beyond the horizon of her life.

Joy turned from that distant *thud* into the silence of freedom, finally unburdened in the small, suffocating room.

Tears streamed down Joy's pale cheeks as she choked on her own blood. *"I see . . . I see . . . "*

Lily nodded, her expression serene. "Do not be afraid. It could only have been what it always was. It has always been, what it will always be,"

They sat together in the stairwell, Joy's broken song fading into silence, leaving nothing but the wailing echo of her sins.

Outside, the moon hung heavy in the Brooklyn skyline, casting a pale glow over the derelict Hotel. The Doorman stood at his post, still as cement, old as time.

Lily stepped out onto the empty street, her dress fluttering slightly in the cold wind.

"Mum, did you make your acquaintance with our new arrival?" the Doorman asked, his voice polite, almost deferential.

"She insisted on an early self-eviction."

The Doorman nodded solemnly. "And to the devil his due."

Lily closed her eyes, catching the beautiful melody that had drawn her before, clearer now, not so far away. She smiled, her expression one of pure delight.

Love.

"Excuse me, sorry to bother you two!"

Richard's tone was laced with urgency. Lily opened her eyes, her smile widening as she took in the sight of him—shivering in the January cold despite his brown sports coat, his gloved hands tucked beneath his armpits in a futile attempt to keep warm. His eyes darted around nervously as if searching for something—or someone.

"Did you happen to see a young woman wandering around out here?" Richard asked, his breath fogging in the frigid air. "I called the cops, but you know how long they take to do anything. She was underdressed for this chill, about this tall, pale-skinned . . . she kept crying for her baby. God, I think she lost her child."

Lily regarded him with a soft, knowing gaze. "Yes, we've seen her," she said gently.

The Doorman, slowly opened the door, "All the children are inside."

The foyer was shrouded in darkness, the air thick with an eerie stillness that pressed in from all sides. Richard moved cautiously, his footsteps echoing on the cracked tiles. Lily followed, her steps light and deliberate, closing the door behind them with a soft click.

ALL THE CHILDREN ARE INSIDE

"She ran in here?" Richard asked, peering into the gloom.

Lily nodded, her expression unreadable. "She did. Together, I think we can find her. Mr?"

"Richard Cormier," he replied, glancing back at her. "What's your name?"

"Lilith. The children call me Lily," She moved ahead of him, leading the way up the stairs, her presence a guiding light in the dark. "Are you family to this girl, a lover, a friend?"

Richard shook his head. "No, nothing like that. She's just someone that needs help, and I can help."

"Most people wouldn't care."

"I work with the type of children the world forgets. We give them a fresh start."

Lily paused on the stairs, turning slightly to look back at him. "That's all anyone can do for someone else," she said, "We're not too different, you and I."

"You work with kids?"

"In a sense. But my heart is with dancing."

As they ascended, Lily's shadow flickered against the walls, twisting and twirling.

They reached the top floor, standing at the precipice of a large, empty hall.

"She's here. Look and see,"

Richard entered the hall, his eyes immediately locking onto Joy's lifeless body sprawled on the floor. He rushed forward, kneeling beside her. "God, she's cold! Shit! Call 911! What's the address to this place?" His voice echoed, frantic and disoriented as he fumbled to help what was beyond help, checking for a pulse, mouth to mouth, trying to revive her.

"Thank you for your goodness, Richard. Thank you for your song."

Richard turned, his confusion deepening. "What are you talking about? She needs help!" His voice rose, edged with frustration and fear. "What the fuck is going on here? Why are you just standing there!"

Shaun emerged from the shadows, his presence sudden and jarring. He wasn't alone. A group gathered behind him, their faces eager. Shaun's knife gleamed in the moonlight, still stained with crusted blood.

"Thank you for your song," Shaun murmured, his voice a low rumble that sent a shiver down Richard's spine.

Richard's instincts screamed at him, the realization dawning too late. He was surrounded—trapped. They ringed him, a sea of tattered men and women, dirty like the homeless but somehow more miserable, more lost. The group moved closer, encircling him like a pack of wolves.

"Thank you for your song! Thank you for your song!" they chanted, their voices rising in a fevered chorus, as they clawed for Richard, hands upon hands, pulling him down, grabbing, smiling, crying, in jubilant elation.

Richard fought, he thrashed and bit, punched smiling faces, kicked at necks and teeth, but it was like struggling against time. Down, down, sinking under the weight of bodies, incapacitated by caressing fingers, their grip unyielding. "Thank you for your song! Thank you for your song!" "Richard! Richard! Richard! Richard!" Lily pranced forward, her delicate arms raised high, her movements graceful and commanding. The crowd parted for her, reverent in their obedience. Joy's body was gone, swept away in the chaos. Richard lay on the floor now, pinned by the weight of the mob, two at each arm, three at each leg, spread like a starfish on his back, his breaths ragged and desperate, as he screamed.

Shaun loomed, the butcher's knife poised.

Lily stood at the center of it all. She gazed down at Richard, happy for him.

"I am a very old story, Richard," Lily said softly, "Neither angel, nor Man, nor Demon. Born of lust & reason. It is REASON that compels me, lust with purpose, purpose without judgment."

Richard's terrified eyes darted around, seeing only the hungry, empty faces of the lost souls around him. Their eyes gleamed with a manic light, their bodies swayed in anticipation.

"If you could see Heaven, if it was guaranteed you would be accepted, wouldn't you leave all your worldly possessions behind? Wouldn't you forsake your eyes, your skin, your bones?"

Richard's voice shook as he pleaded, "Please. Whatever you're doing, please don't! Amy is waiting for me! My students, I have people, I have—"

"Do not be afraid." Lily leaned closer, her voice a soft, relentless

ALL THE CHILDREN ARE INSIDE

whisper. "You're almost there. Almost home. I will send you to your father, Richard, the father of all, before living taints the music of your soul."

Richard's struggles intensified, but the hands holding him down were legion.

"Let me dance for you now."

Shaun's knife descended, the blade slicing through Richard's sternum, carving a path down past his belly and through his groin. Richard's screams ripped through the hall, a raw, primal agony.

"Do not be afraid, you are almost home! Do not be afraid!" Lily reached into the gruesome wounds, her hands coming away slick with Richard's blood. She smeared it across her youthful face, her arms, her legs, savoring the ritual. An orgasmic sigh escaped her lips, her eyes fluttering closed.

Her children fell silent, their collective gaze fixed on Lily as she began to flow, dancing in unnaturally fluid and hypnotic motions, as if she was without a spine, without knees or elbows, her slender body twirling in perfect harmony with the unearthly music that filled the space. Richard's screams gradually faded, overtaken by the haunting melody of his soul, a symphony only Lily could truly hear.

Lilith's children, the lost souls who clung to her purpose, gently touched one another, their fingers tracing intricate patterns in the air as they swayed in time with her dance. Some of their faces painted with Richard's blood, the red smears turning their sorrow into a grotesque perversion of hope.

Richard's vision blurred, the unimaginable pain receding as he watched Lily's shadow stretch over the crowd. Fear ebbed away, replaced by a strange serenity. He saw beyond the crumbling walls, beyond the world itself, to the infinite horizon that lay ahead.

All beauty, all horror, all time.

One. Many. I AM.

His bloody lips curved; the final notes of his soul reverberated softly.

A trumpet sounded.

"Thank you," he whispered.

Jamal Hodge is a multi-award-winning filmmaker and writer from Queens, NYC, who has won over 100 filmmaking awards with

JAMAL HODGE

screenings at the Tribeca Film Festival, Sundance, Chelsea Film Festival, and others. He directed the first season of Investigation Discovery Channel's 'Primal Instinct (2018) and was also a director on the PBS docuseries Southern Storytellers (2023) and Madness & Writers: The Untold Truth, Maybe? (2025). As a writer, Jamal is an active member of The Horror Writer's Association and the SFPA, being nominated for the 2021 & 2022 Rhysling Awards and winning 2nd place at the 2022 Dwarf Stars. Crystal Lake Publishing has published his inaugural poetry collection, The Dark Between The Twilight, *and* The Anthology Bestiary of Blood Modern Fables & Dark Tales, *which boasts 18 Bram Stoker award-winning writers.* Everything Endless, *a collaborative poetry collection with Jamal Hodge and Grand Master Linda D. Addison, will be released by Raw Dog Screaming Press in 2025.*

SMILE

Robin Brown

"**How would you** rate your performance since joining us?"

"How would I rate my performance? Well, I have a pretty good ratio of getting a customer order right, I haven't had any complaints—as far as I'm aware—and I've successfully resisted the urge to eat any of the processed, deep-fried crap we sell. So, I'd say I'm just about hanging on."

I don't say any of that, of course. Instead, I kind of shrug a bit, offer a half-hearted smile, and say "Fine, I guess."

"Satisfactory, I think," my manager nods, circling something on his little form. He's not a bad guy really. I only hate him with all my guts because he represents everything about this place. He's small, a bit grubby, completely charmless, and a rulebook on legs.

"Where do you think you can improve?"

"I suppose I could learn how to use the ice cream machine."

"No, no, no," he shakes his head. "The ice cream machine is only to be operated by shift leaders, team leaders, or management."

"Is it difficult?"

"No, it's rented. It's not company property."

"Oh."

"Let's focus on you, instead," he says, trying to smile sincerely and failing spectacularly. "What is it about your performance that needs improvement?"

"I have a feeling you're going to tell me."

"I'm interested in what you think."

"I got nothing." I shrug, knowing my reluctance to play ball will only infuriate his tiny little corporate-loving brain.

"You don't smile," he snaps. "You need to smile when you serve the customers."

"Have I had any complaints?"

"Actually, you're our leading front-end worker. Customer feedback noted your easy-going nature and readiness to help out. So, you know, you're nearly there." He couldn't sound more condescending even if he tried. "But this is about more than that, this is about delivering the correct Happy Burger experience."

"Okay, I get it," I try to level with him. "I'm not really a smiler, though. I can try but I'll end up looking like a weirdo."

"Well, trying is no longer good enough."

"What does that mean?"

"Starting this week, a new program has been installed into the security cameras. It's going to scan all our faces, all the time, and it will be able to rate our Happy Burger faces."

"What the hell . . . That's a bit *Black Mirror*, isn't it?"

"It's only ensuring we deliver the correct service, as we're supposed to do already."

"So, the cameras are going to be watching us? Every second of the day?"

"They already do that."

"But now they're going to be judging us."

"Judging isn't the right word. They're going to be rating us."

"Oh. That's so much better," I say with a dry tone, but my manager is too wrapped up in himself to notice.

"If you smile, you'll have nothing to worry about."

"And if I don't smile enough?"

"Well, there'll be re-training, and if that doesn't work then you'll get an unofficial warning, and then an official warning, and finally dismissal."

"Bloody hell."

"Look, it's not like we're asking a lot from you. Just smile. It's that easy."

All it took was three months and it's broken me.

The staff toilet is a cupboard-sized room, there's only a toilet and a tiny sink to the side with a small mirror above it. I'm staring

SMILE

into that mirror now, twenty minutes after my shift ended, and I can't get the smile off my face.

My cheeks hurt and my jaw aches, but they won't relax. I can't control them. They're stuck. They won't respond to what my brain wants them to do. With my fingers I pull my cheeks down and force my lips together, but my eyes start watering, and the pain is like a cramp all over my face. I can't hold them there for long.

I let go and my cheeks slap back. My mouth opens again. The smile returns even as I cry out from the pain I just went through.

So, I sit down and I wait. I scroll through my phone, liking photos I barely look at, watching videos I pay no attention to, switching between apps on my phone just for something to do, for something to take my mind away. Half an hour passes by, and I can feel it slowly happening. My face is relaxing. The smile is disappearing. It used to take a minute or two after I clocked off, then it took ten minutes, now it's half an hour. It's alright now, though. I'm done for the day.

"What the hell is wrong with you?" my girlfriend shouts at me.
"What?"
"I asked you to come to bed with me."
"Yeah, I will."
"You asked me if I'd like fries with that!"
"Oh. Sorry."

The cameras are everywhere. Little black orbs hanging from the ceiling, nestled in every corner, watching every move we make, every smile we fake, they're always watching me.

It's chaos. Some of the kitchen staff haven't turned up this morning so there's a backlog of orders, as well as a queue of impatient customers out the door. Manager's scared witless and there's no light at the end of the tunnel. All we can do is put our heads down and do what we can with every order that comes in.

"It's been twenty minutes!"
I smile.
"I only wanted a Happy Muffin and Coffee!"

ROBIN BROWN

I smile.
"This place is rubbish."
I smile.
"What are you smiling for!?"
I have no idea. I smile.

It's been a whole hour, sitting on the toilet scrolling through my phone, and my face still hasn't relaxed. It's like someone's superglued a smile onto my skin and the bloody thing won't peel off.

Someone's knocking at the door. They're knocking loudly, saying something and I think they're angry about it. In fact, I think they've been at the door for ages. There's nothing for it. I stand up, check my smiling face in the mirror, and open the door.

Stepping out into the small corridor is like stepping into a nightmare. Half a dozen of my co-workers, including front-end, kitchen, and drive-thru, are waiting for me. We all have a smile stuck to our faces. We all can't seem to shake it. We all have tired eyes.

It's the middle of the night. My girlfriend's asleep next to me. We hardly spoke all evening and it's been like this for the past couple of months. I can't sleep, though.

When I forget to concentrate, my face pulls back into the Happy Burger smile. It's somehow worse when all the lights are out and there's silence all around. I can feel it underneath my skin, pulling at my cheeks, lifting my lips. It's always there.

I can't stand it any longer. I get out of bed and go to the bathroom. The street lighting outside casts my silhouette against the mirror above the sink. I'm a dark figure, a void cut in the shape of a young man. I turn the bathroom light on. There it is. Stuck to my face. I didn't even realise it had come back this time. Maybe it's always been there. Maybe I've lost all feeling.

I can't go on like this. I can't look at that thing on my face. I can't keep it there anymore.

SMILE

I have an early morning shift so my girlfriend's still asleep when I leave the flat. The streets are practically empty this early too and I don't pass anyone on my short walk to Happy Burger, *where your favourite food is just a smile away.*

I walk in through the front door and head for the staff entrance, but the little black orbs in the ceiling don't bother me anymore. They still see me, of course. They're always watching. But now there's nothing to see.

As if from far away, I hear someone screaming. When I walk into the kitchen, people start backing away from me. It's weird. I guess they want to watch me, as well. They've *all* come to watch me. I don't mind. They can watch me all they like. There's nothing to see. Me and the chef's knife I stole from work saw to that.

Robin Brown *is the author of* The Sworn Sister, *published in the upcoming Dragon Soul Press anthology* The Hunt, *and "The Rising Tide" in* Rogue Waves, *another upcoming Dragon Soul Press anthology. He has recently signed with Wild Ink Publishing to release his debut urban fantasy novel* Vampire Metropolis *in 2025. Robin started writing as a young boy because his dad's old computer could barely play Minesweeper. Despite purchasing a modern gaming computer to play Minesweeper today, it turns out Robin is terrible at it and doesn't understand the rules anyway, so he's taken up writing again. He is over twelve thousand days old and lives somewhere in Manchester, England. He is genuinely not a hundred percent sure exactly where.*

GOODBEAK

Gregg Stewart

THERE HE IS, the sonofabitch, standing on his porch scratching his big, white belly with one grimy hand, the dreaded thunderstick in his other.

Knottie and I exchange a glance across the high branches of the ash tree. "SEE?" he calls to me, and the sound alerts the white-bellied man to our presence. He looks up with a vile sneer and aims his stick. We take off, screaming, "ASSHOLE! ASSHOLE!"

The thunderstick goes off with a ground-shaking *'BOOM-CRACK!'* sending all the forest folk bursting from the trees, raising their angry voices skyward.

It didn't used to be this way. Miss Ravenhair was the mistress here. She was kind and taught us many things. We'd bring her walnuts, and she'd crack them open for us. She showed us how to leave breadcrumbs in the shallows to attract minnows. And she gave me my name: Goodbeak. She was clever and worthy of our admiration, unlike the white-bellied man. He gets no gifts.

We used to bring Miss Ravenhair trinkets from the forest—blue eggs, a lucky rabbit's foot, bright silver cords to braid into her dark hair, and once—a shiny gold earring we discovered near the long stretch of hard, black earth where we found the flat food.

We'd also bring her items for her cupboard, like newt eyes, black-cap mushrooms, and snake skins. She knew the old ways, and it pleased her that we brought these things.

GOODBEAK

Miss Ravenhair showed much respect for our homeland—rare for a human. She would wear black robes and dance under the full moon. We would watch her from the treetops, mesmerized, and when the moon was high, she would strip her robes and run through the forest. We would follow, calling her name and swearing our oaths to protect her. When she reached the glade, she would collapse into the lush grass to lie under the moonlight, breathless, pale and beautiful, while we circled overhead.

One night, someone saw us. Others came the next day. They pushed and shoved into Miss Ravenhair's nest and found the earring we had gifted her. They grew angry and took her away.

They brought her to the human settlement—an awful, filthy place. We followed and that's when we saw the signs stapled to their pretend trees. The signs all read 'MISSING' and showed a golden-haired girl. She wore earrings like the one we gifted to Miss Ravenhair.

That's when I knew this was our fault. I told the others, and we cried from the rooftops and wires all night, "SORRY! SORRY!" but it only made the people angrier.

They put Miss Ravenhair in a cage—a cruel and terrible thing to do. That night, we brought seeds and trinkets to her single window, but the bars prevented us from getting too close. She looked so sad. Outside, people pointed at us and said we were 'proof.' What is proof?

The next day, Miss Ravenhair was gone. She has never returned, and bad luck has plagued our forest ever since. Sick trees, tainted streams, rotten eggs. The worst fate was when the white-bellied man moved into Miss Ravenhair's nest. He began cutting down trees—our homes! We were here first, but he no longer wanted us and tried to drive us away. He set his thunderstick upon us, the coward, and our numbers dwindled. But we have remained, harassing him at every turn.

On one warm afternoon last spring, the man had hung his coat on a tree limb while digging a large hole at the forest's edge. He digs many holes. Knottie and I went snooping, and inside the coat pocket, we discovered an earring. It was the one we'd given Miss Ravenhair—the source of her demise. How did this man get it? But wait! It was not the same earring but the earring's mate. That's when I knew the truth of our betrayal. Proof!

GREGG STEWART

From that moment, we vowed never to stop until we had our revenge.

Today, at long last, we intend to hatch our plan. There is a place beyond the hills where everything is drab green. The people there all carry thundersticks, though they never point them at us. They also have large green eggs that explode in a burst of fire and sharp metal barbs.

We have stolen one. And I, Goodbeak, have learned its secret.

The white-bellied man steps from the porch and walks into the forest, leaving his nest unattended as we'd hoped. Knottie and I circle back, bringing the stolen green egg to his doorstep.

Then, we wait.

A short time later, the white-bellied man returns. Knottie and I stand close together on the porch. The man smirks as he levels his thunderstick at us, but we know he will not fire it toward his nest.

"Only two o' ya left," the man says. "Yer like an attempted murder." He giggles and guffaws at his bad joke. We do not like the sound one bit and Knottie takes a nervous hop to the right, revealing the large green egg behind us.

The white-bellied man's eyes go wide. There is no time to waste. I grab the silver pin with my beak and pull. Knottie pushes on the handlepiece until the pin comes loose. We take to the sky in different directions, screaming our intent, "DIE! DIE! DIE!"

The white-bellied man bellows and points the thunderstick at me, but before he can fire, the egg explodes, alighting the nest in waves of white-hot fire and splintered wood.

We fly far from that place and do not look back. Once we land, Knottie peers at me. "GOOD?"

"YES!" I reply with a trickster's grin.

We will attempt to join a new murder tomorrow, but for now, we will rest knowing that Miss Ravenhair and our brethren have their vengeance.

Gregg Stewart *is an HWA author, award-winning songwriter, film composer, studio and touring musician, journalist, editor, and screenwriter.*

GOODBEAK

He is the author of "Let It Out: Unlocking Creativity to Access Authentic Expression" *(New Fable, 2024), which reached #7 on Amazon's best-seller list for new releases in creativity. His dark fiction tales have appeared in multiple publications, including the Sirens Call and Crimson Quill Quarterly along with short story anthologies from Black Cat Press, Crystal Lake, Hellbound Books, and Sley House Publishing.*

THE HUG

Gary McMahon

THE PARTY WAS OVER; the gathering was disbanding. People were leaving in dribs and drabs: in pairs, small groups, or simply one by one.

"I'll see you next week, at badminton practice," said Joyce, a tired smile on her face.

"Yes, I'll be there." Jane was almost at the door. She'd run the gauntlet of farewells, cheerios, see-you-laters, and had managed to shrug on her coat as Tim grappled with the lock to open the front door. "I'll call you in a couple of days."

Joyce leaned in and held her briefly, kissing the air by her left cheek. "You do that. We can talk about the business deal I mentioned."

Jane smiled, nodded, wished she hadn't mentioned the little windfall she'd come into when her aunt had died last month. She glanced over at Tim; he was shaking hands with Bob, Joyce's husband. Bob was half cut, as usual. He could barely keep his eyes open and was struggling to stand without supporting himself against the wall.

As she turned towards the open door, and the night beyond, a short, stocky man in a dark suit stepped forward, arms open, and lunged towards her for a hug. Taken by surprise, she returned the hug, wondering what he'd whispered quickly and quietly into her ear, and trying to remember if she'd even spoken to him during the party. Then he was gone, darting through the kitchen doorway and into the back of the house. A mild sense of social discomfort remained in his wake. Nothing major. Nothing to lose sleep over.

THE HUG

"Our taxi's here," said Tim, grabbing her upper arm and guiding her over the threshold towards the car waiting at the kerb. The night air was cool. She smiled as it kissed her skin, making her feel more awake than she had in the crowded hallway.

They climbed into the taxi and, as it pulled away from the kerb, Jane waved to the slowly closing front door. At the side of the house, a shadow twitched: a swift, dark movement that she supposed was a cat, or even an urban fox, ducking out of sight.

The streets were empty, so it didn't take them long to get home. She unlocked the door to the house while Tim paid the driver, and as she entered the dark space, she groped reflexively for the light switch. Tim wasn't far behind; he entered and shut the door, securing the locks.

"I'm knackered," he said, kissing her briefly on the neck. "That was such a chore."

"Their parties are *always* a chore," she said, kicking off her shoes at the bottom of the stairs. "Bob gets pissed, Joyce gets weepy, and we end up talking shite with people we'll never meet again."

Tim laughed, which turned into a yawn. "Bedtime," he said, starting to climb the stairs.

"I'll be up in a bit." She went through to the kitchen, grabbed a glass from the draining board, and listened to his heavy, drunken footsteps as he crossed the landing to the bathroom. She turned on the tap to drown out the noise of him pissing, left it running too long so that the water overflowed the glass.

Sitting in the conservatory, she sipped her water. She always liked to hydrate when she'd been drinking. It was one of the few useful things her booze-loving mother had taught her growing up. The lights were off so she sat in the darkness and looked out at the small garden. The fence needed painting. The borders were overgrown with weeds. They'd been living here for over a year and still not got a grip on the outside space.

Closing her eyes, she made a promise to herself that she wouldn't go to the next party hosted by Joyce and Bob. She'd think up a good excuse—a death in the family, a thorn in her side, a sinkhole appearing in the street outside . . .

When she went upstairs to bed, Tim was lying on his back, snoring. It was a soft sound, not at all like the rough-edged wheezing he usually produced after a night of drinking, so she got into bed carefully, not wanting to disturb him.

It took a while for sleep to come. She kept dozing and then twitching awake, as if from a sudden shock. This went on for a long time until, finally, she drifted into a proper sleep state. Her dreams were dark and fuzzy; twisted shapes danced just out of reach, and there were distant cries of what seemed like anguish.

Sunlight woke her. Tim must have got up early, perhaps gone for a run. He liked to do that to clear his head. She had a memory of something stalking her. She didn't know what it was, or why it was hounding her, but the memory was frightening all the same.

She got up, had a cold shower, dressed in clean clothes, and started to make a late breakfast.

Tim came home while she was mixing the eggs and milk for an omelette.

"Good run?"

He was breathing heavily and his face was flushed. "A hard run . . . thought I was going to puke when I got about a mile in, but the feeling passed. I'm off for a quick shower."

"Don't be long. I'm making omelettes."

"Yeah, okay." He left the room.

Ungrateful bastard, she thought, a sudden rage making her head throb.

She stopped whisking the eggs. Where on earth had that thought come from? Okay, Tim hadn't thanked her for making breakfast, but he'd just come back from a tough run, and he was in a rush to bathe. She didn't take the omission personally—he'd merely been distracted.

The shit.

"No," she said, picking up the bowl. "No, that isn't what I think. Not at all."

Upstairs, she could hear the shower spraying. Tim began to hum tunelessly.

The vague anger receded. She felt relaxed again, glad to be preparing food for them both. By the time Tim came down to join her—thanking her for the meal, of course—she'd put the odd incident out of her mind.

After breakfast, she left Tim doing the dishes and drove to the nearby shopping precinct. Traffic was heavy. There were road works on the main road through town, which caused queues on most of the side streets. By the time she reached the car park, she felt anxious and impatient.

THE HUG

After locking the car, she walked the few hundred yards to the shopping precinct. It consisted of a row of independent shops, a nice alternative to the ubiquitous supermarkets that had infested every town and city in the country. There was a butcher, a grocer, a newsagent, a card shop, and a quirky little store called "Bits & Bobs" that sold original artwork, interesting ornaments, and other sundry objects that couldn't be had elsewhere.

As she passed the butcher's window, the meat display caught her eye. There were the usual beef joints, dressed chicken breasts, lamb shanks, and sausages, but in the middle of the display sat something she failed to recognise. It was long and pink, with too many stumps where the limbs had been removed. At first, she thought it must be a whole pig, but as she surveyed the carcass, she realised it wasn't porcine in nature.

What on earth is that?

The head had been cut off so she couldn't identify it that way, and the skin was as smooth as plastic. The ridge of its spine was far too prominent; the bones at its haunches were sharp and protruding; the nub of neck left behind after decapitation was too thin for the rest of the body.

Jane glanced to her side to see if anyone else was looking at this thing, but people seemed not to have noticed the weird display. When she looked back at the window, it was just a pig carcass.

She moved on, walking quickly. Her head felt strange, as if it were filled with water. The weight shifted inside her skull, sloshing around up there.

Sitting down on a nearby bench, she took deep breaths and tried to calm down.

Long ago, when she was still at university, someone had spiked her drink. Luckily, a male friend had spotted the culprit with his fingers in her glass, and dragged him out of the pub to beat him unconscious outside. The police had arrived. An ambulance. She'd spent the night in a hospital ward hallucinating and throwing up in a plastic tray.

Had someone slipped something into her drink at the party last night? And if so, why? And who had done it, anyway? She remembered that little man who'd hugged her at the door. A stranger whose face she couldn't even recall—he was just a short, blocky figure with a blank oval atop his broad shoulders.

Everything was fine now. The hallucination—if that's what it was—had passed. She'd been working long hours at the office for the past month, and financial problems had been surfacing before she'd learned about the small inheritance from her distant aunt.

Stress, that's what it was. Surely, that's all it was.

Abandoning her shopping trip, she walked back to the car park and got into her car. She didn't start the engine immediately. Instead, she leaned back into the seat and closed her eyes, taking deep breaths and thinking calming thoughts. She meditated for a while, allowing her mind to drift, and when she came out of it, there was a figure watching her.

It was a man. Short and stocky. He was standing at the other end of the car park, motionless. His hands were tucked into the pockets of a dark overcoat, and he was too far away for her to make out his features.

A feeling of dread washed over her, taking her by surprise. Negative thoughts filled her head: the dead aunt she'd never really known, the fact that one day Tim would die, and she would die too, the realisation that although they'd never had children, she'd always wanted them, but now it was far too late . . . dark waves, lapping at the shore of her existence. Kept at bay for so long, but now the flood defences had broken and the black water was coming through.

Fumbling for the lock, she tried to open the car door. The figure tensed, then darted away, moving towards the exit at an alarming pace. By the time she'd got out of the car, he was gone. When she went to the exit and opened the heavy fire door, peering into the chilly stairwell and down the concrete stairs, there was no sign of him.

She called Joyce that afternoon.

"Who?"

"He was a short bloke. Stocky, you know. I can't remember much else about him, but he was in the hallway when we left. He hugged me."

Joyce didn't say anything for a moment, and then sighed. "Sorry, I was so drunk last night I can barely even remember you leaving. That could've been anyone. There were people there even I don't know!"

THE HUG

"Are you sure?"

"Why? What's wrong? You sound . . . well, a bit anxious."

Jane paused, wondering how much to say. She didn't want Joyce to think she'd lost her mind. "I think he gave me something. Passed it on."

"Like a virus, you mean? Oh, God, we aren't all going to come down with covid again, are we?"

"No. Not like that. It's more like . . . I don't know, not exactly. But it's as if he passed on a feeling. Like a sense of something."

"Eh? I'm not following you. Are you okay? I know you've been overworked lately, and Tim had some issues with that bank loan. Are you feeling the strain? You can talk to me any time. I hope you know that. You do know that, don't you?"

"Yes. Yes, and thank you. Don't worry. It's fine. I think I've caught the flu, that's all. Listen, I'll call you in a few days, when I'm feeling better."

I fucking hate you, she thought.

"Okay, darling, just—"

But Jane had already put down the phone.

Until now, when she'd verbalised her concerns, she hadn't understood how she felt. Telling Joyce that she thought the man had passed something to her, something had clicked into place.

Darkness shifted at the periphery of her vision. Her head began to ache. Small pink shapes writhed on the walls, but when she looked at them, they were no longer there.

The man. What he'd passed on, it had been a sense of doom.

She went to the conservatory and sat in her favourite chair, looking out at the garden. It looked shabbier now, dirty, and overgrown. The sky had taken on a darker hue. Everything seemed less focused, as if a filter had been placed across her field of vision.

Darkness lapped at the edges of everything.

Catching sight of her reflection in the glass, she was unable to make out her own features. Just a patch of flesh, a blur, a smudge.

Tim was in the garage, working on one of his woodwork projects. He wouldn't even know she was gone. She put on her coat, grabbed her bag, and went out to the car.

She drove to the car park but, of course, the man wasn't there. He'd moved on. There was a black stain on the concrete where he'd been standing, a mark that would never wash off.

Driving around town, she looked at the faces of strangers.

None of them was smiling; everyone walked with slumped shoulders and dour expressions. There was no happiness here, no joy to be experienced, not anymore.

Buildings wavered like faulty projections across her vision; cars seemed to crawl with tiny insects that erupted across their bodywork. The world was changing before her eyes, but in subtle ways that she failed to grasp.

It was dark before she even knew it. The streetlights came on, bulbs opening like the luminous eyes of deep-sea creatures. The streets thinned of pedestrians. Bars filled with desperate drinkers. Shops shut and boarded their windows. The night surged in. The darkness.

She pulled up at the kerb in a rundown part of town, where the edges of a local sink estate marked for demolition met the border of a street of cheap terraced houses. There was litter everywhere—empty beer cans, fast food wrappers, bits of paper and plastic clogging the gutters.

If he was going to be anywhere, it would be here, in this liminal place, where one edge joined another. He would inhabit that space between the two, squatting at the border of what is known and what is merely guessed at—a denizen of the edgelands.

Sitting in her car, she knew that she would see him eventually. These were the streets he walked, the byways he travelled. This was his home.

She wasn't sure how long she waited, but at some point, probably in the early hours, he stepped out into the street. She watched him as he walked slowly towards the quivering tower blocks of the derelict estate, his hands thrust deep into his pockets. His face was a blur; a smudge; a mere suggestion of features.

She got out of the car and followed him. Along the street, down a narrow alley, across a patch of waste ground, until he entered a building through a back door. He needed no key. The door simply opened at his touch.

She followed him through.

Inside, she climbed a grubby, piss-stinking stairway, tracking him. On the third floor, he stopped and opened the door to one of the flats. He slipped inside, leaving the door ajar.

Without thinking, she followed him inside. Splintered wood ran along the edges of the doorway and frame like rows of dirty teeth. She imagined this smirking mouth snapping shut on her

THE HUG

arm, rending flesh and breaking bone, but it simply eased shut behind her.

"I knew you'd find me," he said. "They always do." His voice was nondescript, much like everything else about him. It had no real tone, no memorable timbre. It was just a voice. Barely even that.

He was standing against the wall, half in shadow. Ambient light bled through the window, burnishing his lower half in a sickly luminescence.

"What did you do to me?" She took a step forward, but the light didn't change angle. He was like a picture, a painting, an old piece of graffiti sprayed onto that wall.

"I hugged you," he said in his voiceless voice. "That is all."

"Who are you?"

He didn't answer.

"Tell me who you are."

"I don't know. I think I used to be someone, a long time ago, but now I have no idea. Perhaps that's what I am: an idea. A thought. A feeling. I don't know. I am no one."

Tears ran down her cheeks, unbidden. "You gave me something."

He raised his hand to his hidden face, his fingers dissipating like smoke.

"I gave you nothing."

"No . . . you passed something to me. What was it? What did you give me? What's inside me?" Her eyes stung. Her throat was dry.

He chuckled softly. Black smoke, like a light ash, was exhaled into the room from his lungs. "No, you misunderstand me. I gave you nothing. Nothing is what I gave you. Before that, you were full, and now you are empty."

He was losing his shape. His edges were softening, becoming protean. She didn't have much time. Soon he'd be gone, just another part of the greater darkness.

"Please," she said. "Take it away."

"But how can I?" His voice was quieter now, almost non-existent: a sigh; a belch; a rancid breath taken in an empty room. "How is it possible to take *nothing* away?"

Stepping forward, she reached out to grab him, but her hands closed only on empty air. A fine black powder coated the wall, the ceiling, the skirting board, the floor where he had stood. The air was rich with it.

Jane fell to her knees on the uncarpeted concrete floor, lifting her blackened fists into the air. She felt nothing. She actually *felt* it stirring within her, like a grub waiting to hatch from its pupa and become something else. It was there, deep inside her body, writhing and flexing and desperate to be born.

Nothing.

Nothing was there. She embraced it.

"There, there," she whispered. "Hush, child."

She didn't know what else to do. There was so little of her old self left. She was simply a broken woman kneeling in an empty room on a shabby street in a rough part of town. Whoever she had once been, whatever she had wanted to become, it was all gone. She was slipping into the place between places, the hinterland she'd been glimpsing all along, in the form of visions, feelings, suggestions.

She closed her eyes.

Opened them again.

Then she stood, opening her fists, and relaxing her arms. Carefully, she raised her blouse, placed the palm of her hands against her belly and began to rub the darkening skin.

Feeling nothing, thinking of nothing, she went home to hug her husband.

Gary McMahon *writes intensely personal horror stories. His short fiction has appeared in countless anthologies and magazines and has been reprinted in* The Best Horror of the Year, The Year's Best Fantasy & Horror *and* Best New Horror. *He's been nominated for several awards and even won a couple of obscure ones. He is the author of the Thomas Usher novels,* The Concrete Grove *trilogy,* The End, The Bones of You, *and his novella* The Grieving Stones *was recently adapted into a feature film. He lives with his family in Yorkshire, UK, where he reads, writes, watches far too many films, lifts weights, and trains in Shotokan karate*

THE DULLAHAN'S RECKONING

Claire Davon

Humphrey cursed when his driver stopped. He could think of no reason to halt in the night. Fear-sweat dotted his forehead, his bad heart beating an irregular rhythm in his chest.

He banged on the window.

"Why are we halting? This hour is not safe." His voice quivered despite his efforts. Once it commanded the attention of men; now it sounded as weak as the old man he had become.

The horses let out frightened whinnies. Humphrey clutched the pistol he held in his lap. The driver had a similar gun at his hip. Highwaymen roamed these lanes, prepared to rob the unwary, but Humphrey feared it was no bandit they faced.

He'd been warned this might happen. Still, he'd had no choice but to ride. If he did not, he might be dead by morning. Only his physician could help him.

"My lord, I had to stop. The road is blocked. It is . . . not human."

He had prepared for this. Humphrey Randolph could not be felled by ordinary means—or supernatural ones.

He jerked on the curtains and reeled back. No man could ever be prepared for the Dullahan.

It was at least eight feet tall, a dark figure of screams and nightmares. Humphrey had suspected that he would run into her on this road. It had always been his destiny. He had ways to thwart even such a creature as this.

The Dullahan pulled on the reins and her black mount reared

into the air. Blood trickled from her neck, matched by the ichor on the staring head under her arm. Nothing could be concealed from her vision, not even on the darkest night. The wagon she hauled was decorated with skull candles, the wheel spokes human thigh bones.

"You will not take me this night, devil." Though he spoke in a low tone, she turned and stared directly at him. Her face burned with a red-hot glow and he longed to let the curtain fall but dared not. The Dullahan raised an arm, her blood-red stare fixed on his form. He fought not to shrink from her gaze.

"You will come with me," she said, her voice a thousand screams in the night. Her penetrating gaze left no doubt she saw Humphrey. "Release your hold on your mortal life. It is time."

"Not on your life." A thin stream of phlegm came out of his mouth as he gasped out the words.

"Sir? What is your order?"

Humphrey coughed again, his body aching. The doctor in London would cure him. He had prepared for this. He knew the dark portents well and assumed he would meet this monster on the road.

"The bag I handed you for safekeeping. Throw it to her. Quickly."

"Sir?"

"The bag. Throw it to her. We have no time for foolishness."

The nightmare carriage creaked. The head she carried—her head—looked at him. The horrid jaw moved, its teeth clacking. "You're doomed, old man. Your time is up."

He wanted to flee from the monster but that would only hasten his death. He had a plan. He couldn't let terror rule him.

He had heard it said that when the headless Dullahan called a man's name, the person dropped dead. He had no more time to waste.

"Not today, hellfire creature. Throw the thing, idiot driver. What are you waiting for?"

The candles in the coach beyond flickered but never went out. The head grinned from ear to ear in an impossible smile that split its face in two. Its attention remained on him. Its victim.

As she came forward, Humphrey banged on the carriage wall with his walking stick.

"Throw it now, or I will have you flayed alive."

THE DULLAHAN'S RECKONING

"As you say, sir."

The Dullahan came to a halt as the thrown sack bounced and spun on its edge before a coin tumbled out.

"That's got you now," Humphrey cackled. "You thought to take my soul, but you won't. That," he pointed to the object, "that will take care of you."

The Dullahan opened her mouth to speak, but Humphrey rushed in before she could.

"You're supposed to disappear now. They said that you throw a golden object in front of a Dullahan and they vanish. You need to melt back to the hell you came from."

Mist curled in wisps on the damp ground. The offering lay face up, the image of a woman holding a staff and clad in a robe glittering in the grass. Animals howled in the night, the chittering of bugs adding to the sounds.

The Dullahan patted the horse and it whickered. Humphrey banged on the coach. The driver jerked on the reins and the horses whinnied but didn't move.

"Let's go," Humphrey said.

Through it all the Dullahan stayed in place.

"She is still blocking the way."

"I know. Vanish, damn you!" Fear surged within him, leaving his hands shaking and his body trembling. "Begone. I command it!"

The Dullahan pointed to the coin. "That is not gold."

"What?" Humphrey gasped. "That's impossible. I bit it myself."

The Dullahan's horse pawed the ground, burying the piece.

"If you throw a golden object in my path I vanish. Do otherwise and I have no such compulsion. Your cheap ways have doomed you."

The Dullahan pointed her finger at the coach and said his name. Humphrey uttered a piteous whine as agony flooded his dying body. His mouth peeled back in a rictus when his heart stopped. Humphrey slumped over the seat. The misty form that was his soul flowed into the Dullahan's satchel.

She focused on the driver and gave him an infernal grin. "Next time it might be your name I call." She rode off, leaving the gasping coachman behind.

When the Dullahan had gone, the driver reached into his pocket and pulled out a gold coin.

"Did you think I wasn't aware of what was in the bag? Too bad,

CLAIRE DAVON

old man." He flicked the reins, and the horses trotted forward.

USA Today Bestselling author **Claire Davon** *has written for most of her life, starting with fan fiction when she was very young. She writes across a wide range of genres, and does not consider any of it off limits. Her novels can be found in the paranormal romance and contemporary romance sections, while her short stories run the gamut. If a story calls to her, she will write it. She currently lives in Los Angeles and spends her free time writing novels and short stories, as well as doing animal rescue and enjoying the sunshine. Claire's website is www.clairedavon.com.*

THE LITTLE THIEF

Esteban Vargas

Uncle Gary was actually fun to be around. He made the yearly family trip to Lake Cardinal bearable. He was a quiet man, but not a stranger to talking. He had just this way of enunciating that was so serene. Like if he was waiting for something to happen.

While the others had gone into the lake, I sat next to Uncle Gary, his face covered in sunblock with SPF 3000. I had been reading the third installment of the *Saga of L.O.V.E* trilogy and was telling him all about it.

"Cass, you know you are my favorite niece, right? But you have such a bad taste in books. I am appalled. I sometimes consider changing you for your brother. But then I ask him what was the last thing he read and he always replies with the same crap—"

"The back of the cereal box? Trust me, I am the best thing you've got."

"Yeah," he said, taking a long pause and looking away. "Hey, listen, let's do something different for a change. I want to show you something and you let me know if I am crazy or not."

"Wait, do you hear that? Is that the galloping thunder of the Four Horsemen? Is the Apocalypse finally upon us?"

He pinched my arm and stood up "Let's go, stop being annoying. And go tell your mother."

I followed Uncle Gary through a sinuous path along the lake's shore, until he stopped by an embankment full of reeds and cattails. Strings of tiny fish zigzagged in between the wet forest.

"What are those, uncle?"

"I have been asking myself that question every day for the past thirty years."

I chuckle. "Fuck, you are old."

For the first time in the history of jabs we had thrown at each other, he remained mute and quizzical. *Way to kill the mood*, I thought.

"Has your mother ever told you when I almost drowned in this lake?"

"She has mentioned it before, but it is not something she loves talking about."

"It's because she is scared. Scared of what we saw here. What they showed us."

"What are you even talking about? Who are 'they'?"

"Them," he said, pointing at the fish. "They have powers."

I raised my hands, giving up, surrendering to the prank. "Ha-ha. You got me, it was a nice one. Sparked my interest and then BOOM, the fish are the X-Men. Can we go to back to civilization now?"

But looking at the tremor rising in his eyes, I knew this was no joke. I swallowed hard. My knees turned into ghosts, and I felt weak against the cool breeze.

"I just want you to try it out. I promise they will not hurt you. They will just give you a message. Let me show you."

He bent down and inserted his full arm into the water. Immediately, the entire school gathered around him, forming beautiful conglomerations, symmetrical and asymmetrical.

"They will not speak to you unless you close your eyes," he said, pulling his arm rapidly away. "I just promised myself to never ever use it again."

"You have officially scared me to death, but it is kinda cool. What do you want me to do?"

"Just stick your hand in there, close your eyes, and let me know what you see. I will hold you, so you don't fall down like your stupid uncle did."

"I expect a big payment for this. Double-banana-split-big."

"You got it," he said. "You will also need a drink."

Despite my fear, I trusted Uncle Gary's words. Besides, something deep within me was urging me to know—a desire that to this same day I still question.

THE LITTLE THIEF

I dipped my hand in the water and what seemed like millions of fish started dancing around it. Some were almost microscopic. The water became thicker than I expected, membranous. Then I closed my eyes and they showed me everything.

I was in the backseat of a car on route to Uncle Gary's homestead. My mom was driving. Uncle Gary was riding shotgun, his favorite spot. It was only us three in the car. They were arguing about something, but I was unable to hear anything. It looked like a flashback, but not quite. My mom's usual black hair was now all silver and my uncle was bald and wrinkly. I looked at my own hands too, worn out by old age. A silver ring gleamed on my left hand. It was a sapphire. My birthstone. I was transfixed by its hue. By what it all meant. By—

Suddenly came the bang, the crunching of metal, the squeal of the tires.

And the pain of death. The smell of it.

I cried for them both, sprawled on their seats, covered in shards of glass. I was stuck between the car's metal frame. Blood trickled down my finger, completely swallowing the silver ring. They were no longer *there*. Their fire had been extinguished and I was struggling to keep my last ember burning bright.

Before being yanked out by my uncle, before my end, I remember the white lights coming for me, the fluttering of millions of wings.

I opened my eyes to Uncle Gary's tear-stricken face.

"You were there with us?"

"Yes," I said, letting my own tears flow. "But it was only the three of us, nobody else."

"I have spent my life trying to find out who was back there. Oh, Cass, I am so sorry. I had a feeling it had to be you. I was just hoping you weren't. You don't deserve any of this."

I hugged him with the remaining strength left in my body. Squeezed hard.

"Uncle?"

"What?" He murmured, sniffling.

"No ice cream for me. I will need more than one drink."

We drowned in our own laughter. I now wanted it to last forever.

In the distance, the crashing wave of time whispered my name and I answered back.

ESTEBAN VARGAS

Esteban Vargas *was born in Costa Rica. He began writing in 2010 and has contributed to Crystal Lake and literary magazines like Cecile's Writers and La Marabunta.*

CHECK-IN/CHECK-OUT

Pixie Bruner

The room was indeed handicapped accessible.
Fully in compliance with the accessibility laws and at a reasonable
    rate per night
However her body never was in compliance.
If tendons and ligaments are the rubber bands
holding the skeleton in place of our meat cages,
she was born with them already stretched out,
as if rescued from the outside of a rubber band ball
found in a great aunt's cellar beside the tinfoil ball.

She could partially dislocate a rib sneezing.
Sublux multiple ribs laughing too hard,
She could sublux a shoulder napping,
Put knuckles out of joint signing a contract.
So she braced herself- literally
Ankle to knee, elbows, knees, wrists
multiple joint spanning rings on fingers
to reinforce herself so she was less mobile.

To maintain a human form required an exoskeleton
To maintain mobility braces, a cane, a wheelchair.
A suitcase full of braces, heating pads, ace bandages, first aid
    supplies,
The concierge at the oddly named hotel saw her to her
room and said "call the front desk if you need anything,"
With a perfect seated shower and spacious floor plan

PIXIE BRUNER

she could do wheelies in, everything at arms level-
It was heaven at the Hotel Macabre.

At night, she unlaced, unzipped, unvelcroed, unwrapped,
unraveled, and unwound herself to sleep in a nest of pillows,
(the kind concierge brought her eight plump lovely limb cradling
marshmallows to secure her limbs to her body as she slept.)
It was almost as comfortable as home.
Heating pad outlet easily accessed.
Plush towels rolled into extra comfy tiny bolsters.
Would look for included phone charger in the morning.
Traveling was exhausting. It could wait until morning.
The exoskeleton of DME waited on the dresser.
Her wheelchair was about four steps away.
Great service at the Hotel Macabre.

The curtains remained drawn.
She tapped the lamp bedside groaning
and light of a partial cloudy interior illuminated
with the morning alarm for her first medications—
The empty-stomach-only ones.
She reached to get her phone take her meds and turn off the
    alarm—
her arm cracked like a wishbone as she reached.
The ball popped out from socket. Joint unjoined.
The pain shot to 11.
Breakthrough meds required.
She was still going to make it on time.
Nothing would make her miss the event,
Last ADA accessible room available,
no more overflow vacancies at the Hotel Macabre.

She slowly reassembled herself into a slightly less solid form of
    human being,
and poured her legs off the side of the platform bed,
The pillows slid with her over the high-count crisp cotton duvet,
Knees buckled, bones crunched,
Pelvis side landed on all wrong-
So very wrong.
She landed in a broken pretzel form,

CHECK-IN/CHECK-OUT

broken at the bottom of the bag
Pretzel human on the floor at the Hotel Macabre.

The duvet could not pull her up.
The medication's too high to reach, her wheelchair
three
steps
away,
which she could not take,
as the pain was the whole universe.
The pills didn't mind the gap between the mattress and bed frame,
the handful slid right in and down into the space, lost.
The glass of water was still on the nightstand.
Salt packets out of reach for postural orthostasis,
The phone, even when hyperextending her fingers,
could not reach the hotel phone receiver on the nightstand,
Her phone, which she had still forgotten to plug in
and was at 10% and buried in the lovely snowdrift of
distant pillows, blankets, towels, and fresh crisp linens.
Quality and cleanliness are assured at the Hotel Macabre.

She tried to unfold herself, breathing shallow,
Heart racing from agony. Like a hummingbird inside her.
Get phone. Call for help.
She hooks clawed fingers to phone cord and yanks.
Plastic snaps. Cord comes away in her hand.
Broken off at wrong angle, like her limbs.
Her umbilicus unattached to safety and help.
She passed out again.
Blessed relief and comfort are yours at the Hotel Macabre.

The next alarm never came.
She awoke on the floor
Assembled incorrectly, not knowing if 8 AM or 9 PM.
Her mouth was dried out, dehydration is quick.
Withdrawal had started.
Dependence is not addiction.
Her nose and throat choked by phlegm,
Each cell was screaming in a different octave of agony.
Bumps under velvet skin in strange places,

PIXIE BRUNER

Some reassembly required. Weak and ill -
trapped between hard places at the Hotel Macabre.

"Crawl to survive, crawl,
pull yourself across the patterned carpet,
Just reach the bathroom,
Just reach for the walk-in shower door,
Just wrench the faucet on,
Just drink until soaked." In her head, a looping mantra.
However, it's now apparently a half a mile away.
Each yarn color shift is a mile marker,
voice a desiccated crackle and no louder
than the minimal rasp of the HVAC returns
At the tastefully-decorated Hotel Macabre.

The blackout curtains masquerade time
It passes. She knows it has passed.
It is measured in single inhalations. Single exhalations.
Moments matter. All is in moments now.
Each second a camera burst shot.
Slip a contorted limb forward, squirm to retract up to it,
drag a leg behind. Rest. Other leg. rest. Inhale. Exhale.
But fatigue army crawls up beside her,
They share a reflection in the full-length mirror,
angled perfectly to see full length
seated-user accommodating mirrors.
Hunger and nausea gnaw on her insides.
Fatigue covers her, tucks her in "as-is" and out-cold
On the floor at the Hotel Macabre.

Waking sometime later,
The door lock makes its snapping sound
But she cannot respond,
she feels different. Her body less ill fitting.
It is a cocoon of obsolescence.
She wriggles right out of it,
becoming a spectral butterfly,
A guide to the lost souls, a psychopomp
her psyche freed, her cage emptied,
she takes to the air vents, flowing like air

CHECK-IN/CHECK-OUT

and gradually rises to the roof,
of the highly-recommended Hotel Macabre.

"She's transcendent, wings resplendent,
she rose, peering in rooms and spaces different than hers,
seeing things she shall never experience,
The knife thrower, the lovers, the formless monsters, the night porter parade
harvests the arsonists, freaks and geeks merge in her new form
She gathers the lost souls in her embrace and leads them out—
Late checkout is allowed at the Hotel Macabre.

She hears an ambulance siren rounding the corner,
Sees it pull up to the door, looking down on the city,
lights flashing and lit up like a Vegas strip on wheels
The EMTs and gurney rush out, the concierge awaits,
the gurney goes right to her room, to retrieve her empty shell
as they fly high over the city, joyous at last, unhaunted.
The sun is shining, it is warm, and all is blooming,
It is a perfect day for appreciating
the exceptional hospitality of the Hotel Macabre."

Pixie Bruner *(HWA/SFPA) is a writer, editor, mutant, and cancer survivor. She lives in Atlanta, GA, with her doppelgänger and their alien cats. Her collection* The Body As Haunted *was published in 2024 (Authortunities Press). She co-curated and edited* Nature Triumphs: A Charity Anthology of Dark Speculative Literature *(Dark Moon Rising Publications, September 3, 2024) to benefit The Nature Conservancy. Her words are in Space & Time Magazine, Whispers from Beyond (Crystal Lake Publishing), Star*Line, Sirens Call, Dreams & Nightmares, Punk Noir, and many more. She wrote for White Wolf Gaming Studio. Werespiders ruining LARPs are entirely her fault.*
https://pixiebruner.substack.com/

YOUR SCHEHERAZADE STRATEGEM WON'T WORK ANY LONGER. YOU CAN'T PUT OFF YOUR DEATH BY TELLING US STORIES FOREVER.
AH, BUT HAVE YOU WORKED OUT WHAT THEY ALL SPELL YET, MR DARLING?
HUH? WHAT DO *WHAT* SPELL?
THE TITLES TO ALL THE STORIES. TAKE OUT THE VOWELS AND THE REPEATED CONSONANTS, THEN COMBINE THEM LIKE THIS.
AND YOU HAVE A *SIGIL* FOR RAISING THE VENGEFUL DEAD.
SO, IF YOU HAD A LOAD OF SUITCASES, FILLED WITH THE BODY PARTS OF YOUR VICTIMS...
...THAT WOULD *SPELL* DOOM FOR YOU, MY DARLINGS!

YOU DID SAY YOU WEREN'T STAYING LONG.
HOW RIGHT YOU WERE.

I BELIEVE IT WAS WILLIAM FAULKNER WHO SAID:
"IN WRITING, YOU MUST KILL ALL YOUR DARLINGS."
AND TODAY'S OBJECT LESSON PROVES JUST HOW RIGHT HE WAS!
TRUST YOUR UNCLE JASP ON THIS, YOU KNOW IT MAKES SENSE.

THE END?

Not if you want to dive into more of Crystal Lake Publishing's Tales from the Darkest Depths!

Check out our amazing website and online store
or download our latest catalog here.
https://geni.us/CLPCatalog

Looking for award-winning Dark Fiction?
Download our latest catalog.

Includes our anthologies, novels, novellas, collections, poetry, non-fiction, and specialty projects.

Where Stories Come Alive!

We always have great new projects and content on the website to dive into, as well as a newsletter, behind the scenes options, social media platforms, our own dark fiction shared-world series and our very own webstore. Our webstore even has categories specifically for KU books, non-fiction, anthologies, and of course more novels and novellas.

Readers . . .

Thank you for reading *Hotel Macabre Vol. 1*. We hope you enjoyed this anthology.

If you have a moment, please review *Hotel Macabre Vol. 1* at the store where you bought it.

Help other readers by telling them why you enjoyed this book. No need to write an in-depth discussion. Even a single sentence will be greatly appreciated. Reviews go a long way to helping a book sell, and is great for an author's career. It'll also help us to continue publishing quality books.

Thank you again for taking the time to journey with Crystal Lake Publishing.

Visit our Linktree page for a list of our social media platforms.
https://linktr.ee/CrystalLakePublishing

Follow us on Amazon:

MISSION STATEMENT:

Since its founding in August 2012, Crystal Lake has quickly become one of the world's leading publishers of Dark Fiction and Horror books. In 2023, Crystal Lake officially transitioned into an entertainment company, joining several other divisions, genres, and imprints, including Torrid Waters, Crystal Lake Comics, Crystal Lake Games, Crystal Lake Kids, and many more.

While we strive to present only the highest quality fiction and entertainment, we also endeavour to support authors along their writing journey. We offer our time and experience in non-fiction projects, as well as author mentoring and services, at competitive prices.

With several Bram Stoker Award wins and many other wins and nominations (including the HWA's Specialty Press Award), Crystal Lake Publishing puts integrity, honor, and respect at the forefront of our publishing operations.

We strive for each book and outreach program we spearhead to not only entertain and touch or comment on issues that affect our readers, but also to strengthen and support the Dark Fiction field and its authors.

Not only do we find and publish authors we believe are destined for greatness, but we strive to work with men and women who endeavour to be decent human beings who care more for others than themselves, while still being hard working, driven, and passionate artists and storytellers.

Crystal Lake Publishing is and will always be a beacon of what passion and dedication, combined with overwhelming teamwork and respect, can accomplish. We endeavour to know each and every one of our readers, while building personal relationships with our authors, reviewers, bloggers, podcasters, bookstores, and libraries.

We will be as trustworthy, forthright, and transparent as any business can be, while also keeping most of the headaches away from our authors, since it's our job to solve the problems so they can stay in a creative mind. Which of course also means paying our authors.

We do not just publish books, we present to you worlds within your world, doors within your mind, from talented authors who sacrifice so much for a moment of your time.

There are some amazing small presses out there, and through collaboration and open forums we will continue to support other presses in the goal of helping authors and showing the world what quality small presses are capable of accomplishing. No one wins when a small press goes down, so we will always be there to support hardworking, legitimate presses and their authors. We don't see Crystal Lake as the best press out there, but we will always strive to be the best, strive to be the most interactive and grateful, and even blessed press around. No matter what happens over time, we will also take our mission very seriously while appreciating where we are and enjoying the journey.

What do we offer our authors that they can't do for themselves through self-publishing?

We are big supporters of self-publishing (especially hybrid publishing), if done with care, patience, and planning. However, not every author has the time or inclination to do market research, advertise, and set up book launch strategies. Although a lot of authors are successful in doing it all, strong small presses will always be there for the authors who just want to do what they do best: write.

What we offer is experience, industry knowledge, contacts and trust built up over years. And due to our strong brand and trusting fanbase, every Crystal Lake Publishing book comes with weight of respect. In time our fans begin to trust our judgment and will try a new author purely based on our support of said author.

With each launch we strive to fine-tune our approach, learn from our mistakes, and increase our reach. We continue to assure our authors that we're here for them and that we'll carry the weight of the launch and dealing with third parties while they focus on their strengths—be it writing, interviews, blogs, signings, etc.

We also offer several mentoring packages to authors that include knowledge and skills they can use in both traditional and self-publishing endeavours.

We look forward to launching many new careers.

This is what we believe in. What we stand for. This will be our legacy.

Welcome to Crystal Lake Publishing— Where Stories Come Alive!

Printed in Great Britain
by Amazon